The FOURTH DURANGO

"Nobody plots like Ross Thomas. Nobody writes like Ross Thomas. Do yourself a favor. Read *The Fourth Durango*. Then read the rest of Ross Thomas."

—Miami Herald

*

"A first-rate thriller, one of Thomas' very best... the trip through the usual Thomas labyrinth is a joyful one."

—Chicago Tribune

*

"Nobody blurs the distinctions between good and evil better than Ross Thomas... and it is always so much fun to get wherever he is taking you."

—Washington Post Book World

*

"This is a sleek powerhouse of a novel, funny and pathetic by turns, and irresistible after the first paragraph... *The Fourth Durango* is the best Thomas yet."

—Toronto Globe & Mail

*

"Thomas at the top of his game... fun from start to finish. Thomas is the king of the capers."

—Houston Post

more....

"First-rate entertainment, a delightful diversion in an almost-real place populated by down-to-earth citizens, out-on-a-limb fugitives, out-on-the-rim eccentrics and out-to-lunch loonies."

—*San Diego Tribune*

*

"Ross Thomas just gets better and better."

—*San Francisco Chronicle*

*

"In *The Fourth Durango,* Ross Thomas delivers a fast-moving tale of chicanery and greed that establishes him once and for all as the master."

—*Washington Times*

*

"Vintage Thomas: well written, laconic, amusing, with a cast of gritty characters, all with their own peculiar kinds of integrity."

—*Boston Globe*

*

"The arrival of a new Ross Thomas mystery is an event combining elements of both Thanksgiving and Mardi Gras, creating alternative fits of solemn praise and uncontrollable glee. . . . *The Fourth Durango* is Thomas at the peak of his form."

—*Seattle Times/Post Intelligencer*

*

"The stakes are high, and so is the entertainment value as the scamsters skirmish in *The Fourth Durango.*"

—*Detroit News*

"Ross Thomas is a simply marvelous storyteller. His intricate, unpredictable novels, a unique blend of hardboiled thriller and black comedy, are always among the best of the year. *The Fourth Durango* is no exception."

—San Diego Union

*

"A new Ross Thomas turns me back into a reader who forgets what day it is or how many pages there are to go. That's how it was with *The Fourth Durango,* which I read in great mindless gulps."

—USA Today

*

"A treat is in store for Ross Thomas fans. *The Fourth Durango* is one of his best books to date... for those unfamiliar with Thomas, this book is also a solid way to get acquainted."

—Kansas City Star

*

"Thomas once again proves himself a master of the crime thriller."

—New York Times Book Review

*

"There is a puzzle in *The Fourth Durango,* a mystery. It's couched in a deliciously clever clue. The sort of clue that puts a satisfied smirk on the face of mystery buffs. I wouldn't for the world tell you what this clue is. Only that it's there."

—Los Angeles Times

ALSO BY ROSS THOMAS

The
FOURTH
DURANGO

ROSS THOMAS

THE MYSTERIOUS PRESS

New York • London
Tokyo • Sweden • Milan

MYSTERIOUS PRESS EDITION

Copyright © 1989 by Ross E. Thomas, Inc.
All rights reserved.

Cover illustration by David McKelvey
Hand lettering by Ron Zinn

 Mysterious Press books are published in association with
Warner Books, Inc.
666 Fifth Avenue
New York, N.Y. 10103

A Warner Communications Company

Printed in the United States of America

Originally published in hardcover by The Mysterious Press.
First Mysterious Press Paperback Printing: September, 1990

10 9 8 7 6 5 4 3 2 1

One

When the white bedside telephone rang at 4:03 A.M. on that last Friday in June, the 36-year-old mayor answered the call halfway through its fourth ring and kicked the 39-year-old chief of police on the ankle to make sure he too was awake.

After a muttered hello, the mayor listened silently for a minute and a half. She listened with mouth grim and eyes narrowed, forming what the chief of police had long regarded as her pothole complaint look. Once the ninety seconds were up, the mayor ended the call with a peremptory "Right" that was little more than a farewell grunt.

As the mayor listened, the chief of police had occupied himself with another inspection of the bedroom's textured ceiling, wondering yet again why the sprayed-on stuff always wound up looking like three-week-old cottage cheese. The moment the mayor put down the telephone, the chief closed his eyes and asked, "Dixie?"—sleepiness and the hour robbing the question of any real curiosity.

"Dixie," the mayor agreed.

"And?"

"She just tucked him into bed."

"How much did he drink?"

"Dixie says the bar."

"Then it's all set, isn't it?" the chief said, opening his eyes to give the yellowed ceiling a final inspection while awaiting the mayor's reply. When none came, he nodded—as if at some unspoken but reassuring answer—and apparently went back to sleep.

Lying on her left side, the mayor examined the chief with mingled wonder and resentment. Soon tiring of the examination, she rolled over onto her back and closed her pale gray eyes, but they popped open almost immediately and she found herself posted to ceiling sentry duty from which sleep failed to relieve her until just before dawn.

Kelly Vines awoke at 10:09 A.M. on that same last Friday in June. He looked first for the black cane then for the blond-all-over woman who had said her name was Dixie. Vines couldn't remember her last name or even if she had mentioned it, but he did recall those mocking blue eyes and her wry observation that they were checking into the only money-losing Holiday Inn west of Beirut.

Although the blond Dixie was gone, leaving behind a trace of memorable perfume, the black cane still hung from the shade of the lamp with the chartreuse ceramic base. It was a thick cane, a bit more than an inch and a quarter in diameter, fashioned out of Macassar ebony and decorated at its tip with a chrome ferrule that was now just a bit worn. An inch or so below where the cane's handle began its curve was a silver band with the initials *JA* engraved into it in small interwoven Gothic letters.

The hangover attacked in earnest when Vines sat up in bed. Diagnosing it as a crippler of some rare and possibly fatal strain, he sucked in four deep breaths, praying without faith that the additional oxygen would do what folklore claimed and ease the pain and ·perhaps enable

2

him to go on living. But when the hangover and its attendant despair grew only worse, bringing on vague thoughts about sweet death, Vines rose, steadied himself with a faltering hand on the back of a chair, and made his way to the black cane.

After unhooking it from the lampshade, he gave it a shake, sighed with relief at its faint sound and twisted the curved handle to the right instead of the left. After three full turns the handle came off, revealing the small silver cap that held the cork.

Vines pulled the cork out of the glass tube embedded inside the cane, lifted the no-longer-disguised flask to his mouth and swallowed an ounce or so of Jack Daniel's Black Label whiskey that made him shudder all over with what the cane's rightful owner had liked to call "shame, horror and all-around nastiness."

The morning bourbon reminded Vines of the first time he had ever drunk from the cane. And that, arithmetic told him, was exactly fifteen years ago when he had been a senior at the university. It was in June of 1973 and less than an hour before graduation ceremonies when the three of them had first sipped whiskey from the black cane together, although no one got much more than an ounce because the thing only held four ounces.

Vines recalled how the cane's owner had chuckled his most vindictive chuckle and smiled his most partisan smile as he proposed the prescient toast: "To Watergate, lads, and all who sink with her."

The three of them had then drunk an ounce or so each: Kelly Vines first and after him the man whose cane it was and, finally, the man's son, who was also Vines's college roommate, and who, not quite fourteen years later, would allegedly shoot himself to death in a moderately expensive Tijuana whorehouse.

Vines stood, still naked in the Holiday Inn room, waiting for the whiskey's balm and leaning with both hands on the black cane as he peered out the fourth-floor window at the Pacific Ocean that always had seemed so idle, or maybe only languorous, at least when compared to the busy and constantly grumbling Atlantic.

Then, as he had almost known it would, the drink from the black cane forced his memory back to the much more recent past, to that night more than a year ago when the sorrowful Tijuana homicide detective had telephoned him in La Jolla to say that the ex-roommate was dead.

Vines had driven down to Tijuana in what he still regarded as record time; found the whorehouse after a frustrating twenty-five-minute search, and identified the six-foot four-inch body, noting without any particular revulsion (it would come later) that much of the once handsome head had been splattered across a lithograph of the Virgin of Guadalupe that hung on the room's south wall.

Vines had been staring at the lithograph when the homicide detective began to describe in Spanish how the dead man obviously had poked the old .45-caliber Colt semiautomatic into his mouth and pulled the trigger *dos veces*. Suddenly mistrusting his own usually adequate Spanish, Vines had offered a tentative translation: "Twice?"

The detective's broad Indian face had slipped on a pious mask as he replied, "Yes, twice," in English and, switching back to Spanish, murmured that only God himself could understand to what mad lengths suicides resorted when they truly desired to destroy themselves.

When Kelly Vines asked whether he really believed that shit about the ex-roommate pulling the trigger twice, the detective had closed his eyes and smiled beatifically, as if thinking of God or money or both. The detective had then reopened his eyes to reply that yes, certainly he believed it, as who would not?

Vines at first wasn't sure whether it was the fading

4

memory of his dead ex-roommate's brains and blood or the breakfast bourbon that made him turn from the Holiday Inn's ocean-view window, hang the cane back on the lampshade and not quite hurry into the bathroom where he threw up the Jack Daniel's he had just drunk and much of whatever it was he had drunk the night before. But later, after he was all through throwing up, he quite sensibly blamed it on the Jack Daniel's.

At 11:04 that morning, his stomach soothed by Mylanta-II and his nakedness clothed by a wrinkled beige linen jacket, dark gray worsted slacks, also wrinkled, and a clean but tieless white shirt, Kelly Vines sat on a stool at the bar of the Holiday Inn's almost deserted cocktail lounge, a medicinal bloody mary at his elbow, and carefully poured two two-ounce miniatures of Jack Daniel's into the hollowed-out black cane.

Three stools down a tall man of about Vines's own age sipped a draft beer and watched with undisguised curiosity. Except for the thick side-wings of pewter-gray hair that had been swept back to rest on his ears, the man's head was bald and both it and his long shrewd face were nicely tanned.

Perhaps to compensate for his baldness, the man had grown a pewter-gray mustache that Kelly Vines recognized from old British films as being of the wing commander variety. The man's eyebrows were a matching pewter-gray and almost bushy enough to shade hazel eyes that seemed more brown than green. There was also a fine big nose that poked out and down toward a thin wide mouth that looked, if not generous, at least friendly. Beneath the mouth was the cornerstone chin.

The man with the wing commander mustache pursed his lips and frowned, as if worried lest Vines spill any of the whiskey that was still trickling into the cane. But when Vines, his hands vise-steady, finished without spilling a drop, the man grinned, revealing large off-white teeth that could only have been his own.

"Want to sell me that fool thing?" the man asked in a pleasant baritone.

"It's not mine," Vines said, turning to hang the cane on the bar. After Vines turned back, the man said, "Think whoever owns it might sell it?"

Vines examined the man thoughtfully, as if considering the question. "I could ask."

The man nodded, obviously pleased by the answer. "For some dumb reason, I've just got to have it," he said, reaching into a pocket of a faded blue chambray work shirt that might have been bought years ago at Sears. From the pocket he removed a business card. His work shirt and scuffed driller boots were in studied contrast to his well-tailored blue pinstripe pants that obviously belonged to some absent but equally well tailored vest and coat. Despite the old work shirt and stomp boots, Vines thought the bald man looked like a suit. After reading the business card, Vines discovered he was right:

Sid Fork
Chief of Police
Durango, California
(Pop. 9,861)
The City That God Forgot

Below the motto—or epitaph—in the card's lower left corner were the numbers of a telephone Vines could call and a post office box and zip code he could write to.

Vines looked up from the card with his first smile of the day. "Why would God bother to forget Durango, Chief?"

Sid Fork finished his last inch of beer and wiped the mustache with the back of his hand. "It wasn't God—well, not exactly anyway. It was old Father Serra who passed through here on his way south from Monterey in 1772 and

6

forgot to found us a mission, which we sure as hell could use now to draw the tourists."

"Did he forget—or just not get around to it?"

"You Catholic?"

Vines shook his head.

"When a bunch of Franciscans came back through here ten years later in 1782 and still didn't found a mission, well, that's twice, right? And wouldn't you say that sort of makes it look like God forgot to give Father Serra and them the nudge?"

"It would seem to," said Vines, who long ago had made it a point never to argue in bars about religion, politics or baseball's designated hitter rule.

"The other mistake they made—the Franciscans and God—was founding that mission over there in Santa Barbara where the weather's not all it's cracked up to be."

"I always thought Santa Barbara had great weather," Vines said, almost beginning to enjoy his straight man role.

"Not compared to here," Fork said, signalling for another beer. After the gray-eyed young Mexican bartender served it, Fork drank two swallows, gave the mustache another quick brush and said, "If you want absolutely pluperfect weather, Mr.—uh—don't believe I caught the name?"

"Kelly Vines."

"As I was saying, Mr. Vines, if you're looking for perfect weather, then the hunt's over because this town's got what the World Health Organization itself claims is the most salubrious climate on God's green earth." Fork paused. "Except for some tumbledown village on the Italian Riviera nobody ever heard of."

Vines nodded a polite, even interested nod, took a cautious swallow of his bloody mary and looked around the still almost deserted hotel bar. "I've been to the Durango in Colorado, the one down in Mexico and the one

7

in Spain, but never here to this one, the fourth one—until now."

The corners of Fork's wide mouth turned down, as if at expected bad news. "Well, that's no real bulletin since about the only way to get here—unless you swim—is through the mountains over that killer two-lane state blacktop that peels off of One-Oh-One—providing you spot the turnoff sign in time, which not many folks do." He paused, sipped his beer and asked, "How'd you get here—drive?"

"Drove," Vines said. "But I had a girl guide."

The chief of police grinned. "If you'd said you flew in or took the train or bus, I'd've said you were dreaming because the Feds closed down our so-called airport two years back for what they claimed were safety reasons, and the last passenger train stopped here eleven—no, by God, twelve—years ago now, and even Greyhound called it quits after GE boarded up the steam-iron plant two years ago next month."

"Sounds like splendid isolation," Vines said, this time taking two swallows of his bloody mary.

"You a hermit?"

"Not yet."

"We've got a few of those—folks who don't mind being kind of cut off from the rest of the world."

Vines nodded his sympathetic understanding and waited to see what came next.

"The rest of us keep up pretty good, though," the chief continued after another taste of beer. "We've got our almost daily paper that's owned by some chain out of London, England. For culture, there's our one-hundred-percent automated FM station that plays nothing but commercials and root-canal rock from dawn to dark and then shuts down. As for TV, well, we can't get any reception to speak of because of the mountains and because no sane cable company'll touch us. But a man can

8

always buy a dish to catch the news and maybe rent himself a slasher flick or two for his VCR—or even one about some rich high school kids fucking each other."

Fork stopped, as if curious about what his one-man audience would say. Vines took another sip of his bloody mary and said, "Paradise."

The chief welcomed the comment with a satisfied nod, but his contentment vanished as he ran an appraising eye around the nearly empty lounge. "This place'll probably file for Chapter Eleven once summer's over."

"The hotel or just the bar?"

"The hotel. Want to buy it?"

Vines ignored the question to ask one of his own. "How long've you been chief of police?"

An expression that Vines took for bittersweet nostalgia swept across Fork's face and affected his voice, giving it a reminiscent, even dreamy tone.

"About nine of us back in sixty-eight were driving down from the Haight in an old GM school bus we'd painted up a sort of psychedelic Day-Glo—heading for the Colorado Durango. The Haight was dead or dying by then and we were aiming for the Rockies, heads all messed up with acid and dope and politics and God knows what all. You remember how it was back then."

"Dimly," Vines said.

"Well, sir, I'm driving and our navigator spots this California Durango on the gas station map. It's late and everybody's tired, so we turn off. The next morning after we woke up and saw how fine the weather was and all, we just stayed on. A few of us did anyhow. And ten years ago I got appointed chief of police and the navigator, well, she got herself elected mayor."

"She?"

"Mayor Barbara Diane Huckins," said Fork, finishing his second beer and pushing the glass away with the air of a man who knows his exact limit. "Or B.D. Huckins, which is what she calls herself now and how she signs everything, even though I keep telling her it's reverse sexism or something."

Fork stopped talking and again looked longingly at the black cane that still hung by its crook from the bar. "I swear I've just got to buy that thing off somebody, Mr. Vines. What d'you think the owner might ask for it?"

Vines framed his answer carefully. "I'm not sure he'd want money."

Fork looked surprised. "That a fact? Well, how about a trade?" Before Vines could reply, Fork's glum expression returned. "Trouble is, I haven't got much to swap except climate—and just one hell of a lot of privacy."

Vines seemed to consider the problem for several seconds.

"He might like some of that," he said. "Privacy."

"He here in town?"

"No, but this afternoon, I'm going to help him find a quiet place to stay for a few weeks. Maybe longer. Probably in Santa Barbara." Vines smiled. "Despite its rotten climate."

Fork sent his eyes roaming around the bar as he asked a question that obviously was far too casual. "Just how private has he got to have it?"

"Extremely."

"And where'd you say he is now?"

"I didn't. But it's just north of here."

Fork's eyes stopped their roaming and settled on Vines with a cold and knowing stare. "Lompoc, maybe?"

Vines returned the law's cold stare with an indifferent one of his own. The silent exchange lasted only seconds, which was just long enough to reach a rough accommodation, if not the deal itself. "Would that matter?" Vines said.

The chief replaced his cold stare with a warm and welcoming grin. "Hell, Mr. Vines, we take pride in being the live-and-let-live capital of the Western Hemisphere, especially since attitude's damn near all we've got left to sell except a little weather."

Fork started to go on but hesitated, as if to make sure his next question was as politic and inoffensive as possible. "What line of work was the cane's owner in before he came to be a guest of the Federal government up there in Lompoc—if you don't mind my asking?"

"He was a judge."

"What kind?"

"A state supreme court chief justice."

"Not this state."

"Hardly."

"Think the judge might swap me his cane and a little to boot for just a whole lot of privacy?"

"He might."

Fork cocked his head to the left as if that gave him a truer perspective of Kelly Vines. "And just what line of work are you in, Mr. Vines?"

"I'm a lawyer."

"Which brand? Corporate? Tax? Criminal? Catch-as-catch-can?"

"Disbarred," said Kelly Vines.

Two

For not quite four years during the Carter administration, the name of Jack Adair had been either second or third on a supposedly secret White House list of five names. It was his name and the names of three other men and one woman that were to be given immediate and serious consideration should any of the nine U.S. Supreme Court justices either retire or drop dead while Jimmy Carter was in office.

None did, as it turned out, but if one had, the betting in Washington was 3 to 2 that Adair would be nominated to fill the vacancy. Yet the same political bookies who were laying 3 to 2 on Adair's nomination were also offering 5 to 1 with no takers that, if nominated, he would never be confirmed by the Senate.

The long odds against Jack Adair's confirmation came as no surprise. Although it was conceded he was smart enough to serve on the U.S. Supreme Court—too smart, some said—it was also conceded he was far too partisan, much too witty and, most damning of all, the owner of an acerbic mouth that never shut up about whatever interested or engaged him, which seemed to be almost everything.

His ready wit and readier mouth had made Adair the media's darling and the talk shows' sweetheart. Only ten days before being indicted he had appeared on the Phil Donahue show and staked out a hyperbolic position on capital punishment (borrowed in part from Camus) that had created a political fire storm down home where almost everyone assumed he was dead serious.

"If to deter murder," Adair had said in his gravest judicial tones and with calculated disregard for the Eighth Amendment, "the state must instruct by example, then there is no deterrence more instructive than a public execution—and not just some run-of-the mill public hanging either, Phil—but a kind of old-fashioned drawing and quartering with those great big Budweiser Clydesdales pulling the guy apart on prime-time TV around eight in the evening just before the kiddies are tucked into bed."

The landlocked state that Jack Adair once served as chief justice had always held to the notion that members of its supreme court should run for their terms of office as did the governor, members of the legislature and just about everyone else on the state payroll down to and including the director of weights and measures. This populist method of choosing a supreme court guaranteed that those who sat on the high bench would be glib lawyers of pleasing mien who were also keen students of politics, if not of the law itself.

The often bizarre and always expensive television, radio and print campaigns waged by candidates for the supreme court made further rents and tears in the state's already tattered reputation, which in recent years had suffered a series of embarrassments, not the least being the almost perennial revelations of graft, corruption and bribery. Other assorted stigmata included the state university's doped-up and overpaid football teams; a recent plague of bank and thrift failures for which there seemed to be no known cure; and—on a different level—the annual state-financed Panhandle Rattlesnake Roundup, a revered cultural event that environmentalists and the SPCA set up a squawk about every year, much to the media's delight, and where, on the average, 29.2 persons got snakebit, 9.7 percent of them fatally.

The state's ultimate embarrassment, however, had been its chief justice, Jack Adair. As the Adair scandal (or L'Affaire Adair, as a few immigrants from back East called it) dragged on and on, many a devout Christian fell to his knees and prayed God to send old Jack a ticket home and, if it wasn't too much bother, Lord, maybe take some of those snotty out-of-state TV and newspaper reporters with him.

But as faithless lovers do, the media eventually abandoned Jack Adair, much to the relief of those in the state who, quite properly, had blamed them for his giddy rise to celebrity status and, improperly, for his being where he was at 7:05 A.M. on that last Friday in June, which was in the shower room of the discharge area of the U.S. maximum-security penitentiary just outside Lompoc, California.

Located in a mild coastal valley and laid out on a grid, Lompoc is about ten miles east of both the Pacific Ocean and Vandenberg Air Force Base and a few miles south and east of the U. S. Penitentiary. With a population of 26,267 at last count, Lompoc is also 147 miles north of Los Angeles, 187 miles south of San Francisco and only 26 miles north and east of Durango, California, the city that God forgot.

As the "Flower Seed Capital of the World," many of Lompoc's streets are named Tulip, Sage, Rose and so forth. Most of them run at right angles to streets that are usually numbered or named with letters of the alphabet. The city's avenues, however, apparently have been named after whatever was obvious or handy. For example, convicted felons are driven west on Ocean Avenue, then north six miles or so on Floradale Avenue to the U. S. Penitentiary, where, on that last Friday in June, hot water pounded against Jack Adair's back in the shower room that offered four shower heads on one side, four on the other and was open at both ends.

Located just next to the penitentiary's discharge area, the showers were available to prisoners about to be discharged or parolled. Most usually took one before changing into their new street clothes that came from either J. C. Penney's or Sears and were supplied free by the penitentiary.

When Jack Adair had begun his sentence fifteen months ago he couldn't—when naked—look down and see either his toes or his penis because of the 269 pounds he carried on his five-foot ten-and-a-half-inch frame. Most of this excess lard had settled around his middle, creating the forty six-inch waistline that blocked the view.

But as the hot spray now drummed against his back and neck, he could, if he wished, look down and inspect a flat thirty-four-inch belly, ten unremarkable toes and sexual equipment that furtive comparative glances over the last fifteen months had assured him was still of average size and shape.

He was soaping his crotch when they slipped into the shower room. Both were fully dressed, although the smaller of the pair was already unzipping his fly. In the left hand of the larger one was a knife with a blade fashioned out of a metal spoon and, for a handle, melted plastic from seven toothbrushes.

The smaller one, who falsely claimed to be a member of the Mexican Mafia, was called Loco by everyone because he liked to eat light bulbs and get sent to the penitentiary hospital where he could sometimes steal paregoric and even morphine. His real name was Fortunato Ruiz and he was serving twelve years for car theft and assaulting a Federal officer with a deadly weapon. The weapon had been a Mercedes convertible; the Federal officer was an FBI agent who correctly suspected the car to be stolen.

"Hey, Judgie," Ruiz called in his curiously sweet tenor. "You and me and Bobby here, we gonna have one real fine goodbye party, true?"

Bobby was Robert Dupree, the man with the knife and, by trade, another car thief who had specialized in Peterbilts. He had liked to steal the rigs in his native Arkansas and sell them in either Texas or Missouri. Dupree himself had started the rumor that he carried not one but two concealed weapons, the first being the knife; the other, AIDS.

The knife now moved in slow tight little circles as Dupree grinned and nodded at Adair. "Gonna have us some nice clean shower fun, huh, Judge?"

Adair dropped the soap and backed against the shower wall, covering his genitals with both hands. He also smiled his most ingratiating smile, believing it to be the standard disguise for cowardice and fear. "Thanks, guys, but I really can't spare the time."

"Won't hardly take no time at all," Dupree said, crossing to Adair in three swift steps and pressing the knife point against the throat where a vanished triple chin had once bobbled.

Adair whistled. It was no melodic pursed-lip whistle, but rather that piercing, cab-stopping blast often used by pretty young New York women at rush hour on rainy days—or by activist diehards in convention assembled who still believed it could resurrect lost causes long dead. From a block away, such whistles can summon a child, a fairly bright dog or, in Jack Adair's case, a savior.

He seemed to flow into the shower room, although nothing but quicksilver flows quite that fast. He was the color of lightly creamed coffee and would have stood six-four, except he was bent forward as he feinted right, went left, used both hands to grab Bobby Dupree's left wrist—the knife wrist—and break it over his raised right knee the way he would break a small stick.

The knife dropped to the floor. Bobby Dupree sobbed and sank down beside it, clutching his broken wrist. The man who was the color of lightly creamed coffee kicked the knife away and turned to Loco, the light bulb eater, whose right hand seemed trapped inside his open fly where he had been fondling himself.

"Go jack off someplace else, sweet thing," the man said.

Loco started backing toward the shower room's far exit. He suddenly seemed to remember where his right hand was, jerked it from the open fly as if it were scalded, blew a wet kiss at Jack Adair and said in Spanish to the man who had broken Bobby Dupree's left wrist: "Fuck your mother, crazy goat." After that, Loco turned and skipped like a child from the shower room.

"Let's go, Jack," said the rescue man, whose name was Blessing Nelson and who weighed just under 215 pounds and had a Stanford-Binet-measured IQ of 142, which, Adair had assured him, was only eight points shy of perceived genius.

"By the use of some rather restrained mayhem," said Adair with no hint of a smile, "you just broke up what could well've been my last romance—for which, needless to say, I'm goddamned grateful."

Blessing Nelson shook his head in wonder. "Never shuts down for rest or repair, does it—that mouth of yours? Just goes on and on, night and day."

"What about him?" Adair said, using a nod to indicate the still kneeling, still whimpering Bobby Dupree.

"Fuck him."

"Speaking again of romance, they'll both try and clean your plow but good," the former chief justice said, wondering whether his grammar would ever return from its long AWOL.

"Loco might," Nelson said, "on account of Loco's stone crazy. But old Bobby here won't try nothing else." He kicked Dupree in the stomach. The hard kick knocked the breath out of Dupree and turned his whimperings into wheezing sobs.

"How much, Bobby?" Nelson said.

Dupree only shook his head and kept on wheezing and sobbing until Nelson threatened with his foot again. Dupree twisted his head around until he could look up at Nelson. "Twenty," he said, gasping it out between the sobs and wheezes.

"Twenty thousand," Adair said, as if almost pleased by the price tag that had been hung on his life.

Blessing Nelson's long calculating look drove the price down. "Shit, Jack, somebody offer me half that in real money, you already be dead and gone."

"Despite what we've meant to each other," Adair said with a half-mocking smile.

Nelson nodded. "Despite that."

Before being arrested, indicted and sentenced to a plea-bargained four years in Federal prison, the 29-year-old Blessing Nelson—by his own secret count—had robbed thirty-four banks and nineteen savings and loan institutions, eight of them twice, all of them located in Los Angeles's San Fernando Valley and none of them more than 180 seconds by stolen getaway car from either the Ventura or San Diego Freeways, his two preferred escape routes.

It was on the advice of an aged journeyman thief whom he had twice represented as a young defense lawyer that Adair had retained Blessing Nelson's services. The old thief, Harry Means, had spent twenty-three of his seventy-two years behind bars and was only seventeen months out of his last cell when Adair—less than ten days away from his own incarceration in Lompoc—had telephoned for advice on how to survive inside a prison.

"You want it without horseshit and feathers, Jack?" the old thief had asked.

"I really do, Harry."

"Well, pick out the biggest, baddest nigger you can find, jump right in his arms and tell him, 'Honey, I'm yours.'" And with that the old ex-con had cackled merrily and hung up.

Adair more or less had followed the advice, retaining Blessing Nelson's services as protector and physical therapist for $500 a month in lieu of sexual favors. And since he was leaving the penitentiary alive, unraped, eighty-six pounds lighter and relatively sane, Adair regarded the money spent as an extremely prudent investment.

Inside the small mirrorless and doorless changing room in the discharge area, Blessing Nelson watched Adair dress. After stuffing the tails of a green J. C. Penney long-sleeved shirt into a pair of gray wash-and-wear pants with a thirty-six-inch waist, Adair held the pants' waistband an inch or so away from his own thirty-four-inch waist and said, "Amazing what a sensible diet'll do."

"What a hundred sit-ups a day'll do," Blessing Nelson said.

"Well, yes; that too."

Adair picked up a red and orange tie, grimaced at it briefly, slipped it beneath the shirt collar and, sawing it back and forth, said, "I'll send word to your mother where I'll be."

"Mama'd like you to keep on sending that five hundred a month you been sending more'n she would a word."

Adair slipped on a short tan rain jacket that reminded him of those once worn by filling station attendants and looked around for a mirror although he knew there wasn't one.

"Can't afford it anymore, Blessing," he said with what sounded like genuine regret. "But I am grateful. Very. If it hadn't been for you, I'd be leaving here with scrambled brains and a distribution franchise for AIDS. Instead, I leave unsullied and—in a certain sense of the word, virginal—save for that unpleasant experience with old Uncle Ralph when I was six and he was what—thirty? Thirty-two?"

Vexation bordering on anger spread across Blessing Nelson's almost too regular features and made no effort to move on. Adair had managed to provoke that same expression at least twice a day, sometimes three, for the last fifteen months. Accustomed by now to Nelson's fits of exasperation, Adair still couldn't predict what would cause one.

"Can we just get the fuck outa here?" Nelson said.

"What about next month when you get out?"

"Next month you be saying, 'Blessing? Blessing who?'"

Adair denied the charge with a solemn headshake. "I remember my friends, Blessing; as well as my enemies."

"You got too many of one and not enough of the other and it ain't hard to figure where you're short. So maybe I'll look you up and maybe I won't. But right now, let's go." He grabbed Adair by the left arm and steered him out of the dressing room and almost into the arms of a senior guard who dyed his hair yellow and whose left blue eye looked frozen.

"You," the hack said, glaring at Blessing Nelson with his one good eye. "Administrative detention."

"Got me a pass."

"Had you a pass. What you got now is the hole." The guard turned on Adair with a kind of fond vindictiveness. "As for you, Mr. Chief Justice, well, you got a treat coming."

Three

Jack Adair stood patiently in front of the large gray metal desk and examined the wall-mounted head of the slain black bear, deciding once again it had been much too small when shot and, therefore, far too young. Both desk and bear belonged to Darwin Loom, an associate warden, who was using a twenty-six-year-old Waterman fountain pen to initial all nine pages of a requisition form.

Loom was a barrel-bodied man in his late forties with thyroidic brown eyes, a curiously unlined face and silvery hair thin enough to reveal a candy-cane-pink scalp. He finished his initialing, recapped the pen, squared the form's nine pages, looked up and pointed at a molded plastic chair.

Adair sat down on the chair and waited to hear what the associate warden had to say. Loom said nothing for nine or ten seconds, letting a scowl and an unblinking stare speak for him. Then came the accusatory demand.

"I still want a straight answer to why you refused parole seven months ago."

"We've been over all that."

"Humor me."

Adair sighed. "Maybe this time we should try the catechistic approach."

"Fine. I always liked my catechism. Simple answers to hard questions."

"The first question," Adair said. "Why am I here?"

"You're a felon convicted of Federal income tax evasion."

"Are such tax evaders usually confined to maximum-security Federal prisons?"

"Not unless they hope to squeeze something else out of them."

"Where are such tax evaders usually sent?"

"To Club Feds in Pennsylvania, Florida, Texas and Alabama—except the one in Alabama's kind of crummy."

"So why am I really here?"

"Because they couldn't prove you took a million dollars under the table—or half of it anyhow."

"What happened after all that was dropped?"

"They hit you with the tax evasion thing and you noloed it."

"Why would I do that?"

"Because they had you cold and you didn't have any choice."

Adair was again studying the head of the black bear who had been shot too young when he said, "Let's go back to your original question."

"Why you refused parole?"

Adair nodded and looked back at Loom. "After I leave here today, to whom do I report?"

"Nobody."

"And to whom would I report if I'd accepted parole seven months ago?"

"To some Federal parole officer maybe half your age."

"And what would've happened if I'd been charged with parole violation—no matter how minor?"

A fresh scowl rewrinkled Loom's forehead as he leaned back in his swivel chair. "You're saying they'd've faked a parole violation so they could squeeze you some more on what that bribe thing was all about, right?"

Adair only smiled. Loom looked away and said, "Well, if they'd stuck you with a phony parole violation, and I'm not saying it could've happened, but if it had, then you'd have been right back here for another nice visit." He looked at Adair and almost smiled himself. "This is where you're supposed to say, 'I rest my case.'"

"I rest my case," said Adair.

In the silence that followed, Loom's expression went from one of near friendliness to total indifference. When he finally spoke it was off to the left in a monotone from lips that scarcely moved. He's been here so long, Adair realized, that now and then he even talks like some old lag.

"Tell me about you and Bobby Dupree," Loom said through ventriloquistic lips.

"Who?"

"That razorback who hangs out with Loco of the light bulbs."

"What about him?"

Loom snapped his gaze back to Adair and made his voice crisp. "He's in the hospital with a broken left wrist and possible internal injuries."

"Then it's sorry I am to learn of his troubles," Adair said with no hint of a brogue.

"We found him in the discharge area shower."

"So?"

"So the last guy to use that shower before we found him was you."

"Impossible."

"Why?"

"Because the last guy to use that shower must've been

the guy who broke Mr. Dupree's wrist, which couldn't have been me, taking my advanced age into consideration and also Mr. Dupree's considerable size."

"Fucking lawyer talk."

Adair nodded politely, as if acknowledging some small but gracious compliment. "What does Mr. Dupree say?"

"That there were four of them and they all wore masks."

Adair rose from the plastic chair. "Then I don't see we have anything more to discuss."

"Sit down."

Adair sat down. Loom leaned far back in his executive swivel chair, placed both feet on the desk, locked his hands behind his neck and examined the ceiling.

"A rumor," he said. "We can discuss a rumor."

"Concerning?"

"Somebody offering twenty thousand cash money to make sure you don't make it out the front gate. Not alive anyhow." The associate warden's gaze fell from the ceiling and landed on Adair. "And since your mouth's not exactly hanging open—and since even I heard it—it must be kind of old and stale as rumors go."

"Not so old," Adair said. "And not particularly stale."

"Whose money?"

"No idea."

"Bullshit."

Adair shrugged. "But rumor or no, I presume you'd rather have me walk out the front gate than be carried out all zipped up in a bodybag."

Loom apparently had to think about what he really wanted but finally nodded his agreement.

"Then I have a proposal."

The associate warden glanced at the oak-encased Regulator clock that resembled those that once hung from schoolroom walls. "Think you might slice a little off its end?"

"Condense my argument?"

"Try."

"All right. I want Blessing Nelson to see me through the gate and all the way to the visitors' parking lot."

Loom rejected the proposal with a shake of his head. "I'll give you two guards instead."

"How much're you paying hacks these days?"

"A princely sum like always. That's why I've got a whole file drawer full of Federal job applications filled out in pencil by guys who don't spell too good."

"For half of that rumored twenty thousand," Adair said, "all two guards would have to do is look left instead of right for two seconds, maybe three, and snicker-snack, I'm dead and they're each five thousand richer, if you follow my math."

Loom's mouth was already open, a rebuttal obviously prepared, when the green telephone rang. There were two phones on his desk: a cream console model with twelve clear-plastic buttons, indicating twelve lines, and the green phone, which had no buttons at all, not even an anachronistic dial. Loom dropped his feet to the floor, snatched up the green phone and barked his surname into it.

After listening for less than five seconds, he gave Adair a bleak look, picked up his fountain pen, used his teeth and right hand to uncap it, and began jotting down notes on the answers he got to his mostly one-word questions that dealt with where, when and how, but not with who or why. After promising to be right there, Loom hung up the phone, recapped his pen, rose quickly and stared down at Adair with a curious mixture of embarrassment and accusation.

"Somebody just did Blessing Nelson," Loom said, his tone matching his face's mixed expression.

"Did?" Adair said, condemning the word's imprecision by spitting out its consonants.

25

"Killed. Speared him. With a mop handle—or something that had a sharp point."

As part of Adair instantly rejected the notion that Blessing Nelson was dead at 29, another part counselled that his rejection was merely the automatic denial that accompanies grief. But when Adair went probing for grief, he discovered only shame caused by grief's absence. Yet he did turn up sorrow, regret and a sense of utter waste. And because he despised waste, anger turned Adair's next question into a near indictment. "You weren't by any chance waiting for that call, were you?"

All sympathy vanished from Loom's expression, replaced by total indifference. "No more than Blessing expected to get speared six times. Maybe seven. They're still counting." Loom started for the door but turned back. "Stay put. Understand?"

"Here?"

"Right here. Don't even stir until you get four guards I'll pick myself." Loom again started for the door and again turned back. "Who's meeting you in the parking lot?"

"Kelly Vines."

Loom recognized the name. "That high-priced lawyer of yours that got himself disbarred?"

"And consequently, my former lawyer."

Curiosity made Loom almost forget his hurry. "Why'd he get disbarred anyway?"

Adair looked at the schoolroom clock, disliking its contrived nostalgia and suspecting it of quartz innards.

"Turpitude," he said to the clock and looked back at Loom with a faint smile. "But fiscal, not moral, although I suspect, like most of us, he's quite capable of either."

Four

Kelly Vines reached the city limits of Lompoc at 2:27 P.M. on that last Friday in June and drove the four-year-old Mercedes 450 SEL sedan west on Ocean Avenue until he found a full-service UNOCAL gas station where he could pay twenty cents a gallon extra to have the tank filled, the windshield washed and the oil and tires checked.

As the attendant busied himself with the tires, Vines noticed that across the street Lompoc police were blocking off an intersection with black and white sawhorse barricades. When the attendant said his oil and tires were okay and that he owed $13.27 for the gas, Vines handed him a twenty, indicated the police and asked, "What's all the excitement?"

The attendant turned, looked, turned back and began handing Vines his change. "Flower Festival parade," the attendant said. "Happens every year and it's about all the excitement we can stand."

The colors struck Vines as he turned north on Floradale

Avenue, which led to the penitentiary. Quarter acres of gold and red, pink and blue, purple and orange blazed at him from both sides of the two-lane blacktop. He slowed the Mercedes to 15 miles per hour and stared at the commercial plots of lobelia, nasturtium, sweet peas, marigolds and verbena.

In his former life Kelly Vines had been an inexpert but enthusiastic weekend gardener. He now noticed flowers he couldn't identify and wished there were time to ask someone what they were. But there was no time and Vines suspected that if he lingered, sniffing at fields of flowers, it would only drag him down Might-Have-Been Lane, an emotional dead end he had no wish to explore. He pressed down on the accelerator. The Mercedes quickly reached 60 miles per hour and sped Vines toward a speculative future that went by the name of Jack Adair.

Vines drove slowly along the pine-shaded drive that led into the penitentiary grounds, counting the four speed bumps that lay between Floradale Avenue and the visitors' parking lot. He drove past the parking lot on the left and the family visiting center on the right, past the gymnasium and the penitentiary administration building, which resembled a college dormitory. He turned right into a long U-shaped drive, drove by some low-lying junipers, a flagpole and on up to the three-story space-age guard tower and the double row of high steel chain link fences that were topped with concertinas of razor wire.

To Vines, the prison seemed to lurk behind the two high fences with their razor-wire toppings. The main building had been built of pale yellow stone with wings that pointed toward the gate like false "This Way Out" signposts. Assuming the Federal government had wanted the place to look as forbidding and threatening as possible, Vines judged it a brilliant success since he could think of nothing more threatening or forbidding than an enormous steel and stone box the state could drop its felons into, lock them up and keep them there for years on end, sometimes even forever.

The Mercedes crept around the curve at the top of the U-shaped drive until a guard in the tower glared down at Vines, who speeded up slightly and headed back to the visitors' parking lot. It was not quite a third full and Vines parked six spaces away from the nearest car.

When his watch said it was 2:59 P.M., he got out of the Mercedes, opened its trunk and removed the black cane. He closed the trunk lid, moved to the car's left front fender and, once more leaning on the cane with both hands, waited for Jack Adair.

Six of them came out of the family visiting center that was across the drive from the parking lot. In the lead was a man with silver hair and a barrel build. Behind him came a middle-aged guard, armed with a Springfield '03 at port arms, who quartered the parking lot, missing nothing.

Kelly Vines stood very still, not moving anything except his eyes. He thought the guard with the '03 looked like a retired marine who had put in twenty years, maybe even thirty. Right behind the guard came Jack Adair, much, much thinner than when Vines last had seen him fifteen months ago. Adair now walked with a new spring to his step that was nearly a bounce and for a moment Vines almost missed the ex-fat man's gliding quick-step that had been virtually a trademark.

Flanking Adair were two young guards in their mid-twenties, one of them a mouth-breather, both of them armed with shotguns. Back at trail was a gloomy-looking guard of about Vines's age who had a hunter's look and an M-16 that he handled with the easy familiarity of someone who has been around guns since he was six.

The man with the thin silvery hair didn't speak until he was less than thirty feet away. "Mr. Vines?"

Vines nodded, stopped leaning on the black cane and hooked it over his left arm.

"Darwin Loom. Associate warden."

"Why the firepower, Warden?"

"Disturbing rumors and a . . . mishap. An inmate died."

"Killed?"

"Yes."

Although still looking at the associate warden, Vines spoke to Adair. "Somebody you knew, Jack?"

"Blessing Nelson."

"I'm sorry," Vines said, looking now at Adair. "What rumors?"

"There seems to be a price on my head."

"A price on your head," Vines said, almost savoring the phrase. "How much?"

"Twenty thousand, I'm told."

"You should be flattered," Vines said. "Ready to go?"

"More than ready."

Adair started for the Mercedes but the associate warden turned quickly to block his way. "Not just yet," Loom said, taking out a small notebook and the old Waterman pen. Over his shoulder he said, "You can help us with this, Mr. Vines."

With the black cane still hooked over his left forearm, Vines walked quickly over to Adair and stood beside him. He unhooked the cane, again leaned on it with both hands and examined Loom with polite interest.

"Help you with what?"

"With where the judge can be reached," Loom said. "Look. Because of his—well, his informal business arrangement with Blessing Nelson, both the sheriff and the FBI'll probably want to talk to him—or to his lawyer at least."

"I'm no longer his lawyer."

"I know. But you could give me some idea of where we could get in touch with you or him if— "

Vines interrupted. "I don't know where we'll be." He smiled a crooked boyish grin, full of charm, that Jack Adair knew to be a disguise. "Until earlier this month I lived in La Jolla," Vines said. "But I now have no fixed address and, consequently, no phone."

Loom frowned, as if Vines's lack of a fixed address made him automatically suspect. "What about your wife or a close relative? Maybe your lawyer or accountant? Just anybody you keep in touch with."

Vines shook his head regretfully. "My finances are such that I don't need an accountant. And even if I needed a lawyer, I couldn't afford one. My wife is in a private psychiatric hospital and divorced from reality, if not from me. My parents are dead. I have no children or other close relatives."

"What about a friend?"

Vines gave Adair a nod. "You're looking at him."

Loom turned to Adair with yet another scowl. "No idea where you'll be staying either, right?"

"A motel tonight, I suspect. After that—well, who can say?"

"Parents? Wife? Children? Old friends—besides him?" said Loom, giving Vines a dismissive nod.

"That's all in my records," Adair said. "But to save time, both parents are dead. My son, as you know, died fourteen months ago in Mexico while I was here. A suicide. My wife and I were divorced in seventy-two and she's long since remarried. My daughter's confined to a private psychiatric hospital."

Loom's eyes leaped back to Vines. "The same one your wife's in?"

"His daughter is my wife," said Kelly Vines.

31

Five

Four miles south on Floradale Avenue, Vines pulled the Mercedes to a stop on the road's shoulder next to a quarter acre of blazing scarlet flowers. Jack Adair stared at them, fascinated, as he slowly twisted the curved handle of the black cane to the right rather than the left.

"What are they?" he asked as the cane's handle came off.

"Iceland poppies."

Still staring at the field of scarlet, Adair placed the cane's curved handle in his lap, removed the silver cap that held the cork, lifted the glass tube flask out of the cane and drank. At the taste of the whiskey, he closed his eyes and sighed. A moment later he opened his eyes and smiled, as if enormously relieved that the scarlet poppies were still there and the whiskey was just as he remembered it.

"After we left Loom and them back there," Adair said, "and after it finally struck me that it really was adiós to durance vile, guess what I smelled?"

"Good intentions."

"No, by God, ripe persimmons. And I haven't smelled a ripe persimmon in fifteen, twenty years."

"I've heard good intentions can smell like almost anything. Even ripe persimmons."

Adair nodded and passed Vines the glass tube flask. The drink that Vines took was scarcely a sip.

"So tell me about it," Adair said. "This city that God forgot."

"Durango," said Vines, handing back the glass tube. "About nine thousand souls, give or take a few hundred, who're scratching out a living with no industry to speak of and some magnificent weather they can't eat or pay their bills with."

"What about tourists?"

"There's no Spanish mission because of an oversight by Father Serra—and God, of course. Consequently, no tourists."

"He a saint yet?"

"Father Serra? Rome's still mulling it over but the odds are he's a shoo-in."

"Well, if the weather's so great and it's right on the ocean, why no tourists?"

"Because there's no beach," Vines said. "The Southern Pacific railroad tracks hug the coastline along that stretch and what beach there was, the storms ate."

After nodding his understanding, Adair had a small swallow from the flask and asked, "How'd you send out the feeler?"

Vines started the engine and glanced into the rearview mirror before pulling out onto the road. "It came to me through Soldier Sloan."

"Sweet Jesus," Adair said, his eyes wide, his tone almost reverent. "What is he now—seventy, seventy-one?"

"Seventy-one."

"Still a bird colonel?"

"Promoted himself to brigadier."

"That must impress the widow women."

"At his age, Soldier says, being a mere retired colonel won't hack it anymore. So this time he retired himself from the Royal Canadian Air Force as a brigadier and affects a very slight British accent that must charm the hell out of the widows down in La Costa, Palm Springs and especially La Jolla, which is where I ran into him."

"How much is he charging us?"

"Five thousand."

"How'd you work it?"

"I followed Soldier's surprisingly explicit instructions and turned off U. S. One-Oh-One at exactly ten P.M. and onto a state blacktop that's the only way in and out of Durango."

"When? Last night?"

"Last night. Eight minutes later, just as Soldier promised, I spotted a disabled car. I knew it was disabled because the hood was up—or bonnet, I suppose—and Dixie was staring down at the engine as though she'd never seen one before."

"Dixie the fair, I presume."

"Dixie was blond and more than fair. The car was an Aston Martin."

Jack Adair had a small final swallow from the glass tube and chuckled with pleasure. "Spare me no details, Kelly," he said. "Not even the dirty stuff."

Kelly Vines got out of the Mercedes and walked slowly toward the woman who was illuminated by the headlights of both cars. She looked up from the Aston Martin's engine with no sign of alarm. "If you're thinking of bopping me over the head and taking my money, I've got six dollars and change."

"I'm not the highwayman."

"The mechanic?"

"Not him either."

"Then you must be the Samaritan who knows damn all about cars."

"I can drive one," said Vines. "Although I've never driven one of these."

"It's simple," she said. "You just put it in second and keep it there—unless you want to back up, of course."

"What happened?"

"It coughed once, sputtered twice, died and no, I'm not out of gas."

"You going to leave it here?"

She shrugged. "If you'll give me a ride into town."

"Which town?"

"Durango."

"All right."

"I'm Dixie," she said, holding out her hand.

"Kelly Vines," he said, taking her hand and finding it to be cool and dry and surprisingly strong.

The only customers in the Holiday Inn's bar and cocktail lounge that night—other than Vines and the blond Dixie—were two serious male drinkers, one white, the other black, both in their mid-forties, who sat at the bar well separated from each other. As mute testimony to their solvency, both kept piles of wet change and damp bills in front of them, silently paying for each drink as it came.

Vines sat at a banquette, an untasted bourbon and water in front of him, waiting for the blond Dixie to complete a call to the Triple-A in Santa Barbara, which she thought might send a tow truck for the crippled Aston Martin.

As Vines waited, the white man at the bar gathered up his bills, leaving the pile of wet change for the gray-eyed Mexican bartender. The man climbed carefully down from his stool. Once safely on the floor, he looked around the room, a thoughtful expression on his face, and said in a clear and pleasant voice, "Fuck California."

As the man left the lounge, his tread a bit measured,

Dixie returned and slipped into the banquette next to Vines. Watching her cross the room, Vines realized she was older than he had first thought. If looks alone were the gauge, she could easily be 25. But Vines had found her mind older than 25, at least ten years older, and her attitude even older than that. She had that hard gloss of women who travel into their forties over rotten roads all the way but arrive more burnished than bruised. So he put her real age at 32 or 33 and wondered about her past.

After two sips of a Scotch Mist, Dixie put the drink down and said, "They're sending the tow truck."

"Good."

"Now I have to find a place to stay."

"You don't live in Durango?"

"God, no. Do you?"

"No."

She glanced around the room. "I suppose I could stay here."

"Think they'd have a room?"

She smiled—a very wry smile. "In the only money-losing Holiday Inn west of Beirut there's always a room."

"Want me to see about a room for you when I see about mine?"

"Why, yes. Thank you."

"Any preference?"

"An ocean view would be nice."

"What if they have only one ocean-view room left?"

"Then we'll just have to share it, won't we?" she said.

After Vines returned from the registration desk, he lied without shame and told her there was only one ocean-view room available. She smiled, as though welcoming the lie, gathered up her purse, rose and crossed to the bar, where she reached into the purse, brought out a fifty-dollar bill, said something to the gray-eyed bartender and handed him the money. The bartender smiled happily, pocketed the bill and handed her a bottle of Scotch whisky. Holding the bottle by its neck down at her left side, she walked back to Vines and said, "No need to go thirsty, is there?"

They ate room-service hamburgers and drank a third of the bottle with their clothes on. They drank another third with their clothes off. Vines discovered that Dixie was indeed blond all over and she apparently discovered all she wanted or needed to know about him—not because the liquor made him talkative, but because he replied frankly and more or less honestly to whatever she asked, assuming the questions were a necessary part of her task, assignment—perhaps even her calling.

The questions were casual, sometimes mere afterthoughts, and she often seemed not to listen to his answers, especially after their clothes were off and she was sitting on his lap, nibbling at his right ear. The only time she listened intently was when she asked Vines about the black cane and whether he had served in Vietnam.

"No," he said. "Why?"

"That cane."

"It's not mine."

"Well, it can't be a present. You don't giftwrap a cane and give it to somebody."

"It belongs to the guy in Lompoc I told you about."

"Is he lame?"

"No."

"Then what's he need a cane for?"

"He hides his booze in it."

Dixie rose from Vines's lap, went to the bed and picked up the cane. She gave it a hard shake, laughed at its telltale gurgle, twirled it like a baton—passing it expertly behind her naked back—pranced over to the lamp with the chartreuse ceramic base, where, with exaggerated care, she hooked the cane over the lampshade, turned to Vines with a grin and said, "Let's try the bed."

Seconds later they were not quite under the bedcovers,

legs intertwined, hands busy, tongues exploring new territory. Later, during recess, Vines said, "If you were me, what would you do tomorrow—first thing?"

"For your hangover? I'd try the bar downstairs and a bloody mary around—well, say, eleven." She paused. "And I'd bring the cane along."

"Around eleven and bring the cane," Vines said. "What time is it now?"

"Who cares?"

By the time Vines had finished his tale about the blond Dixie and his meeting the following morning with Durango's chief of police, Sid Fork, they had reached Ocean Avenue in Lompoc. The annual Flower Festival parade seemed to have ended but the avenue was still jammed with locals, tourists, uniformed high school band members, good natured police, cars and a large number of florist delivery vans from out of town.

One of them, a pink Ford van with a scripted green sign on its rear door that read, "Floradora Flowers, Santa Barbara," darted around the Mercedes on the left, horn bleating. The pink van almost clipped the sedan's front left fender as it veered back into the lane and slammed on its brakes for a red light. Vines sounded his own horn in a disapproving honk.

As if on signal, the rear door of the van flew open and something black and round and shiny pointed itself at the Mercedes. Vines instinctively began to duck, but when he saw that the black, round, shiny thing was a 35mm camera with a moderately long lens, he instead covered his face with both hands, peering between his fingers at the photographer.

Jack Adair had jumped with a noticeable start when the pink van's rear door banged open. But he didn't bother to hide his face. Instead, he tilted his head back to eliminate any trace of the vanished triple chin, smiled a beaming, practiced smile, quickly erased it and stuck out his tongue.

The photographer was a dark-haired woman who, from her quick sure movements, Vines guessed to be in her late twenties. She wore pale blue coveralls and enormous dark glasses with white plastic frames. Her camera was obviously motor-driven and Vines estimated she had had time to expose at least six frames, maybe even seven.

After Adair stuck out his tongue, the woman lowered her camera and grinned at him. She slammed the rear door shut as the van made a fast right turn on red, causing a few pedestrians to jump back. The pink van sped off down the side street. Vines made no attempt to follow. When the car behind him honked, he noticed the light had changed to green, took his foot off the brake and drove straight ahead.

Neither Vines nor Adair said anything for half a block. It was then that Adair cleared his throat and said, "I don't suppose she was from *People* magazine?"

"No."

"Somebody needed proof of what—us being back in harness?"

"I think they were just dropping a hint."

"What kind?"

"That they know where we're going."

"Well, that's part of the plan, isn't it?"

"That's part of the plan," Vines agreed. "Such as it is."

They drove in silence for nearly five minutes until they reached Lompoc's eastern edge and turned right onto a state highway with a poppy-decorated road sign that designated it as the scenic route to U.S. 101. Adair looked at Vines and said, "This the shortest way?"

"The prettiest anyhow."

Adair smiled contentedly, said, "Much obliged," and for almost ten minutes silently admired the rolling green and tan foothills that boasted scattered stands of fine old oaks and, here and there, some dairy cows, all of them black-

and-white Jerseys. Deciding that cows still looked as bored silly as ever, Adair said, "We meet this guy Fork and the mayor for dinner, right?"

"At her place."

"How'd you size him up—the chief?"

"Ever met a slightly bent Zen-Rotarian?"

"Don't think so."

"You will tonight."

"You haven't met her honor, B. D. Huckins, yet?"

"Not yet."

"What's the B. D. stand for?"

"Barbara Diane."

"She the brains, you think?"

Vines sighed. "Let's hope so."

Six

To reach Mayor B.D. Huckins's two-bedroom frame bungalow on the cul-de-sac called Don Emilio Drive, it was necessary to travel up Garner Road into the sand, shale and clay foothills of the faintly forbidding mountains that helped isolate Durango from the commercial rewards of tourism and the cultural benefits of free television.

Named after an almost forgotten U.S. Vice President by a totally forgotten developer, Garner Road consisted mainly of seven hairpin turns. Mayor Huckins lived just off the seventh hairpin and Sid Fork, the chief of police, lived two hairpins down on Don Domingo Drive, another cul-de-sac, in a two-bedroom house whose floor plan was identical to the mayor's.

The mayor's house was painted sky-blue with dark blue trim that complemented a fine stand of jacaranda. The chief's house, which should have been repainted, was described as "measle white" by the mayor because its flaking paint exposed a rash of strange pink spots that she said looked contagious.

Fork had landscaped his house with rocks and cactus. The rocks were six extremely large and ugly igneous boulders, weighing anywhere from a quarter to a half ton, that had been dumped on the chief's property by a disgruntled and illegal Mexican alien.

When Fork had first noticed the boulders and decided he absolutely had to have them, the Mexican alien was hauling them away from a blasting site in a dump truck. The chief had promptly arrested him for driving two miles over Durango's 25-mile-per-hour speed limit, which nobody in living memory had ever observed. In exchange for his liberty, the Mexican had agreed to haul the boulders up to the chief's house and arrange them nicely in what Fork described as a *jardín de piedras*. Instead, the Mexican had dumped them all up against the chief's front door.

The door stayed sealed for two days until Fork could hire six other illegal Mexican aliens at six dollars an hour each to arrange the boulders into a garden of stone. He then had the same Mexican aliens plant twelve immense cacti—or cactuses as Fork, the contrarian, called them— that he had confiscated from a professional Arizona cactus rustler who had strayed into Durango by misadventure.

Intended for the rustler's wealthy Santa Barbara client who, the chief claimed, was "some dipshit who poisoned coyotes for a hobby," the stately saguaro cacti now seemed to be dying in the moist ocean air although Sid Fork said it just made them look even more noble and tragic.

After work, Mayor Huckins and Chief Fork often met at Norm Trice's Blue Eagle Bar on North Fifth Street to compare civic notes, drink a glass or two of wine or beer and determine whether the mayor felt like inviting the chief home for dinner and bed. Two out of five nights she usually did, but on the other three nights and most weekends she told him not to bother.

When banished by the mayor, the chief would sometimes call the blond Dixie in Santa Barbara and offer to take her out for a pizza or a Mexican dinner, providing her husband was in New York or Tegucigalpa, London or Istanbul, or wherever it was that he went to make—in Fork's opinion—more money than he and Dixie could ever spend.

On that last Friday in June, B.D. Huckins and Sid Fork met in the corner booth of the Blue Eagle after work and ordered two gin martinis, causing Norm Trice to ask what the occasion was.

"We just felt like it, Norm," said the mayor.

"Just felt like it?" Trice said to Fork, as though seeking a second opinion.

Fork stared at him coldly and nodded.

"You two come in here every night," said Trice, "well, three or four nights a week anyhow, and B.D. here has her glass of white wine, maybe two, and you your couple of beers, and the only time either of you ever order a martini is when B.D. gets reelected every two years, or when you collar some guy's wanted down in L.A. and get your picture in the paper and, come to think of it, that's about every couple of years too. So when I say, 'What's up?' I'm asking if maybe Iacocca's called to say he's gonna start making DeSotos again in a brand-new plant in our fine new industrial park that's been growing weeds for three years. And if so, well, the gin's on me and let's all get shitfaced."

As Trice talked, the mayor stared down at the fifty-three-year-old wooden tabletop and the dozens of initials and dates that had been carved into it. The earliest date, she knew from previous inspections, was 12-3-35, which was the day Norm Trice's father had opened the bar, naming it for the blue eagle that then symbolized Roosevelt's National Recovery Administration. In fact, a large old plywood NRA blue eagle, its paint fading, still hung behind the bar, clutching a gear with a few missing teeth in one claw, two and a half bolts of lightning in the other, and pointing its beak forever to the customer's left.

When she was sure Norm Trice was through talking, the mayor stared up at him with winter-rain eyes that, if soft and brown, would have been far too large for the delicate chin, full mouth, not quite perfect nose and a forehead that seven years ago Sid Fork had warned her was a mile too high and made her look about 19 instead of 29.

B.D. Huckins's hair, which was a bit darker than honey, had then hung straight down, almost to her waist. The following morning she had had it hacked off into a Dutch-boy bob with bangs that ended just above the chilly gray eyes and camouflaged the smart high forehead. In her next campaign for mayor, she won by 56.9 percent—up 3.6 percent from the previous election. Sid Fork gave all the credit to the haircut.

The mayor pinned Norm Trice with her gray stare for several seconds before she said, "Nobody's called, Norm. Not Lee. Not Ronnie. Not even Mayor Sonny from down in the Springs. Nothing good's happened. So if it's not too much trouble, would you please go get the drinks?"

After Trice left, mumbling about a guy having a right to ask, Sid Fork said, "I got four real nice T-bones at the Alpha Beta since he's just out of the joint and I thought he might like a good steak."

"You get any charcoal?"

"Sure."

"What else?"

"Baked potatoes—big Idaho bastards."

"They'll take an hour."

Fork nodded his agreement. "And I thought one of my Caesar salads and maybe some scratch biscuits."

"What about dessert?"

"Vines doesn't much look like a dessert eater. I don't know about Adair."

44

"Okay. Let's skip dessert. If they want sugar, I think I've got some B and B left."

A sullen Norm Trice returned and silently served the two martinis. After he went away, B.D. Huckins tasted hers, sighed and said, "What's he like?"

"Vines?"

She nodded.

"Well, he's kind of low-key, more smooth than slick, and he's still got all his hair." Fork ran a palm over his own bald head. "About my age. Pretty good bones but not much meat on 'em. Real dark eyes, maybe black, and real dark hair with a nose not near as bad as mine or the eagle's over there. He's tall enough and looks—well, cagey-smart, the way a one-eyed jack looks."

"How long do they need?"

"He didn't say."

"What about money?"

"Vines won't deal till he talks to Adair."

B.D. Huckins finished her martini, put the glass down and said, "Why was he disbarred?"

"Some money disappeared."

"Whose?"

"Adair's."

"How much?"

"They're not sure but they say it was close to half a million. Just before the state started investigating Adair on that bribe thing, he put every dime into a blind trust and made Vines the administrator or trustee or whatever you call it."

"Administrator."

"After the bribe thing was dropped, the Feds went after Adair on tax evasion. But when they went to freeze his assets, they found he didn't have any. Or hardly any. Vines swore he'd lost it all through imprudent investments. He even had records to show how he'd lost a lot of his own money along with Adair's. But they brought Vines up before a hearing panel of the state bar court anyway and nailed him on four separate counts of misconduct that, from what I hear, were pretty vague. Then the state supreme court—the same one Adair'd been chief justice of—disbarred Vines. Just like that."

"None of them recused themselves?"

"Nope."

"What really happened to the money?" the mayor said.

"Who knows?"

"Guess."

"I'd guess Vines managed to squirrel it away out of the country."

"Where?"

"Jesus, B.D., I was on the phone long-distance part of the morning and most of the afternoon, finding out what I just told you. How the hell do I know what country?"

"Okay," she said. "Let's assume they've got money somewhere. The next question: who's after Adair?"

"That's easy. Somebody who doesn't want him to tell what he knows."

"Which is what?"

Fork replied with a shrug and finished his martini.

"Suppose you knew something you could blackmail somebody with," B.D. Huckins said. "Somebody nasty as lye. You'd need a safe place to operate from, wouldn't you? A sanctuary."

Fork's mouth went down at the corners as he shook his head. "I wouldn't want any sanctuary," he said. "Sanctuary always sounds to me like some little locked room in the church basement with maybe an army cot and a slop jar. Or like some wildlife preserve with a 'Keep Out—No Hunting' sign that's been all shot to hell. So if I was them, Vines and Adair, I wouldn't be looking for any sanctuary."

"Right," B.D. Huckins said. "So we'll offer them just what we offered all the others. A hideout."

Seven

After parking the blue Mercedes in one of the four empty metered spaces in front of Figgs' department store on Main Street in Durango, they went in just before closing and bought Jack Adair four Arrow shirts, two pairs of Levi corduroy pants, four pairs of socks and six pairs of Jockey shorts, Adair taking great pleasure in specifying his fifteen-and-a-half-inch neck and thirty-four-inch waist sizes.

Vines paid in cash as a bemused Adair watched the fiftyish woman salesclerk with the golden beehive hairdo wrap the sales slip around the twenty-dollar bills, stick everything into a metal cylinder and pop the cylinder into a pneumatic tube that shot it up to the cashier's office on either the second or third floor.

When they were again in the Mercedes, Adair said, "Makes you believe in time travel, doesn't it? What do you think we warped into back there—nineteen fifty?"

"Fifty-three," Vines said, "since that's as far back as I can remember."

After a last stop at a liquor store, where Vines bought

two bottles of Jack Daniel's, they drove to the Holiday Inn and went up to adjoining oceanside rooms on the fourth floor. Vines stood at the window in Adair's room, again staring out at the Pacific that now seemed more green than blue. From the bathroom he could hear Adair splashing around in the tub, taking his first bath in fifteen months and singing in a surprisingly true baritone about leaving on a jet plane.

Vines turned from the window when Adair came out of the bathroom, wearing gray corduroy pants and a blue oxford-cloth shirt that still had the fold creases in it. Adair joined Vines at the window, where they stared out at the ocean for nearly a minute. When the minute was almost up, Adair turned and went to the desk, where the whiskey stood next to the bucket of ice that Vines had fetched from the machine down the hall.

"Want one?" Adair said as he dropped ice cubes into a glass and poured in the bourbon.

"Not yet," Vines said, still staring at the ocean.

"So. When'd you last see her?"

"Two weeks ago."

"And?"

Vines turned. "I drove up to Agoura from La Jolla to pay the monthly bill. I pay it in cash every month on the fifteenth."

Adair nodded. "Where's Agoura exactly—in relation to L.A.?"

"North end of the San Fernando Valley. It's hilly out there—low round hills that're turning brown now but'll turn green again when it rains. Some nice old oaks. It's all very—" Vines searched for the word the doctor had used. "Nonthreatening."

"Soothing," Adair translated.

"Soothing. From her window she sometimes can see deer and even a coyote or two."

"Dannie always did like coyotes for some reason," Adair

said. Dannie was Danielle Adair Vines, wife of the disbarred lawyer; daughter of the jailbird justice. The topic of coyotes exhausted, Vines waited for Adair's next question, confident of what it would be since it was the logical one to ask.

"What do the doctors say?"

"They're guardedly optimistic," Vines said. "But they're being paid six thousand in cash each month, so they would be, wouldn't they?"

"But you're not."

"What I am, Jack," said Vines, his voice resigned, "is the messenger. I drive up there every month on the fifteenth and hand over the money envelope they're too polite to count in my presence. While they're counting it, I go sit in a nice little conference room with a big picture window. They bring Dannie in. She sits at the far end of the table and smiles the way she always smiled, as if you're the most wonderful thing in her life. Then she says, 'Who're you? I don't think I know you.'"

Adair closed his eyes so he could rub them and the bridge of his meandering nose with thumb and middle finger. "No possibility of her faking it, is there?" he asked, opening his eyes and wincing as he realized that a yes would be worse than a no.

"I wasn't sure," Vines said. "So after a couple of months of that who-are-you stuff, I started telling her I was Warren Beatty or Jerry Brown—who she always had half a crush on—or even Springsteen. But all she ever said was, 'I don't think I know you.'"

"Well, shit, Kelly," Adair said, turned back to the desk, started to pour himself more bourbon, thought better of it, put the glass down and again faced Vines. "Think she'd know me?"

"We could find out."

"I take that for a no."

Vines nodded.

Deciding he wanted another drink after all, Adair turned, picked up the glass and dropped more ice cubes into it. As he poured the bourbon, he said, "You tell her about Paul?"

"On April thirteenth last year—one day after it happened—I drove up and handed over the money envelope two days early. She and I sat at the table in the little conference room again. There were two deer about thirty yards away and she was looking at them and smiling."

"When you said what?"

"Something like, 'Your brother, Paul, shot himself to death last night in a Tijuana whorehouse.'"

"And?"

"Nothing."

Adair sighed and sat down in a chair, slowly and carefully, as if in great and unfamiliar pain. He sat leaning forward, arms on his knees, holding the glass in both hands and staring at the carpet.

"Darwin Loom," Adair said.

"The associate warden."

Adair nodded, not looking up. "He told me it was suicide before he even let me take that La Jolla call from you. Preparing me for the shock, I guess. Know what I told him?" Adair looked up from the carpet and cruelly parodied his own voice. "My son'd never take his own life. Not my son." He gave his head a self-accusatory shake and resumed his examination of the carpet. After a long silence Adair again looked up and said in a suddenly weary voice, "So tell me what happened, Kelly. Not that crap you told me over the phone."

"You're right. It was crap."

"Afraid you were being taped?"

"Or that you were."

"Your letters weren't any better. Same reason?"

"Same reason."

Adair sighed. "Let's hear it."

"The cops in Tijuana claim Paul was alone in an upstairs room when it happened. They also claimed he'd ordered up two girls. After I drove down there from La Jolla, one of the cops showed me what he said were sworn statements from both girls, who by then'd disappeared, apparently forever. The statements said the girls were on their way up to Paul's room when they heard the shots."

"Why'd they call you—the Tijuana police?"

"Paul had one of those 'in case of emergency notify' cards in his billfold. Your name, old address and phone number had been typed in and crossed out. Mine was written on the back of the card."

"So how'd they lay it out for you—the Tijuana cops?"

"They said he poked a forty-five in his mouth and pulled the trigger twice."

"Twice?" Adair said.

Vines nodded.

"You saw him, I guess."

. "I saw him, Jack. Most days I still see him. It was twice."

Shaking his head in disbelief, Adair gave the carpet a final inspection with blue eyes that once had seemed as innocent as a 9-day-old kitten's. But when he looked up now it was obvious all innocence had either died or moved away. They look like blue dry ice, Vines thought, and if he moves them fast enough, I'll get to hear them click.

Below the bleak eyes and the meandering nose was Adair's wide mouth that, in the past, was always twitching its ends up, as if at some cosmic joke. Now the joke was over and the mouth was clamped into a thin line that Adair pried open just wide enough to say, "Okay, Kelly, now you can tell me the real bad stuff."

Eight

The real bad stuff began a little less than fifteen months ago just after Vines was disbarred and Adair was sent to prison. It was then that Vines had packed one large suitcase, left his native state and driven the blue Mercedes to La Jolla, California, where he moved into a more or less rent-free beachfront condominium at Coast Boulevard and Pearl Street.

The expensively furnished two-bedroom apartment belonged to a former client, the oil exploration firm of Sanchez & Maloney—usually referred to by those in the oil business as Short Mex and Big Mick. When oil was nudging $30 a barrel the firm had bought the condominium as a weekend retreat the two partners could be whisked to by company jet.

They had managed to use it three times before offering it to Kelly Vines at the bargain rent of $3,000 a month, which he was to deduct from the $39,000 the wildcatters' firm still owed him but couldn't pay because oil by then was around $15 a barrel.

The $39,000 fee was what Vines—prior to his disbarment—had billed Sanchez & Maloney for persuading a vice-president of one of the majors to drop a $5-million lawsuit. The suit charged that Joe Maloney had knocked the vice-president down in the Petroleum Club bar and stomped him with an almost brand-new pair of lizardskin cowboy boots as a half-drunk Paco Sanchez had olé-ed his partner on.

The major oil company vice-president withdrew his suit after Kelly Vines let him examine photocopies of registration forms obtained from a motel down in Houston near the Intercontinental Airport.

"The young woman who shared these rooms with you on seven different occasions," Vines had said in what he always thought of as his iced-snot voice, "does, in fact, bear your surname, although she would seem to have been not your wife, but your sixteen-year-old niece."

Six months after the suit was dropped, which was two days after Vines's disbarment, Paco Sanchez and Joe Maloney came by to offer him the keys to the condominium.

"You can stay there as long as talk's cheap and shit stinks," Sanchez had said.

"Or until oil's back up to twenty-five a barrel," said Maloney.

Sanchez smiled sadly. "Like I said, Kelly. Forever."

Kelly Vines gave away or abandoned most of what he still owned, packed the one large suitcase and drove to California. This was a month after Jack Adair had entered the Federal penitentiary at Lompoc and two weeks and three days after Vines's wife had emptied her personal E. F. Hutton Cash Management fund of $43,912 and told friends, if not Vines, that she was flying to Las Vegas for a divorce.

She spent only four hours in Las Vegas—just long

enough to buy twenty-four Seconal capsules from a hotel bellhop and lose $4,350 at blackjack—before flying on to Los Angeles, where she checked into the Beverly Wilshire. Up in her room she searched the telephone directory and called the first psychiatrist she found who had a Beverly Hills address. With the use of only minimum guile, she talked him into giving her a same-day appointment.

Danielle Vines convinced the psychiatrist during their nine-minute session that she was very nervous, extremely depressed and unable to sleep because of her father's imprisonment and her husband's disgrace. The psychiatrist gave her an evaluation appointment for 7 A.M. the following Tuesday, his first free hour, and wrote her a prescription for twenty-four Seconal capsules.

Danielle Vines thanked him, had the prescription filled at the nearest pharmacy, returned to her room at the Beverly Wilshire and ordered up cinnamon toast, a bottle of wine and some Dramamine, the sea- and motion-sickness remedy. She ate the toast first, washing it down with the wine. Then she swallowed some Dramamine. After that she used what was left of the wine to wash down her hoard of four dozen Seconals, confident that the toast and Dramamine would help keep them down. After that she picked up the phone and called her brother, Paul Adair, in Washington, D.C., to tell him exactly what she had done.

Adair said, "So after she called Paul, he called you."

"No. He called the hotel back and got it organized. Doctor. Ambulance. Name of a hospital. No cops. No press."

Adair nodded. "I can almost hear him."

"He called the hospital then, which turned out to be in Santa Monica, and started out by talking money to them, which he said they seemed to appreciate. Once Paul had the hospital squared away—private room, round-the-clock nurses, a specialist, no visitors and all—then he called me."

Adair examined Vines thoughtfully. "First he told you about Dannie. And after that I'd say he got around to what was really on his mind."

Vines sighed. "He parceled out the blame, Jack."

"Who got the most—me?"

"He was very even-handed. We each got half."

"Then he flew out here?"

"That same night. I met him at LAX and we went to St. John's in Santa Monica."

"The hospital."

Vines nodded. "They'd pumped her stomach by then and she was out of intensive care and in the private room with a private nurse. But something had snapped or popped or fused because she didn't know me and she didn't know Paul. So after a few minutes we left and Paul went apeshit again."

"Still carrying on about you and me?"

"Still. But by then I was numb and the more he ranted, the more numb I got. It was almost pleasant—something like codeine. Finally, I got tired of listening and told him to fuck off."

Adair rose, walked to the window and looked out. "This the longest day of the year?"

"Tuesday was."

Adair turned. "What'd Paul say exactly, during his ranting and raving—as near as you can recollect?"

"He said he was going to ask them for a six-month leave of absence and if they wouldn't give it to him, fuck 'em, he'd quit. He said he'd use the leave to get to the bottom of the cesspool that you and I'd dragged Dannie down into. He also went on and on about the bribe and old Justice Fuller—but especially the bribe. How much was it really, and did somebody really take it, and who'd I really think put up the money? He used 'really' a lot."

"So what'd you say?"

"I told him I really didn't know, wished him well, drove back down to La Jolla and waited upon events."

Adair again turned to the window. "I think we're going to have one spectacular sunset." Still staring at the ocean, he said, "How long did it take exactly?"

"To kill him? Thirty-two days."

Adair turned from the window with a frown that was more thoughtful than puzzled. "Then he must've been getting somewhere."

"That occurred to me."

"He didn't do anything half-smart like sending you a report or a letter about what he was up to?"

"He called once."

"When?"

"Two days before he was killed. He said he was going to meet some guy in Tijuana who claimed to know something. I suggested he meet him instead at the San Diego zoo near the koalas with about five hundred witnesses around. Paul said he couldn't do that because the guy said La Migra was looking for him at all border checks. I suggested a nice long phone call. He said a phone call was never as good as a face-to-face. I asked if the guy had a name. He said it was Mr. Smith, laughed, hung up and that's the last thing he ever said to me."

"So he went down to Tijuana and somebody shot him twice and fixed it up as a suicide," Adair said. "If they'd shot him once, it might've worked, but twice meant they wanted to make it a statement—a declaration."

"That also occurred to me."

"Then there's poor Blessing Nelson and that price on my head."

"Another statement," Vines said. "And certainly a declaration."

"Plus the girl photographer in the back of the pink van. Floradora Flowers of Santa Barbara. When're we going to check them out?"

"First thing tomorrow."

Adair looked down at the carpet again. "Was there an autopsy on Paul?"

"A perfunctory one in T.J. I claimed his body. After I called his lawyer in Washington, I had it cremated. It was in his will."

"Who got the ashes?"

Vines nodded at the window. "The ocean. That was also in his will, although he probably meant the Atlantic. But since he didn't specify, he wound up in the Pacific. He didn't leave much—about ten thousand in a checking account, a two-year-old BMW and a hundred-thousand whole life policy some friend had sold him. He left it all to one of those Washington think tanks that's still trying to decide whether it's neo-conservative or neo-liberal."

"Not that it matters much anymore," Adair said, turning yet again to look at the ocean. "Funny about Paul, though. He never got interested in money—at least, not the way you and I did. If he hadn't gone into government, he could've made himself a ton of it."

"Maybe."

Adair turned to examine Vines with undisguised curiosity. "You ever like Paul?"

"I grew up with him and roomed with him for four years."

"Evasive."

Vines looked at something just beyond Adair's left ear. "I don't suppose I ever liked him. Not really. I respected his mind, envied his looks, despised his politics and very much wanted to fuck his sister."

"Which you eventually did."

"Which I eventually did."

Adair, his curiosity again evident, asked, "You ever like Dannie?"

"Very much."

"And now?"

"And now, Jack, I just love her."

Nine

It was still light that last Friday evening in June when they stopped along the outer edge of the seventh hairpin turn up on Garner Road. By raising himself slightly in the front seat of the Mercedes, Jack Adair could inspect most of Durango down below, including its five-block-long, three-block-wide business district, or downtown, which was bounded on the west by the Southern Pacific tracks. Just beyond the tracks were the ocean and what Chief Sid Fork liked to call "the longest one-foot-wide sharp-rock beach in the entire state of California."

As Adair had predicted, the sunset was spectacular, its last rays bathing the business district, including the lone seven-story skyscraper, in a soft warm light a stranger might have compared to gold—a more knowledgeable native to brass.

Adair was still taking in the view when he asked, "How much've we got left in that Bahamian bank?"

"Around three hundred thousand."

Adair turned to stare at Vines with disbelief and even shock.

"We had expenses, Jack. Your legal fees. The high cost of money laundering. Dannie's treatment. Blessing Nelson's mother. And me—since I ate and drank some of it up."

"We'll just have to make do then," Adair said, remembered something and added, "Keep sending that five hundred a month to Blessing's mother."

"For how long?"

"Until we run out of money," said Adair, and resumed his inspection of Durango down below.

Five blocks east of the SP tracks, the city's business district had failed in its attempt, many years ago, to flow around Handshaw Park, which was two city blocks of pines, magnolias, coral trees, eucalyptus, green grass when it rained, nine concrete picnic tables, a children's broken slide, some swings and a gray bandstand that once had been painted a glistening white.

Back when the bandstand still glistened, select members of the Durango High School marching band made a few vacation dollars by playing concerts in the park on summer Sunday afternoons. But as the city's tax base shrank, the budget ax fell first on the summer concerts, then on the marching band itself and, finally, on its director, Milt Steed, who had also taught art and, when last heard from, was playing cornet down in Disneyland.

Handshaw Park had been called simply City Park until B.D. Huckins was elected mayor. She renamed it after Dicky Handshaw, who had served four terms as mayor until Huckins beat him in the 1978 election, which was still remembered as the most vicious in the city's 148-year history.

Renaming the park had seemed at first like a nice conciliatory gesture. But that was before word got around of an exchange in the Blue Eagle Bar between Norm Trice and a prominent local attorney who regarded himself as a budding political savant. The attorney had claimed that next time out B.D. Huckins could easily be defeated by almost any candidate with balls and a few brains.

"Like you, huh?" Trice had asked.

"Sure. Like me. Why not?"

"Because," Trice had explained in a patient voice, "B.D. didn't name that park after Dicky Handshaw so folks'd remember him. She did it so guys like you'd remember what happened to him."

Kelly Vines said, "Seen enough?"

Jack Adair nodded, took one last look and settled back down into the leather seat. "About two dozen streets running east and west," he said, "and maybe two and a half dozen running north and south. Too many vacant lots. No architectural landmarks to speak of, unless you count a lot of Victorian piles all tarted up in that green and cream they like to use. Probably bed-and-breakfast inns now—or lawyers' offices. Wonder why they always use cream and green?"

After Vines said he didn't know, Adair asked another question. "And since I sure as hell didn't see any of them down by the tracks, where do you think the rich folks live?"

"Up here in the hills," Vines said as he drove slowly down the cul-de-sac called Don Emilio Drive. "Where they always live."

At the end of the dead-end street they could see Mayor Huckins's neat blue two-bedroom bungalow and admire her fine stand of jacarandas. The other six houses that lined the short drive were no more grand than the mayor's. Appraising each house as they drove by, Jack Adair said, "Well, if this is how the rich live, God help the poor."

It was the mayor herself who opened the door after Vines rang the bell. She wore a black skirt, a gray silk blouse and not much makeup. Her jewelry consisted of a man's gold tank watch that may have come from Cartier and a pair of plain gold earrings that may have come from a drugstore. Vines thought she looked as though she didn't much care where either came from.

B.D. Huckins looked first at Adair, then at Vines and back at the older man. "You're Jack Adair," she said, holding out her hand. As they shook hands, she said, "How'd you like to be called—Judge, Mr. Chief Justice or Mr. Adair?"

"Jack, if it won't make you uncomfortable."

Huckins smiled a noncommittal smile and looked at Kelly Vines. "Mr. Vines," she said, holding out her hand.

"Mayor Huckins," said Vines, accepting the hand and finding that it reminded him strangely of the blond Dixie's. The mayor's hand was as slim and cool and firm as Dixie's, but the handshake didn't last nearly as long because it was of the quick squeeze and even quicker release variety favored by seasoned campaigners.

She led them from a small foyer into the living room, whose principal piece of furniture was a long cream couch from the 1930s in remarkable repair. There was also a chocolate-brown leather club chair, which, from a carefully positioned brass floor lamp, was obviously where she did her reading. Both chair and couch were drawn up to a coffee table that was actually an old steamer trunk, laid on its side and plastered with bright labels from ancient European hotels and extinct steamship lines.

On the well-polished oak floor was a large and gaudy woven wool rug that Vines suspected of being from the Yucatán. There was no television set but plenty of books and on the walls were three Monet prints and two posters.

One of the posters displayed a tasty-looking bunch of wet purple grapes with a slogan that read: "The Wrath of Grapes. Join the Boycott . . . Again!" The other poster showed a highly stylized worker banging away at something with a couple of hammers. Below him was Bertolt Brecht's forlorn hope: "Art is not a mirror held up to reality, but a hammer with which to shape it."

Vines followed Adair and Huckins around the dining area's glass and chrome table, into the kitchen, out the back door and onto a used-brick patio where Chief of Police Sid Fork, wearing an apron made out of what looked like mattress ticking, presided over the charcoal grill.

They talked first about the weather and, after exhausting that, turned to the presidential primary campaigns whose earlier stages Adair said he had followed from behind the penitentiary walls. He introduced his fifteen-month stay in Lompoc by referring to it as, "When I was in jail." With that out of the way, Vines noticed that both Fork and Huckins relaxed, although he thought the bourbon everyone was drinking could have had something to do with it.

"When I was in jail," Adair had said, and went on to describe his informal, admittedly unscientific sampling of the inmates' political preferences. He confessed he was somewhat surprised to find an overwhelming majority rigidly conservative and almost morbidly patriotic.

Sid Fork said he wasn't surprised. "If you'd've asked them to come up with an ideal ticket for either party, they'd've said John Wayne for President and Clint Eastwood for Vice President. And if you'd've mentioned that Wayne was dead, they'd've said that's all you know because of what they'd heard from a guy who knows a cousin of Wayne's bodyguard. And this guy who knows the bodyguard's cousin swore on a stack of Bibles that the Duke's holed up in Rio Lobo, not dead at all, but just waiting for the right moment. And if you'd've asked them where the hell Rio Lobo is, they'd've said exactly twenty-nine point four miles west of Fargo."

His analysis delivered, the chief took a long drink of his whiskey and water, set the glass down, turned to the grill, gave one of the steaks an almost vicious stab with a fork, flipped it over and turned back to Adair.

"What'd you really think of those assholes they had you locked up with?"

"I sometimes found their thought processes interesting and oddly entertaining. But then I'm partial to the odd."

"Most of 'em stupid?"

"None too bright anyway."

"Any of 'em smart—maybe even brilliant?"

"A few."

"How about charming? You run into any charming assholes?"

"An even rarer bird."

Fork seemed prepared to continue the colloquy but changed his mind when B.D. Huckins asked whether the steaks were ready yet.

"If everyone likes 'em rare, they are," Fork said and looked at Kelly Vines, as if daring him to ask for well done. But Vines said he liked his steak rare and the ex-Chief Justice said he never ate his any other way.

They ate at the redwood trestle table on the patio, not talking much except to compliment Fork on the steaks, the Caesar salad, his scratch biscuits and the baked Idaho potatoes. When Jack Adair, a master of small talk, asked whether the potatoes had been baked in a real oven or in a microwave, Fork said a real oven because B.D. wouldn't have a microwave in the house. He said she still thought they caused cancer although he'd bought one for his own house because who the hell wants to wait sixty minutes for a potato to bake when a microwave'll do it in ten?

Conversation died then and nobody, not even Adair, could think of anything pertinent to say. Just before the silence grew uncomfortable, B.D. Huckins rose and asked whether everyone wanted coffee. Everyone did, so she went into the kitchen and returned a few minutes later with a tray that held a Thermos carafe, four tan mugs, cream and sugar. As she poured she announced without apology that there was no dessert, although if they'd like something sweet, she could offer Benedictine and brandy. No one wanted any.

Mayor Huckins sat back down at the trestle table, had a sip of her coffee and smiled politely at Kelly Vines. "I believe you ran into my sister, Dixie."

Vines tried, with fair success, to conceal shock behind mild surprise. "I don't think she said her name was Huckins."

"Well, she wouldn't, of course, since her name is Mansur. Dixie Mansur. She married an Iranian. One of the rich ones, thank God."

Vines nodded, as if approving of Dixie's wise choice and good fortune. "There's not a lot of family resemblance."

"We had different fathers. Mine was Huckins; hers was Venable."

"I assume Dixie turned in a report."

"She gave you an A-plus. If she hadn't, we wouldn't be talking."

Sid Fork rested his elbows on the table and leaned toward Vines, his expression perhaps a trifle too friendly. "Soldier Sloan claims you're okay, too," he said and leaned back to wait for Vines's reaction.

Without expression and using only enough inflection to make it a question, Vines said, "Does he, now?"

Fork nodded. "I guess Soldier'd qualify as one of those guys I mentioned earlier—a smart and charming asshole."

"Extremely charming, but not too smart. Where'd you meet him?"

"Mutual friends. Soldier says both you and the judge here represented him at different times. But it's sort of hard to tell when Soldier's lying."

"You can believe him, at least on that point," Adair said. "I did represent him long ago when I was still in private practice and when, I should add, both Soldier and I were considerably younger. Years after I went on the bench I heard he was in some kind of trouble whose exact nature escapes me. So I sent word for him to get in touch with Kelly, who, if memory serves, managed to get him out of whatever mess he was in."

Turning to the mayor, Adair gave her his most winning smile and said, "So it would seem we are who we claim to be." The smile vanished. "Are you?"

"You mean have we ever done this kind of thing before?" she said.

"Yes," Jack Adair said. "That's exactly what I mean."

Ten

According to the mayor, it had begun ten years ago with the passage of Proposition 13 that rolled back California property taxes and virtually wrecked the budgets of many of the state's cities, particularly the smaller ones.

"Thirteen wouldn't even let a city like Durango issue general obligation bonds until a couple of years ago," she said. "Not that there was anybody jumping up and down to buy them."

"How bad did it get?" Adair asked.

"We almost went broke. And we would've if the economy hadn't picked up a little, at least for a while there, and if it hadn't been for the donations from, well, from certain benefactors."

Adair nodded, his eyes curious, his expression bland. "How many benefactors have lined up, cash in hand, over the last nine or ten years?"

She looked at Fork. "A dozen?"

"An even dozen."

"How much did each one—donate?" Vines asked. "On the average?"

"The first four, one hundred thousand," Huckins said. "Then inflation kicked in so the next eight had to come up with two hundred thousand."

"Each?"

"Each."

"Two million all told then," Adair said. "And in exchange for this generosity, each philanthropist was provided with a safe haven? A sanctuary?"

"A hideout," said the mayor.

"Were any of them avoiding the law?" Vines said. "Or is that any of my business?"

"One was sort of avoiding the law," Fork said. "But it was some weird kind of CIA thing, so B.D. and I said to hell with it and let him buy in. The rest of them were all dodging the opposition."

"Business rivals?"

"Guys who wanted to kill 'em," Fork said.

"Did they ever succeed?" Adair asked with obvious interest.

"Never," the chief said.

"Never in Durango," B. D. Huckins corrected him. "But two of them got antsy, a couple of years apart, and left before they should've although we tried to talk them both out of it. The one who left first fell off a building in L. A. Mid-Wilshire, I think. The other got hit by a car in north Dallas that backed up over him just to make sure he was dead. The other ten are all okay as far as we know, but . . ." She shrugged.

"They don't write," Fork said.

"They don't even call," said the mayor with a small smile.

"And the two million dollars?" Adair asked, looking around as though hoping to find something it had been spent on.

"It helped keep things going," the mayor said. "The frills anyhow. The library stayed open, just barely, and so did the VD clinic and the day-care center, at least until GE pulled out and we had to close it. The center, I mean, not the clinic. The rest of the money, what there was, went for police and maintenance."

"Nobody ever questioned these—donations?" Adair asked.

"We've got a mayor-city council type of government here," she said. "And since I've been mayor each new council member has been, well, carefully elected."

Although Adair nodded approvingly, she volunteered nothing else. Another silence threatened, but Vines fended it off with a question to Fork. "What about your cops, Chief?"

"Mind if I do a little bragging?"

"Why not?"

"Well, I'd say we've got one of the best small-city forces going. There's me, four detectives, twelve uniforms and three clerks who double at the jail when they have to. There's also a county deputy sheriff, Henry Quirt, who's got a whole lot of other ground to cover so we make sure he doesn't waste any time around here."

"*Four* detectives?" Adair said, raising an eyebrow.

"Four. And every last one of 'em personally recruited by me. Tell you how I did it. I went looking for experience— guys that'd put in their twenty years and had their pensions and maybe a little baksheesh salted away, but were only forty-one, forty-five, around in there, maybe even fifty and kind of bored with sitting around the house. So I offered 'em thirty a year, God's own climate, great hunting and fishing, cheap housing, free dental and health, light work and long vacations."

"And they jumped at it," Vines said.

"Who wouldn't? Two of them're out of homicide in Chicago and Detroit; one's out of Dallas bunco and fraud, and the other's a narc who wanted to get out of Miami in one piece. They've got about eighty-five years' worth of collective experience and nobody slips by." He smiled knowingly at Vines. "Absolutely nobody."

Vines thought back to the previous night and the blond Dixie. Dixie Mansur. "Those two drunks at the bar in the Holiday Inn, right?"

Fork gave him a small proud nod.

"Congratulations," Vines said.

It was then that Jack Adair decided to find out whether he could close the deal. Turning to the mayor and forcing a certain amount of unfelt heartiness into his voice, he said, "Well, it would seem that we are indeed in most capable hands."

"Not yet," she said, ignoring both the compliment and the heartiness. "Not till we discuss money."

"Yes. Of course. How much would, say, a month or two cost us?"

"Two hundred and fifty thousand regardless of whether it's a week, a month or a year. If somebody else is after Vines, the rate doubles. If the same guys who're after you are after him, you get a two-fer."

Since hearty had won him nothing, Adair turned grave and judicious, nodding at Huckins as if the sum she had mentioned, although not inconsequential, was by no means staggering. "Suppose," he said, "your fee were to be increased substantially for only slight additional effort on your part?"

"We don't do takeouts," the chief said, his voice firm, his expression forbidding.

The mayor gave the chief an exasperated look, then studied Adair for several seconds. "Go on," she said.

"I have to confess something first," he said. "I don't know who wants to kill me or have me killed."

Huckins nodded impatiently. "That's standard. None of them ever seems to know who'll be sent to do it."

"I can only presume," Adair said, "that it'll be arranged by whoever attempted to make it appear that I and another justice on the court accepted substantial bribes. He was Justice Mark T. Fuller. The 'T' was for Tyson."

Sid Fork stretched, yawned without apology and gave the night sky an inspection. "We heard about that. We also heard about your son—Paul, wasn't it? A suicide down in T.J. And just this afternoon up there in Lompoc some dude with a funny name got it. From what I hear, he was your baby-sitter." Fork brought his gaze down from the stars. "Blessing something."

"Blessing Nelson," said Adair. "A friend and associate."

Resting her elbows on the trestle table and her chin on her right fist, B.D. Huckins examined Adair curiously. "Maybe I'm just not tracking you," she said.

"How so?"

"You're not offering us a lot of money to do almost nothing extra."

"No. What I'm proposing—" Adair broke off to look at Vines. "Since it's your grand design, perhaps you'd best explain it."

Vines nodded, stared at Fork for several seconds, nodded again, as if at some inevitable conclusion, and turned his stare on B.D. Huckins, who grew impatient and said, "I'm listening."

Directing his remarks solely at the mayor, and choosing each phrase with care, Vines said, "What we want you to do—is send out word—that you'll sell Jack Adair—to whoever wants him—for one million dollars."

The mayor leaned back, picked up her tan coffee mug, had a swallow of cold coffee and put the mug down, not taking her eyes off Kelly Vines. "You want us to fake an offer—"

"The million will be real."

"—that could damage our reputations."

"Who with?" Vines asked.

"He's got a point, B.D.," Fork said.

"Tell me this," she said. "Why would anybody pay a million for a Jack Adair?"

"Because of what he knows," Vines said.

She looked skeptically at Adair. "Which is what?"

Adair sighed. "I don't know what it is. Or maybe it's something I do know but haven't sufficiently analyzed."

"Must be worth a lot—whatever it is that you don't know you know."

"Obviously."

"Have you thought of faking a blackmail pass at them?"

"Alas, I'm not a blackmailer and I don't know who they are."

"I said *fake* a blackmail pass."

"I heard what you said."

She turned from Adair to Sid Fork. "Then it'd be up to us to set it up, wouldn't it?"

Fork frowned. "Won't be easy."

She turned next to Kelly Vines, her delicate chin thrust out, her gray eyes calculating. "So how do we split the million?"

"We don't," Vines said.

It was obvious to Vines that the mayor didn't like surprises, pleasant or unpleasant. She narrowed her eyes until they were almost closed and pressed her lips into their grimmest line. If she frowns, Vines thought, the deal's off. But Huckins didn't frown. Instead, she opened her eyes wide and let her mouth relax into a faint smile.

"We get it all then—Sid, the city and me."

Vines nodded. "If you succeed."

"And if we don't?"

"You get nothing and Jack here probably gets a poorly attended memorial service."

"Then it's on what you lawyers call a contingency basis."

"Which is how we lawyers get rich."

The mayor's faint smile was still in place as she turned to the chief of police. "Well?"

Fork gave his wing commander mustache a thoughtful brush with his left thumb, frowned at Vines and said, "I still get the cane, no matter what?"

"No matter what," Vines said.

The chief turned to B.D. Huckins with a grin. "I think it sounds rich."

A silence developed, which no one tried to end. It was finally broken when the mayor again looked at the chief of police and gave him an order in the form of a suggestion.

"Why not take Mr. Vines down to the Blue Eagle for a drink while the judge and I go over a few details?"

It was obvious that Fork could think of several reasons why not, but he made no protest. He merely turned to Kelly Vines and said, "Like to go have a couple of quick ones?"

Vines thought of asking if they had any choice, but what he said was, "The quicker the better."

Eleven

At 11:26 P.M. on that last Friday in June, the pink Ford van, now stripped of all commercial identification, deposited a short thick man with a clerical collar in front of Felipe's Pet shop at 532 North Fifth Street, just four doors down from the Blue Eagle Bar's corner location.

The pet shop had closed at its usual time of 6 P.M. In its window was a jumbled pile of four puppies asleep on their bed of shredded newspaper. The puppies were a mixed breed the pet shop owner was advertising as Sheplabs. As the pink van sped away, the man in the clerical collar glanced up and down Fifth Street, saw nothing of interest and turned to the pet shop window.

He smiled at the sleeping puppies, ignoring his reflection in the glass that revealed small, rather gray teeth and a mouth so thin it seemed almost lipless. The mouth was much too close to his small snout of a nose whose right nostril seemed half again as large as the left one. He was bareheaded and his thick black hair was going gray and had been cut, or clippered, into an uneven flattop by an apparently unsteady hand.

To complement his clerical collar he wore black shoes and a too-tight black suit made from a dull synthetic material. The suit was almost the same shade of black as his eyes, which could have been those of some old and unrepentant libertine, dying alone and bored by the process.

The man flicked his middle fingernail twice against the shop window. But when the sleeping puppies continued to ignore him, he stopped smiling, turned left, away from the Blue Eagle Bar, and hurried down the sidewalk on uncommonly short legs. After forty or fifty feet his fast walk slowed to a normal stroll, then to a hesitant saunter and finally to a full stop.

He turned quickly, not quite spinning around, his eyes raking both sides of Fifth Street. He nodded then, as if remembering the cigarettes or the dozen eggs he had forgotten to buy, and retraced his steps, hurrying past the sleeping puppies without a glance. When he reached the corner, he took one last rapid look around and ducked into Norm Trice's Blue Eagle Bar.

Although 2 A.M. was the legal closing hour, Trice often closed his bar and grill around midnight because by then most of his customers had run out of money and gone home. But if it was payday, or the second or third of the month when the welfare, unemployment, disability and Social Security checks arrived, Trice would stay open until two and sometimes even three or, as he put it, until they drank up the government money.

There were no customers in the Blue Eagle when the man in the clerical collar walked in, took a seat at the bar and ordered a glass of beer. After Trice served him, the man paid and said in a cold thin tenor, "They say the mayor drops by here once in a while."

"Who's they?" said Trice, who never gave away anything except unsolicited advice.

"And the chief of police. I hear he drops in sometimes, too."

"So?"

The man took a swallow of beer and smiled his gray smile. "So this friend of hers, the mayor's, asked me to give her a letter and I thought maybe I'd give it to you and you could give it to her."

"Give it to her yourself down at City Hall tomorrow."

"I'm leaving town tonight."

Trice sighed. "Okay, but next time buy one of those things they sell at the post office. You know—stamps."

The man nodded, smiling his thanks, reached into the right pocket of his black suit and withdrew a five-by-seven-inch sealed manila envelope. He slid it across the bar to Trice, who looked down to read the white peel-off label. On it someone had typed: Mayor B. D. Huckins, Durango, California.

Trice picked up the envelope, noticing it contained some kind of stiffening, cardboard probably, and placed it on a shelf beneath the bar. "I'll see she gets it."

"You won't forget?"

"I just said she'd get it."

The man with the clerical collar smiled, nodded his thanks again and said, "Maybe you could do me another little favor?"

"What?"

"Could you cash this?"

He handed Trice a personal check made out to cash for $50 and drawn on a Wells Fargo bank in San Francisco. The name signed to the check was Ralph B. Farr. Up in the left-hand corner, the same name was printed above a San Francisco address that Trice thought was probably in the Mission District.

Still staring down at the check with something akin to

revulsion, Trice said, "Well, maybe if you could get the Pope to endorse it, Padre, or even just a bishop, I might see my way clear to— "

Trice's elaborate refusal collapsed as he looked up from the check and saw the .22-caliber semiautomatic in the false priest's left hand.

"I'll just take what's in the register then," the man said in his thin tenor that Trice decided was the only thin thing about him except his lips. Two hundred pounds at least, Trice memorized, maybe two-ten and no more'n five-one, if that. The fucker looks like an eight ball in that priest suit—like Father fucking Eight Ball.

Pretending to consider the demand for the cash register's contents, Trice frowned with unfelt regret and said, "Well, Your Eminence, there's really not a hell of a lot in there, not much more'n you'd find in Saint Maggie's poor box, if that—fifty, maybe fifty-two bucks."

"That'll do nicely," the false priest said and shot Norm Trice in the face, once just below the left eye, and once just above the mouth, the .22 short rounds making scarcely any more noise than two doors slamming.

The short man in the clerical collar hurried out of the Blue Eagle and into the waiting pink van. Diagonally across the street from the bar, another man stepped out of the dark recessed doorway of Marvin's Jewelry. The other man was in his mid-thirties and had graying hair. He wore a white shirt, faded blue jeans and old high-top Converse basketball shoes, the pro model, even though he was an inch or so under six feet. He also wore a sad, almost resigned look.

After he watched the speeding pink van disappear down North Fifth Street, the man stuck his hands in his pockets, turned and, with head bowed and sad expression still in place, walked slowly in the opposite direction.

Twelve

Kelly Vines and Sid Fork walked into the empty Blue Eagle Bar eight minutes later. Fork looked around for Norm Trice, called his name, even looked in the men's toilet and, finally, behind the bar, where Trice lay dead on the duckboards, the $50 check, made out to cash and signed by Ralph B. Farr, still clutched in his right hand.

The chief of police said, "Aw shit, Norm," and knelt beside the body. He noticed the check and removed it from Trice's hand by pinching a corner of it with the nails of his right thumb and forefinger. Rising, Fork carefully laid the check on the bar and warned Vines not to touch it.

Kelly Vines twisted his head around to read what was written and printed on the check. "Fifty dollars, made out to cash and signed by a Ralph B. Farr. Wells Fargo bank in San Francisco."

"Don't touch it," Fork warned again, turned to the old mechanical cash register, hit the no-sale key and glanced at the cash drawer's contents. "About a hundred and fifty, around in there," he said, closed the drawer and picked up the bar phone. "You want to get back here and pour us a couple?"

"Sure," Vines said and went around the bar as Fork tapped out a number on the phone. Vines selected a bottle of Wild Turkey, found two glasses and was looking for the ice when he noticed the manila envelope. He read the mayor's name on the peel-off label, dropped ice into the glasses, poured in the whiskey, added tap water and turned to tell Fork what he had found.

The chief of police was still on the phone, talking in that low and confidential tone often used either to announce deaths or spread rumors. After Fork hung up, Vines handed him a drink and said, "I found an envelope addressed to the mayor."

"Where?"

Vines pointed. "You touch it?" Fork asked.

"No."

Fork walked over and bent down to read the stick-on label. "It's to B.D, all right." He straightened and had a long swallow of his drink. "Maybe I oughta open it."

"You're the chief of police."

"I don't want to mess up any fingerprints."

"There won't be any fingerprints," Vines said.

"Why not?"

"Let's say the shooter comes in and orders a beer."

"Why a beer?"

Vines pointed to the two-thirds-full glass of beer on the bar that still had condensed water beads on it. Fork gave the glass a grudging nod. Vines said, "He orders the beer, drinks some of it, hands the bartender—"

"The owner," Fork said. "Norm Trice."

"He hands the owner the envelope and—"

"How do you know about the envelope?"

"I'm guessing," Vines said. "Anyway, he hands it to him and now we're supposed to have fingerprints on a manila envelope and maybe on a beer glass. Then he asks the owner to cash a check. More fingerprints on the check—plus yours all over the phone and the cash register. When the owner tells him he won't cash his rotten check, the guy shoots him. Twice. In the face. The shots go in six inches apart, maybe five, which tells us the shooter's either very lucky or very good. The owner drops and the shooter empties the cash register."

"Except he didn't."

"I know," Vines said. "Which means that although he may've left the mayor a message—the envelope and the body—I wouldn't bet on any fingerprints."

"A pro, huh?"

"Open the envelope and find out."

"It's evidence."

"That's why you should open it," Vines said. "Before somebody else does."

Fork put his glass down, picked up the manila envelope and ripped its flap open with a thumb. He pulled out a piece of gray cardboard with six glossy black-and-white photographs bound to it by a tan rubber band. Fork stripped away the rubber band and, one by one, dealt the photographs onto the bar.

Five of the six photographs had been taken through the windshield of Vines's blue Mercedes. The first showed a startled Vines, raising his hands to his face. The second showed him with his hands over his face, peering through his fingers. The third showed a startled Jack Adair. The fourth showed Adair smiling. The fifth showed Jack Adair sticking out his tongue. The sixth and final photograph showed Sid Fork and B. D. Huckins standing beside a car, the driver door open, deep in conversation, Fork doing the talking and Huckins looking up at him.

"Whose car?" Vines asked.

"B. D.'s."

"When was it taken?"

"Beats me," Fork said. "When'd they take the ones of you?"

"Today."

"Where?"

"Lompoc."

"Who took 'em?"

"A girl photographer from the back of a pink Ford van with a green sign on it that said, 'Floradora Flowers, Santa Barbara.'"

"You hid and Adair stuck out his tongue."

"A metaphor, you think?" Vines said.

"Beats me," said Fork and bent over to look more closely at the photographs of Mayor Huckins and himself. "This one of me and B. D.'s not bad."

Vines heard a car door slam, then another one. He scooped up the photographs, stuffed them into the ripped-open manila envelope and shoved it down into his right hip pocket just before the Blue Eagle's front door banged open and two men in their forties strode in, wearing the proprietary air that marks a policeman almost as plainly as his badge or uniform.

Vines assumed they were the two homicide detectives Fork had recruited from Detroit and Chicago. He also recognized them as the pair of mock-drunks from the Holiday Inn cocktail lounge. One was of average height, black, scholarly-looking and egg-bald. A leather gadget bag hung by a strap from his left shoulder. The other resembled a too-tall elf with nimble brown eyes and a long sly face. The brown eyes walked up and down Vines as the man moved slowly toward Fork. Vines remembered the too-tall man as the one who had climbed down from the barstool and said, "Fuck California," in a clear and pleasant voice.

When the tall man reached Sid Fork, he said, "Old Norm, huh?"

"Shot," Fork said. "Twice."

The detective leaned over the bar and peered down at the body on the duckboards. The bald detective didn't bother to look. Instead, he put the gadget bag on the bar, unzipped it and took out a Minolta camera with a built-in flash. He went behind the bar and began photographing the dead Norm Trice. After taking six or seven photographs, he looked at the tall detective and said, "Looks like somebody with a twenty-two."

Fork decided it was time for introductions. He indicated the detective with the camera and said, "Joe Huff, Kelly Vines." They nodded at each other. Fork then introduced the too-tall detective as Wade Bryant. After the tall detective and Vines exchanged hellos, Fork said, "We got here about seven, maybe eight minutes ago."

"Where was the check then?" Bryant asked. Although the check still lay on the bar, Vines couldn't recall Bryant even giving it a glance.

"It was in Norm's hand," Fork said. "The right one."

"Take a look in the till?"

Fork nodded. "About a hundred and fifty there."

Bryant shook his head and frowned, as if disappointed so far by what he had seen and heard. He reached into the pocket of his white short-sleeved shirt, took out a pack of Lucky Strikes and lit one, blowing the smoke to his left and away from the others. "It doesn't parse," he said.

"Why not?" said Fork.

"Guy comes in and orders a beer," Bryant said, giving the two-thirds-full glass of beer a brief look. "He drinks a swallow or two and then asks to cash a personal out-of-town check. That means he sure as shit didn't know Norm. So when Norm turns him down, the guy takes out a twenty-two or maybe even a twenty-five and plinks Norm twice in the face, which is pretty fair country shooting. Then the guy takes off, leaving behind what's in the till and also the check with his name, address and phone number on it just in case we want to call the San Francisco cops and have 'em go pick him up."

Joe Huff, the detective with the camera, came around the bar, glanced at Vines, started putting the Minolta back into the gadget bag and said, "You have any theories, Mr. Vines?"

"Does Trice have a wife?" Vines said, more or less answering the question with one of his own.

"He's got a wife," Sid Fork said and looked at Huff. "You want to go tell Virginia?"

"Not me," Huff said.

"That's what they pay chiefs of police for," Bryant said. "To bear the bad news—especially when it's to Virginia Trice."

Fork looked at Vines. "You want to come along?"

"No, but I will."

"Before you go, Sid," Bryant said, looked closely at the Wells Fargo check, went around the bar, picked up the phone and tapped out a long-distance number. He waited through what Vines decided were five rings before the call was answered.

"May I speak to Ralph B. Farr, please? . . . Mr. Farr, this is Detective Bryant with the Durango police department . . . Durango, *California* . . . I'm calling to ask if any of your Wells Fargo checks were lost or stolen recently?"

After five minutes of conversation, most of it spent reassuring Ralph B. Farr that if his stolen wallet and checkbook were found, they would be promptly returned, the call ended. Bryant turned to Sid Fork.

"Somebody lifted them out of his hip pocket somewhere on Geary two weeks ago. He reported it to the cops. Which means what we've got here is either a wacko or a pro. If it's a pro, he's long gone. If it's a wacko, well, who knows?"

"Maybe he's both," Vines said.

Bryant's eyes again made their trip up and down Kelly

Vines. "A professional wacko? Now that's something to bite into."

"I like it," Joe Huff said.

Fork looked at his watch. "Well, we've got to go. You guys know what to do."

"Yeah, we know."

"While I'm consoling the widow Trice, get Jacoby down here and see if he can lift some prints."

"Prints," Bryant said and chuckled. "Prints," he said again, as if repeating a punch line, and laughed out loud as he turned to Joe Huff. "Hear that, Joe? The chief just got off another of his zingers."

"I'm not laughing," Huff said, "but only because a loud laugh bespeaks a vacant mind." He paused. "Goldsmith."

"Paraphrased," Vines said.

"And improved," said Joe Huff with no trace of a smile.

Thirteen

When they went from the kitchen into the living room after doing the dishes—he washed, she dried—B.D. Huckins waved Adair to the long cream couch and asked whether he'd like a brandy.

"No, thanks."

Adair waited until she was seated in the chocolate-brown leather club chair before he lowered himself to the couch. When she crossed her legs, not carelessly, but indifferently, he glimpsed the tops of the stockings she wore instead of panty hose, which made him wonder whether garter belts had made a comeback during his fifteen months in prison.

"Tell me about that cane," she said. "The one Sid wants."

"It was my grandfather's."

"An heirloom?"

"A curiosity. He won it off a gambler in nineteen twenty just after Prohibition began. The handle unscrews and there's a stoppered glass tube inside that holds about four ounces of hooch. That's what he always called his liquor—

hooch. After repeal in thirty-three our state stayed dry and my grandfather passed the cane on to my old man, who eventually passed it on to me. I would've given it to my son except he thought it was dumb."

"So you passed it on to Vines."

"For safekeeping."

"He was more reliable than your son?"

"Just closer. Geographically. My son was in Washington; Kelly was in La Jolla."

"And you were in Lompoc."

"I was in Lompoc."

"What business was he in?"

"Paul? He was a lawyer like Kelly and I, but he was never in private practice. By the time he was eighteen, maybe nineteen, he'd already decided on a career with the Federal government."

"Your going to jail couldn't have helped his career much."

"Didn't hurt it. Right after I was sentenced he got jumped up from the civil service equivalent of light colonel to brigadier general."

Huckins's full mouth went into its wry smile. "Washington must've liked his politics."

"The current brand and Paul's made a snug fit."

"And yours?"

"In my family the politics of the sons has always been opposite their fathers'. My grandfather, who won the cane off the gambler, was a Debs socialist. His son—my old man—sat down and cried when Taft lost the nomination to Eisenhower in fifty-two."

She leaned back in the leather chair. "So when did the vote bug bite?"

"In high school. I was a pretty fair debater and I got the notion of becoming a lawyer and maybe going into politics after I discovered how good winning made me feel. Win-

86

ning anything. Later, I discovered there's nothing like winning an election. Absolutely nothing."

"How old were you?"

"When I first ran? Twenty-seven. I got elected county attorney, served a couple of two-year terms, sent some rich crooks to jail, got my name in the paper and then went back into private practice where I made a nice living defending the same kind of rich crooks I'd once prosecuted. When I thought I'd made enough money, I ran for the supreme court and won."

"How much was enough?"

Adair shrugged. "Two or three million, around in there."

"How'd you get to be chief justice?"

"The members of the court elect one of their own every four years."

"Sounds weird."

"It's a weird state. After I'd served on the court four years, they always elected me for some reason."

"For some reason," she said.

Adair nodded and leaned forward, elbows on his knees. He made no attempt to hide his curiosity when he said, "I'm obliged to hear about it."

"About what?"

"How you really got elected mayor."

Huckins examined Adair dispassionately, as if he were some just-caught fish that she could either keep or toss back into the lake. Finally, after almost twenty seconds, she said, "All right."

Adair edged forward on the couch and used his gravest voice to say, "When you come to the part where it gets nasty, Mayor, as it always does, just keep on going and don't worry about my sensibilities." He gave her a small smile. "Such as they are."

B.D. Huckins said there were nine of them in the Day-Glo General Motors school bus that pulled into Durango that night in 1968. The next morning, four of them decided to stay. The other five wanted to keep heading for the Rocky Mountain Durango in Colorado. A coin was tossed. Those who were Colorado-bound called heads and won both the toss and the psychedelic bus.

Staying on in the California Durango, she said, were herself, then 16; her 12-year-old half sister, Dixie Venable; Sid Fork, 18; and a 20-year-old nut case who some days said his name was Teddy Jones and other days Teddy Smith.

Huckins said Teddy was a drinker and a doper who fried and pickled his brain with acid and gin and anything else he could inhale, swallow or stick in his arm. But Teddy was also the only one who had any money. When he rented a four-room house (more shack than house, she claimed) on Boatright Street out on the eastern edge of Durango in what even then was a rural slum, the other three moved in with him.

She said the communal living lasted three weeks, maybe four. It ended when she and Fork came back from the beach one afternoon. It was a real beach then, she said, with plenty of sand and not anything like it is now. Anyway, she and Fork went in the house and found the 12-year-old Dixie naked and tied to the bed. Teddy was equally naked and drunk on gin and apparently trying to do it to Dixie with the gin bottle because, Huckins said, he probably couldn't do it any other way.

Sid Fork picked up something, a sash weight, she thought, and knocked Teddy down with it and kicked him senseless. When he woke up, Fork had all of Teddy's money, which she remembered as being about $300— almost a thousand in today's dollars. Fork told Teddy he could have his money back after he got the next bus out of town. She said there were still two bus lines serving Durango then—Greyhound and Trailways.

So that's what Teddy did, she said. Sid Fork walked him

into town, bought his ticket, put him on the bus, gave him back his money and told him if he ever saw him in Durango again, he'd drown him in the ocean.

Although that was the last of Teddy Jones or Smith, she, Fork and Dixie still had to eat. So she and Fork got jobs—he in a gas station and she in a drugstore where the owner-pharmacist, a nice enough old guy of about 45, started hitting on her until she told him if he didn't cut it out, she'd tell his wife.

The three of them managed to get by until late August of 1968 when the gas station where Fork worked was burgled. The owner suspected Fork, of course, she said. But being a class-A shit, didn't accuse him or fire him or even go to the cops. What he did, she said, was worse. Much worse.

Huckins thought it was two or possibly three weeks later when two FBI suits from Santa Barbara drove up to a gas pump. Sid came out and they asked him for his draft card. That tore it, she said. The gas station owner had turned Fork in for draft evasion and three weeks later he was in the Army and four or five months after that he was an MP in Saigon.

After Fork left, Huckins said she went to the owner of the drugstore and told him if he still wanted to go to bed with her on a regular basis, it would cost him $200 a month on top of what he was already paying her. The pharmacist-owner said he'd like to think about it. Three days later, he asked her to stay after work.

The pharmacist told her he'd maybe come up with a solution. There were these two friends of his, both real nice guys, one of them a lawyer and the other a CPA, and both of them, like him, members of the Durango City Council. And they, all three of them, he meant, were willing to set up a kind of cooperative.

What they wanted to do, she said, was pay her $150 a month each. The pharmacist would get Monday and

Wednesday nights; the lawyer, Tuesdays and Fridays; and the CPA, Thursdays and Saturdays. Huckins said they thought she ought to have Sundays off.

Huckins said she made the pharmacist a counterproposal. She told him she'd agree, providing they'd fix it so Dixie could enter school in September without any hassle about a transcript of previous school records. Her second condition was that since she didn't see any future in selling aspirins and Kotex, she wanted a job with either the lawyer or the CPA so she could learn something practical.

She said it took a week of negotiations before they agreed. The CPA gave her a job as file clerk and relief receptionist and Dixie enrolled in the seventh grade. Later, she said, when the CPA noticed his new file clerk's head for figures, he started teaching her basic bookkeeping and even sent her to shorthand and typing classes at the Durango High School's afternoon continuation program that, due to Proposition 13, got discontinued nine years ago.

After she'd been with the CPA for about three years, Huckins said, he made her office manager. And it was just about then that Sid Fork came back from Vietnam.

"This would be when?" Adair asked. "Seventy-one?"

"Late seventy-one."

"And you were nineteen or twenty then?"

"Just turned twenty."

"So how'd it go after he got back?"

"We had a talk and after that it went okay."

When Sid Fork returned from his three one-year tours with the Military Police in Saigon, she said he had a specialist 6 rank on his sleeve and a money belt around his waist that contained $15,000 in black market profits. Adair guessed that a specialist 6 was the equivalent of a staff sergeant in the Army he had once served in long ago. Three stripes and a rocker, he remembered.

"Why'd the chief sign over for those two extra tours?" Adair asked.

"He liked being an MP. He also liked that black market money."

Huckins said Fork wanted to pick up right where they'd left off. He even wanted to move down to Los Angeles, where he figured he could join its police department. She asked him what he thought he'd be in ten years—an LAPD sergeant? Fork said he didn't see anything wrong with that until she told him he could be Durango's chief of police in six or seven years if they followed her plan.

B.D. Huckins broke off again to ask Adair whether he would like a brandy or something. Adair said he didn't want any brandy, but he certainly did want to hear how she'd managed the rest of it.

Huckins said she'd managed it by making herself indispensable to the three members of the sex co-op. All three were still city councilmen, so after she'd learned enough shorthand, she offered to take the minutes of the weekly council meetings. Until then the chore had been rotated among the five members. All of them hated it, she said, because it meant the note-taker had to listen to what the others said.

They snapped up her offer, Huckins recalled, and told her how much they appreciated it, especially since it didn't cost the city anything. She told them she liked doing them a favor and if they wanted to do the old chief of police one, they ought to tell him how he could hire himself a big tough ex-MP and Vietnam vet for almost next to nothing. And that, she said, was how Sid Fork joined the Durango police force.

Jack Adair decided to ask some more questions. "Who served as city treasurer? That CPA you worked for?"

"Yes. It was a part-time job. Now it's full-time."

"He turn a lot of the routine stuff over to you?"

"As much as he could get away with."

"So you took the council minutes and, in effect, kept the city's books."

She nodded.

"Was that sex co-op still in operation?"

"They all still paid and dropped by once or twice a week. But by then it was more therapy than sex. They liked talking to me about almost everything."

"And everybody."

"And everybody," she agreed.

"I assume you remembered what was said."

"I wrote it down."

"A CPA, a lawyer and a pharmacist," Adair said, as if thinking aloud. "They must've poked their noses into the closets of every skeleton in town."

"If they missed any, Sid didn't."

"You two were still close?"

"He got Sunday nights."

Adair nodded his appreciation, if not approval, of the arrangement, looked at her shrewdly and asked, "So which one of them died on you?"

"The pharmacist."

She said he died in 1973 of an aneurysm not long after her twenty-first birthday. Because it was an off-year, the city charter required the mayor to appoint a successor to the unexpired term, although a majority of the council had to approve the mayor's choice.

"With only a four-man council left, there could've been a tie vote," Adair said.

"The mayor could break a tie."

"You must've had yourself two solid votes on the council—the CPA and the lawyer."

"I also had the mayor. The other two council members wanted him to nominate some young, sharp and ambitious lawyer. But my two guys told him he'd be smart to nominate a very young female who'd go on taking the minutes and totting up the books like always."

"So how long'd it take to dump the mayor?"

Huckins said it took her five years. She served out her appointed term and was reelected to the council in 1974 and 1976. In 1978, she formed a slate and ran against the incumbent mayor, Richard Handshaw, charging that he was superannuated, negligent and incompetent until Sid Fork advised her to boil it down to baby talk.

After that she called Dicky Handshaw old, slow and lazy. She also beat him with a 52.3 percent of the vote and renamed City Park after him just three days before she fired the old chief of police and appointed Sid Fork in his place.

Adair shook his head in awe and admiration. "Named a park after him, by God."

"It had been a rough election and I thought it would calm things down a little."

"And maybe serve as a constant reminder of what happened to poor old Dicky."

B.D. Huckins smiled for the first time in what must have been thirty minutes. "Yes, I suppose it could, but I never really thought of it that way."

"Of course not," said Jack Adair.

Fourteen

Shortly before midnight on that last Friday in June, Kelly Vines and Sid Fork pulled up in front of a floodlit three-storied Victorian showplace that boasted two scalloped cupolas, eight gables (by Vines's quick count) and a veranda that wrapped around two sides of the house and part of a third.

"What's she do," Vines asked, "charge admission?"

"The floodlights stay on till he gets home. She's in there all by herself and the lights are sort of burglar insurance. Besides, the place is on the city's scenic tour."

"You have a scenic tour?"

"Yeah, but it only takes ten minutes."

The floodlights revealed a new coat of rich cream paint that contrasted rather biliously, in Vines's opinion, with the two shades of dark green that had been applied to the trim. A fairly new shingle roof had been left to the weather. The house itself sat well back on a deep two-hundred-foot-wide lot and was surrounded by a carefully thinned-out forest of elderly pines. At the rear on the alley was a two-story building, also floodlit, that Vines assumed had once been the stable and was now the garage.

As they followed a serpentine brick walk to the veranda, Sid Fork explained how Norm Trice had inherited the house from his father, who had inherited it from *his* father, who had built the place in 1903.

Fork rang the bell. The woman who opened the door was younger than Vines had expected. When she saw that her late night callers were the chief of police and a stranger, she assumed the worst and automatically denied it by slowly shaking her head. It was an "I don't want any whatever it is" gesture that went on and on until Sid Fork said, "I'm sorry, Virginia, but I've got bad news. Norm's been shot and he's—well, he's dead."

At the word "dead," Virginia Trice's head stopped shaking and her eyes began to blink rapidly as she fought the tears. They were large dark brown eyes, very wet now, and spaced far apart in a narrow tanned face that was crowned with short thick straw-colored hair. The face also offered a small, possibly pert nose and a firm, possibly stubborn chin. In between nose and chin was a perfect mouth whose full lower lip was being bitten. Virginia Trice stopped biting her lip, opened her mouth, sucked in an enormous breath, stopped blinking and held the breath until it finally escaped in a long sad sigh. When the sigh was over, she said, "Come on in."

They followed her down a wide hall, past an elaborately carved oak staircase, through a pair of sliding doors carved from the same wood, and into what Vines thought must once have been the parlor. Much of the polished oak floor was covered with a red and purple rug—the purple so dark it seemed almost black. The red in the rug clashed with the pink in the tiny climbing roses that formed the pattern on the wallpaper.

Also on the walls were what Vines assumed to be California seascapes, painted in oils by obvious amateurs who, while competent, were less than gifted. In two corners of the room were heavy carved tables with ball-and-claw feet and round marble tops. Fat porcelain lamps sat on both tables, wearing orange silk shades that had faded and now looked more quaint than gaudy.

Virginia Trice was tall, at least five-ten, and wore tight old jeans that made her long legs look even longer. She also wore a man's white button-down shirt with its tails out and its sleeves rolled up above her elbows. The collar was frayed. On her bare feet were scuffed Topsiders.

She lowered herself slowly into an armless chair with a worn plush seat. With knees together and hands folded primly in her lap she seemed to listen carefully as Sid Fork introduced Kelly Vines as "a friend of mine." She greeted Vines in an almost inaudible voice as he and Fork sat down side by side on a couch with a cane back.

The short silence that followed ended when Virginia Trice cleared her throat and said, "Who shot him?"

"We don't know yet," Fork said.

"Was it a stickup—a robbery?"

"I don't think so, but it could've been."

"Well, was he shot once, twice, lots of times—what?"

"Two times. In the head."

"Must've been quick then. I mean, Norm didn't have to lie there, hurting and bleeding and yelling for help."

"It was quick, Virginia."

She sighed again. "What a shitty thing to happen."

Fork nodded his solemn agreement and asked, "Is there anyone you'd like me to call? Maybe somebody you'd like to come over and stay with you."

Instead of answering Fork, she looked at Kelly Vines. "You and Sid old friends?"

"Not really."

"I've lived here four years and I don't know hardly anybody I'd like to come over and stay with me. We've only been married three years. I'm his second wife. What he calls squaw number two. I used to be the waitress at the Eagle and I guess that's why people didn't like us getting married."

"Who didn't like it?" Fork said in mild protest.

She ignored him and continued speaking to Vines. "They didn't like it because of me being a waitress and our ages. I was twenty-three and Norm was forty-three. Twenty years difference. You think that's too much?"

Vines said no, he didn't think it was too much.

There was a silence until she looked at Fork and said, "Now what the fuck do I do, Sid?"

Fork edged forward on the couch, rested his elbows on his knees and let a look of compassion spread over his long face. "First thing you do is get a good night's sleep."

"What's sleep?"

"I'll get Joe Emory to send over some pills."

"Even with pills I won't sleep."

"You've got to so you can get up in the morning."

"What for?"

"I don't much like mentioning money at a time like this, but everyone's gonna want to see where Norm got killed. You go down there and open up in the morning and you'll take in a thousand, even fifteen hundred."

Not even avarice could erase the grief and sadness from her face. "That much?" she said and quickly answered her own question. "Yeah, I guess maybe we could take in that much." She frowned at Fork. "You think Norm'd mind?"

"Virginia," Fork said, his tone kind and patient, "Norm won't give a damn one way or the other."

Fifteen

Fork and Vines entered Mayor B.D. Huckins's house without knocking at 12:46 A.M. to find Jack Adair on the cream couch with a bottle of beer and the mayor in her chocolate-brown leather chair. She turned to say something as they came in but Sid Fork preempted her with: "Somebody shot Norm Trice dead about an hour ago and left us a message."

Huckins nodded, as if at some mildly interesting news, and rose slowly, turning away from the three men. She walked over to one of her Monet prints and seemed to examine it carefully. Still staring at the print, she said, "How's Virginia taking it?"

"Hard."

"You get somebody to stay with her?"

"She didn't want anybody."

Huckins turned from the slice of "On the Seine at Bennecourt," her face composed, eyes almost dry, voice steady. "I'll call her. See if she'd like to stay here a few days."

The mayor moved to the rear of the leather chair and

leaned her thighs against its low back, as if she found the support reassuring. Folding her arms across her chest, she said, "What message?"

Vines took the five-by-seven-inch manila envelope from his hip pocket, crossed the room and handed it to Huckins. "It's addressed to you," he said, "but it concerns all four of us."

"I see you opened it," the mayor said, her tone making it clear she didn't like anyone opening her mail. She removed the photographs and examined them quickly. When she began to go through them more slowly, Jack Adair asked, "Who're Norm and Virginia?"

"Virginia's the wife of Norm Trice," she said, putting the photographs back in the envelope. "He owned the Blue Eagle Bar and some other property around town. He was also my earliest backer." She looked at Adair. "Financial backer."

Adair used a sympathetic headshake to demonstrate how fully he appreciated the mayor's loss. She walked around the leather chair to hand him the envelope. "I'll miss Norm," she said.

"I can imagine," said Adair as he removed the photographs and went through them slowly. When he finished he looked up at Vines. "You hid and I stuck out my tongue."

"The chief thinks it's a metaphor."

Fork shook his head. "You said that, not me."

Adair looked at B.D. Huckins, who had moved over to a window and was staring out at the night. "Where and when did they take this one of you and the chief?" he asked.

Without turning, she said, "Just after six in the evening two days ago in the parking lot behind City Hall."

Adair looked at Fork for confirmation. The chief tugged at an earlobe, frowned and said, "By God, that's right."

B.D. Huckins turned from the window to look at Adair.

"Sid and I were talking—maybe even arguing—about whether to have a drink. We didn't. Have a drink, I mean."

"You didn't notice the photographer either," Vines said.

The mayor shook her head. "Those pictures of you two. Where were they taken?"

"Downtown Lompoc," Vines said. "Less than an hour after Jack got out of jail."

She looked at Fork. "I'd like a drink, Sid. Some brandy."

"Anybody else?" Fork asked. Vines said he'd like a beer and Adair said he'd finish what he had. After Fork left for the kitchen, the mayor sat back down in her favorite chair, tucked both feet up beneath her and smoothed the black skirt down over her knees.

No one said anything until Fork returned with two beers and the brandy. He served Huckins, handed Vines an open bottle and asked if he needed a glass. Vines said he didn't.

After she tasted her brandy, B.D. Huckins asked the room at large, "What could be the point of killing Norm?"

"To make sure we understand the message," Vines said.

"Which is what—in plain English?"

"That's easy," Fork said, taking the only other chair in the room, which was really more stool than chair. "They used those photos to tell us they know all about how you and I're going to supply the judge and Vines here with a hideout. Then they killed poor old Norm to tell us they're the worst kind of folks to fuck with." He looked at Vines. "That about it?"

"Just about."

In the silence that followed, Jack Adair leaned back on the couch's cushions and examined the ceiling. Finally, he said, "I wonder how they discovered the connection between you and us so quickly."

After another, briefer silence, B.D. Huckins said, "Somebody talked."

"I told no one," Adair said. "And Kelly spoke only to Soldier Sloan."

"Then he talked to one person too many," she said.

"Who'd you tell?" Vines asked her. "Other than your sister?"

"Nobody."

Vines and Adair looked at Sid Fork, who said he hadn't told anyone either.

Adair returned his gaze to the mayor. "And who would your sister tell?"

"Her husband," Fork said before the mayor could say anything.

"I hope she did," B.D. Huckins said, indifferent to the three bleak stares she drew. When she spoke again, it was to Jack Adair. She leaned forward a little and stared at him with cool gray eyes that—Adair later swore to Vines— "peeped right down into the basement of my soul where it's all dark and dirty and crawling with bugs."

"Understand this," she said. "If I'm to negotiate with these people—whoever they are—I'll need an intermediary. A go-between."

"Makes sense," Adair said.

"And a rich go-between's far better than a poor one because a rich one won't be nearly so tempted to cross us, if the occasion presents itself—which, in this case, it sure as hell will. And God knows Parvis is rich enough."

"Parvis your brother-in-law?" Adair asked.

"Yes."

"Thought you said his name was Mansur."

"Parvis Mansur."

"When do Kelly and I get to meet him?"

"What about tomorrow?"

"Are you talking about Saturday or Sunday?"

"Saturday. Today."

"Today'd be fine," said Jack Adair.

Sixteen

Although the name chiselled into the polished granite slab above the entrance read, "Durango Civic Center," no one ever called it anything except City Hall. Built on the site of the old City Hall, which went up in 1887 and fell down in 1935 during the earthquake, the new City Hall had been completed with WPA money in June of 1938, its golden anniversary now slipping by ignored and unremarked.

It was a solid-looking three-story granite building that B.D. Huckins liked to describe as a gray footlocker with windows. Including its parking lot and Fire Engine Co. No. 1 (there was no Engine Co. No. 2), the Civic Center took up nearly half a block of prime real estate on Noble's Trace.

The Trace, as everyone called it, was the only thoroughfare in Durango that resembled a boulevard and the only one that curved, twisted and wandered through the city from its eastern limits to the Southern Pacific tracks on the west. All other streets—except those up in the foothills—ran straight as a stripe from east to west and north to south.

Noble's Trace took its name from a Louisiana gambler called Noble Clark, who, with his Mexican prostitute wife, Lupe, had founded the settlement 148 years ago, naming it Durango after the one in Mexico from which Lupe had fled during the 1835 plague of scorpions.

With the reluctant and lackadaisical help of some Chumash Indians, the couple built the first structure in Durango to have four walls and a roof. It was a half-timber, half-adobe building that contained a combination trading post, tavern and bawdy house. It burned to the ground under mysterious circumstances twenty-three months later, roasting to death both Noble and Lupe Clark and two unidentified male customers.

The old trail that had wound through the mountains, the foothills and down to the ocean was still called the Trace because no one had ever thought there was any real need to name it anything else.

As its chiselled-in-stone name asserted, the Civic Center was home to all of Durango's municipal services. The mayor, the chief of police and the city treasurer were all up on the third floor along with the treasurer's hive of bookkeepers. On the second floor were the courtroom and the chambers of the city's municipal judge who was elected every four years. Down the hall from him were the elected city attorney and his two appointed deputies— plus two clerks, a bailiff, three secretaries and the aging part-time court reporter and full-time gay activist who, although growing deaf, was still too vain to wear a hearing aid. The fire chief worked out of his office in Fire Engine Co. No. 1.

The Civic Center's ground floor was reserved for the city's walk-in trade. Nearly a third of it was occupied by the police force and the jail itself, which afforded six cells and a drunk tank. The rest was given over to bureaus where citizens could pay taxes, fines and water bills; obtain marriage licenses and file for divorce; register births and deaths; apply for building permits and easements; and, if so inclined, which few were, attend the weekly meetings of the Durango City Council.

Shortly after 9:30 A.M. on that last Saturday in June, Chief of Police Sid Fork was leaning back in his banker's swivel chair, his feet up on his walnut desk, listening to a report from his two homicide detectives, Wade Bryant, the too-tall elf, and Joe Huff, who, to Sid Fork, was always the professor.

After Bryant stopped talking, the chief said, "Twenty-twos, huh?"

"First choice of the dedicated professional," said Huff.

"It'd kind of help if we had a motive," Fork said. "I mean, why would some pro-hitter, up from L.A. or maybe down from San Francisco, pump a couple of rounds into old Norm and not even bother to empty the register?"

"What a good question," Bryant said.

"My, yes," said Huff.

"Well?"

"Because somebody paid him to," Huff said.

"So who's the somebody?"

"Now there you've got us," Bryant said. "Joe and I've been worrying about that very thing. So this morning we get up early, even though it's Saturday, and drop in on the new widow to, you know, make sure she's okay and hasn't stuck her head in the oven or anything, and maybe even ask her a question or two. Well, we get there about eight this morning and guess what?"

Fork yawned. "She wasn't there."

"Right," said Bryant. "So Joe here says, 'Let's try the Blue Eagle because maybe she's down there either going over the books or drowning her sorrows.' So we drive down to the Blue Eagle and guess what?"

"That's guess what number two," Fork said.

"We almost couldn't get in is what," Huff said.

Fork nodded, as if pleased. "Packed, huh?"

"Four deep at the bar," said Bryant. "Well, two anyway. And behind it was Virginia herself, drawing beers, pouring shots, smiling through her tears and playing a lively tune on the cash register."

"I told her she'd probably take in at least a thousand," Fork said. "Maybe even fifteen hundred."

"Your idea then?"

"Better than staying home, wandering around those fourteen rooms and chewing holes in her hankie."

"Well, we finally make it up to the bar," Huff said, "catch Virginia's eye and Wade says something commiserative such as 'How's tricks, Ginny?' and she tells us how grateful she is we've dropped by and that the first round's on the house."

"So you never got around to asking her about who might've sent the shooter?"

"Didn't seem like the moment," Bryant said, "what with Condor State Bank on one side of us and Regent Chevrolet on the other."

"Kind of a wake, was it?" Fork said.

"Kind of."

Sid Fork turned his head to stare out the window. "I can remember when a guy died, his relatives and neighbors and friends'd gather round after the funeral with a ton of food, a lot of it fried chicken and baked ham, and the widow'd be standing there, all in black, shaking every hand and agreeing that yes, indeed, the late Tom or Harry sure did look natural and weren't the flowers just beautiful?"

"When the hell was this?" Bryant asked.

"Twenty-five, thirty years ago," Fork said, turned his gaze from the window and asked Bryant, "So what'd you come up with—if anything?"

Bryant licked his lips, as if pre-tasting his answer. "A possible eyewitness."

Fork dropped his feet to the floor and leaned forward. "Who?"

"Father Frank from St. Maggie's."

"Wonderful," Fork said, putting his feet back up on the desk. "Our whiskey priest."

"He's been dry awhile," Joe Huff said. "Going to AA and everything."

"How'd you get on to him?"

"He was hanging around outside the Eagle this morning, afraid to go in, when Wade and I came out."

"Afraid of the booze, huh?"

"Probably," Bryant said. "So Joe asks how's it going, Father? And he says just fine except he thinks maybe he'll come back and pay his respects when Virginia's not so busy. Then he looks at me and I can see him telling himself no, yes, no, yes—until finally he says he thinks he noticed something oddish last night. Don't think I ever heard anybody say oddish before."

"Me either," Joe Huff said.

"Anyway, it seems he'd been to a meeting—"

"AA meeting?" Fork said.

Bryant nodded. "But it didn't take, or something somebody said rubbed him the wrong way, or maybe the bishop'd sent him a cross little note. Who knows? But anyhow he was kind of upset so he decided to walk off whatever was bothering him. And he's down there on North Fifth when he sees this other priest looking at the puppies in Felipe's window."

"Sheplabs, aren't they?" Fork said. "Cute little fellows."

Joe Huff took over the report. "Well, you know how Father Frank goes around in a T-shirt and jeans most of the time. But he says this other priest is all in black and has a wrong-way collar on and everything. So Father Frank thinks the other guy's visiting or just passing through because he's never seen him before. And he also thinks the other priest might like to drop by Pretty Polly's for coffee and doughnuts. So he's about to cross the street and invite him when the other priest turns and almost runs the other way."

"Toward the Eagle?"

"Away from it. So Father Frank sort of steps back into Klein's doorway, which is pretty deep, because he doesn't want the other priest to get the wrong idea."

"What wrong idea?"

"I'm a Baptist," Huff said. "How the hell should I know? You want to hear some Bible Belt stuff about what priests and nuns do? Curl your toenails."

"Just tell me what happened, according to Father Frank."

"What he claims he saw and heard is this," Wade Bryant said. "He says the other priest scoots down the sidewalk, stops, spins around like he's just remembered something, then makes a beeline for the Blue Eagle."

"What time is this?"

"He thinks about eleven-twenty."

"What time the AA meeting end?"

"Nine-thirty, but he hung around another half an hour or so for the cookies and coffee."

"And then went on his hour-and-a-half walk."

"Walking past bars, I expect," Huff said. "Testing temptation."

"But this other priest," Fork said. "He went in the Blue Eagle."

Huff nodded.

"So what'd Father Frank do?"

"He hung around some more," Bryant said, "waiting for the other guy to come out because he still thought they might go have coffee and doughnuts together."

"Where'd he hang around?"

"Cattawampus across the street from the Eagle," Huff said.

Fork closed his eyes, as if drawing himself a map of the intersection. "Marvin's Jewelry," he said. "Another deep doorway."

"Father Frank says he uses doorways like that because he doesn't like to be seen hanging around street corners at night," Bryant said.

"Let's get to the odd stuff," Fork said. "He see anything?"

Bryant shook his head.

"He hear anything?"

"He thought he heard somebody clap inside the Eagle."

"Clap?"

"Clap."

"Once?" Fork asked. "Five times? Fifty times? What?"

Bryant grinned. "You know, Sid, that's exactly what I asked him myself."

"And?"

"And he said they clapped just twice."

"Then what?"

Then the stranger-priest hurries out of the Eagle and jumps in a van that drives off in a hurry."

"What'd Father Frank do then?"

"He says since he didn't have anybody to drink coffee with, he went home and went to bed."

"What'd this other priest look like?"

Bryant nodded at Joe Huff, who pulled out a small notebook, turned some pages and read what he had written. "Short. Very short legs. About five-one. Forty to forty-five. Also fat. Round like a ball. Gray hair, cut short. And ugly. Porcine."

"Porcine?"

"Piggy-looking. He had one of the noses that turn up and aim their nostrils right at you."

"What color were his eyes?"

"Father Frank says he wasn't close enough to tell," Bryant said. "But he was close enough to see that the guy looked piggy."

"What about the van?"

Bryant shook his head with regret. "No license number or make because Father Frank says he can't tell a Buick from a Ford. But he did say it was pink."

"Pink?"

Bryant nodded.

"Well," Fork said. "That's something."

Seventeen

The roadhouse where Adair, Vines and B. D. Huckins were to meet the mayor's rich Iranian brother-in-law at 1 P.M. that Saturday was four miles east of Durango on the south side of Noble's Trace which, once past the city limits, changed from a boulevard into the two-lane blacktop that curved and twisted its way to U.S. 101.

The roadhouse was called Cousin Mary's and owned by Merriman Dorr, who insisted it was a supper club and not a roadhouse at all. Dorr was a fairly recent immigrant from Florida who claimed to have taught geography at the University of Arkansas, flown as copilot for something called Trans-Caribbean Air Freight and, before all that, played two seasons at second base for the Savannah Indians in the double-A Southern League.

Not long after Dorr materialized in Durango, the ever dubious Sid Fork made a series of long-distance calls and discovered Dorr had done everything he claimed and more. The more included being held without bail for three months in the West Palm Beach jail on a vaguely worded fraud charge.

The alleged fraud had involved two and possibly three shipments of M-16 rifles and M-60 mortars. Dorr was said to have been paid for them by a Miami export-import firm called Midway There, Inc. The firm claimed it had never received shipment.

All charges against Dorr were suddenly dropped when Midway There, Inc., went out of business one Thanksgiving weekend, never to be heard from again.

After that, Sid Fork made no more investigatory long-distance calls about Merriman Dorr because, as he told the mayor, "It was all beginning to sound pretty much like spook stuff." But Fork still considered it his civic duty to preserve Cousin Mary's excellent menu and reasonable prices even though the roadhouse lay just outside his jurisdiction. So he paid Dorr a cautionary semi-official visit eight weeks after the roadhouse opened for business.

"Why here?" he asked Dorr.

"When I was down in that West Palm Beach jail, I heard talk about your easy ways."

"You hear about our rules?"

"No."

"Well, the rules are no dope and no whores unless you want the Feds or the deputy sheriffs dropping by."

"What about a nice quiet table-stakes poker game on weekends?"

"That's different," Sid Fork said.

B. D. Huckins drove her three-year-old gray Volvo sedan into the roadhouse parking lot and followed the gravel drive that led to the rear. Kelly Vines, noticing the small blue Neon sign that spelled out "Cousin Mary's," asked if there was indeed a Mary who was somebody's cousin.

"Merriman Dorr," said Huckins. "He owns the place."

"Food any good?" Jack Adair asked from the back seat.

"The portions are too big."

The final question came from Vines, who asked why there were no customers' cars in the front parking lot.

"Because he doesn't open till six," the mayor said.

Cousin Mary's had been an abandoned eighty-one-year-old two-room schoolhouse until Merriman Dorr bought and remodeled it, doing much of the work himself, even the wiring. He also added two wings and painted the place barn-red except for the roof. Every morning—although often it was barely before noon— Dorr ran the Stars and Stripes up the old but newly painted and still sturdy flagpole. When he first opened the place, Dorr had rung the old school bell at sunrise on all holidays. And even though his nearest neighbors lived a quarter of a mile away, all of them (except for one deaf woman) had called, written or come by to protest the dawn clangor. After that, Dorr rang the bell only on the Fourth of July and Veterans Day.

He also kept a wide yellow ribbon, almost a sash, tied around the trunk of the huge old oak that still grew in the middle of what had been the school playground but was now the roadhouse parking lot. The yellow ribbon, Dorr had told a 23-year-old reporter from *The Durango Times*, memorialized all Americans still held hostage by assorted terrorists and "every other American who languishes in some foreign prison just because those airheads in Washington forgot to juice the right people."

Some considered Dorr a patriot. Others thought he was a nut. He did a nice business.

Huckins parked her Volvo behind the roadhouse at the end of a row of five almost new and remarkably plain sedans of various American manufacture. Kelly Vines thought all the sedans might as well have worn vanity license plates that read: RENTED. B. D. Huckins caught his inspection of the overly anonymous cars and answered his unasked question. "They're what the players drive."

"Poker?"

"Poker."

The back door of the roadhouse was familiar to Vines because he had had one just like it installed in the apartment of a client who had had good reason to believe that someone was trying to kill him. The door was at least two inches thick and consisted of a solid aluminum core wrapped with steel sheathing.

Huckins raised her fist to knock but before she could the door was opened by a lean six-footer with lively green eyes and a face rescued from male-model insipidness by a thin eggshell-white scar that ran from his left eye back to his left earlobe. The scar gave him a pleasantly sinister look that Vines thought was probably good for business.

Merriman Dorr's green eyes flickered over Vines, tarried on Adair and came to rest on B. D. Huckins. He smiled then, letting perfect teeth gleam, and said, "I swear, B. D., you get prettier each and every time I see you and that surely's not often enough."

It was nicely put and softly said, but Huckins ignored the compliment and instead made minimal introductions. "Jack and Kelly. Merriman."

"Gentlemen," said Dorr, turning sideways so his guests could enter. As Huckins went by him she said, "I don't see Parvis's car."

"Must be because he's not here yet."

Dorr and the mayor went down a hall, followed by Vines and Adair. They passed a closed door. In front of it in an armless wooden chair sat a watchful man in his fifties who rested a pump shotgun across his knees. From behind the door came the unmistakable click of poker chips being stacked or tossed into the pot.

Halfway down the hall they stopped at another closed door, which their host opened, almost bowing them into the room. "What an extraordinary cane," Dorr said as Adair went by.

"An heirloom," said Adair.

Dorr entered the room as B. D. Huckins was turning to inspect the large round table with its starched linen cloth, artfully folded napkins and four place settings of heavy silver, gold-rimmed china and crystal goblets, into which the napkins had been tucked. Vines noticed the room had no windows and guessed the almost silent air-conditioning kept the temperature at a permanent 72 degrees.

In one corner of the room were three tan easy chairs, a dark green couch and a coffee table. On the floor was a brown carpet woven out of a synthetic fiber. On the pale cream walls were seven interesting watercolors of the old schoolhouse. Not far from the couch and easy chairs was a wet bar. A half-open door advertised the bathroom.

"How's this sound, B. D.?" Dorr asked. "Some really great trout, wild rice, maybe a little broccoli and a Cousin Mary salad followed by a flan for dessert?"

"Fine," she said.

"Chief Fork not joining us?"

"No."

Dorr nodded, as if at mildly disappointing news, and gave the wet bar a wave. "You all just help yourselves," he said and left.

The mayor was examining a fingernail on her left hand, Kelly Vines was inspecting one of the schoolhouse water-colors and Jack Adair was sipping a glass of beer when the door opened nine minutes later and the blond Dixie Mansur entered, followed by an elegant man in his late thirties who, for some reason, made Vines think of a ceremonial dagger, just waiting to be drawn.

Dixie Mansur wore fawn slacks that looked expensive and a dark brown silk blouse whose price, Vines guessed, had been exorbitant. Her eyes skipped over Vines and

114

Adair and stopped at her half-sister, the mayor. "I invited myself along," she said.

"I'm glad," Huckins said and turned up her cheek for the kiss her sister bent down to give her. "I don't think you've met Judge Adair. My sister, Dixie Mansur."

After they shook hands and said hello, Huckins said, "You know Kelly Vines, of course."

"Of course."

B. D. Huckins smiled up at her brother-in-law, who stood with a pleasant, if unsmiling expression, his right hand deep into the pocket of his tan raw-silk bush jacket, his left hand holding a cigarette down at his side. "How are you, Parvis?" Huckins said.

"Splendid, B. D. You keeping well?"

The mayor nodded her answer and introduced him to Jack Adair and Kelly Vines. Parvis Mansur shook hands first with Adair and then with Vines, thanking him for "rescuing my wife."

"It was nothing," Vines said.

"I'm in your debt."

"Not at all."

"At least accept my gratitude."

"Of course," said Vines, wondering whether the pleasantries would ever end. They did when the door opened and a Mexican busboy hurried in with a new place setting. Right behind him came a frowning Merriman Dorr, who glared at Mansur's wife and said, "You could've at least called, Dixie."

She ignored both the scolding and Dorr, who was now supervising the busboy. After the place setting was laid, Dorr moved a salad fork a quarter of an inch to the left, turned to give no one in particular a charming-host smile and said, "I do hope you all enjoy your lunch."

"I'm sure we will," B. D. Huckins said.

"Good," Dorr said and left, shooing the busboy ahead of him.

After the door closed Parvis Mansur turned to the mayor and asked, "Have we time for a drink?"

Huckins indicated the wet bar. "Help yourself."

On his way to the bar Mansur asked, "Dixie?"

"Sure."

All watched as Mansur dropped ice cubes into a pair of glasses, poured the Scotch and added the water. He did it with an economy of movement that was almost miserly. Vines suspected it was how he did everything, except talk, since Vines also suspected Mansur enjoyed the sound of his own voice, which was a deep baritone, verging on bass, and unaccented except for its British vowels and inflection. Wondering how early the British overtones had been acquired, Vines had a sudden mental picture, not quite a vision, of an elderly retired British Army officer, eking out his pension by spending long afternoons in Teheran, teaching received pronunciation to a squirming 6-year-old Parvis Mansur, who never forgot anything.

After everyone was settled into either the easy chairs or the long couch, Mansur looked at Adair and said, "Tell us about it."

"Hard to say where to begin."

"Perhaps with the case itself—the one involving the million-dollar bribe."

"The false bribe," Adair said.

"Very well. The false bribe."

Jack Adair drank the rest of his beer, put the glass down, clasped his hands over the black cane's curved handle and examined the ceiling for a moment or two, as if gathering the threads of his narrative. He then looked at Parvis Mansur.

"Well, sir, it came to us on appeal, of course, and it involved murder, a touch of incest and maybe a few trillion or so cubic feet of natural gas. So you could say, as such cases go, this one was kind of interesting."

"Yes," Mansur said. "I can see how one might say that."

Eighteen

Jack Adair began his tale with Delano Maytubby, the 52-year-old Osage Indian doodle-bugger who, equipped with nothing more than two wands of willow, had established a reputation for finding oil and gas beneath land the major oil companies had either ignored or written off. If things were slow, Maytubby, when pressed, would also look for water. But he first made it clear to whoever hired him that he was a genuine professional doodle-bugger and not some goddamn amateur dowser who believed in wood sprites and stuff.

Maytubby had been hired to look for either gas or oil beneath the five square miles of blackjack oaks and cockleburs that 63-year-old Obie Jimson ran cattle on down in the southeast corner of Adair's state.

The two of them would drive around the ranch in Jimson's ancient Ford pickup until Maytubby said stop. He would then get out, armed with his two willow wands, and head off in a direction of his own choosing, Jimson following along in low gear in the pickup. They did this for nearly a month until the crossed willow wands dipped and bobbed three times, pointed straight down and Delano Maytubby said, "Oh-oh."

Jimson climbed down from the pickup and looked around skeptically. "Here, you reckon?"

"Here."

"So what is it?"

"Well, it ain't oil so it must be gas."

"How can you tell the difference?"

Maytubby pointed his right hand straight up. "What color's that?"

"What?"

"The sky, goddamnit."

"Blue."

"How do you know?"

"I can see it."

"How do you know you can see it?"

"Well, shit, Del, I just know."

"And that's how I can tell it's gas instead of oil," the doodle-bugger said. "I just know."

The primary reason Obie Jimson had hired Maytubby, other than for his reputation as the state's preeminent oil and gas diviner, was that Maytubby couldn't keep his mouth shut. A leasehound for one of the majors, sitting in Crazy Kate's Coffee Shop two days later, overheard Maytubby boasting about his alleged find on Jimson's ranch.

The leasehound mentioned it casually to his boss, who told him to run a swab on the folks at the courthouse to see whether anyone else, besides a doodle-bugger, had been nosing around the area. When the leasehound reported back that a guy he knew from Phillips Petroleum had suddenly shown up in town, his boss told him to get out to Jimson's place and see how hard a nut he'd be to crack.

Obie Jimson proved to be a real tuf nut, as the oil fraternity usually spelled it. He hemmed and he hawed and he mumbled about how cattle and oil don't mix, and about protecting the land that'd been in his family for three generations and about how disappointed he was that that doodle-bugger he'd hired didn't find any water because cows sure as hell can't drink oil or gas.

After the leasehound left, promising to return with what might be an interesting proposition, Jimson telephoned Continental Airlines, which was the cheapest, and made a reservation for a flight to New Orleans. He then dug out a clipping from *The Wall Street Journal*, which had named the twenty best tax lawyers in the nation, and called Randolph Parmenter in New Orleans, who was listed as number sixteen.

Jimson flew down to New Orleans the next day, had a few drinks and a good dinner, wandered around the French Quarter until 3 A.M. and showed up for his 10 A.M. appointment with Parmenter, looking relaxed and rested.

Parmenter asked the initial question that most lawyers and doctors ask: "What seems to be the problem?"

"The problem," Jimson said, "is there's a chance of me getting stinking rich and I don't want those socialist nut cases up in Washington to get their hands on it. Well, not on most of it, anyhow."

Parmenter's office was just off Canal in one of the older downtown buildings that prided itself on the respectability and stuffiness of its tenants. Its coffee shop was said to serve the best chicken salad sandwiches in town and its cigar stand prided itself on the quality of its contraband Cuban cigars.

The lawyer gave Obie Jimson a patronizing old-money smile and asked, "And just what do you consider to be stinking rich, Mr. Jimson?"

"Sixty, seventy million maybe—around in there. But not all at once, of course."

Parmenter abandoned his patronizing air. "And the source of all this new wealth?"

"Natural gas."

"Well, the deep stuff is bringing nine dollars per thousand cubic feet now," Parmenter admitted.

(*"You have to remember," Jack Adair told his audience, "that this was all back in early nineteen eighty-four."*)

"Won't stay up near that high," Jimson said.

"Oh?"

"It's gonna come down ass over teacup 'fore long."

"What makes you think so?"

"Read in *The Wall Street Journal* where that Saudi Arabia guy, what's his name, Sheek Yamani's predicting it, and I figure he's gotta know something I don't."

"The geology on your land's been done, of course."

"Don't think I said that."

"Then how can you be certain the gas is there?"

"Because the best doodle-bugger in the Osage Nation says so."

"A doodle-bugger," Parmenter said. "I see."

"No, you don't, Mr. Parmenter. It just so happens I've got me a fairly new wife, although it turns out I don't much like her, and I also got me two young kids, a boy and a girl by my first marriage—she died, my first wife, ten years ago—and I had to raise Jack and Jill practically by myself—at least until I married Contrary Mary two years back. And I'm much obliged to you for not smiling at my kids' names the way most folks do. Jack's twenty and Jill's eighteen—I married late the first time and not late enough the second—and I wanta divide up the revenue source before the gas gets proved out because I read in *Money* magazine that if you do that, you can save a ton on taxes."

Parmenter leaned back in his tall wood and leather chair and peered at Jimson through a pair of horn-rimmed glasses. Jimson, who had never worn glasses, noticed they were trifocals. "*Money* magazine?" Parmenter said, unable to keep the horror out of his voice.

Jimson nodded.

"Well, it is true that if you distribute your real property

before certain natural resources are proved to be within or beneath it, you can avoid significant taxes. However, the IRS regards such prior distribution schemes with considerable skepticism. Are you quite sure there haven't been other geological explorations or seismographic surveys done of your property?"

"Not that I remember," Jimson said.

"Has there been any recent interest?"

"Well, some old boy from a wildcat outfit they call Short Mex and Big Mick dropped by the other day. But I played the fool and he went away."

"So you flew down to see me solely on the faith you have placed in this Osage doodle-bugger's proficiency?"

"It's not a question of me having faith in him, Mr. Parmenter. The question seems to be if the IRS would."

When he finally understood the elegance of Obie Jimson's reply, Parmenter allowed himself the day's first smile. Still smiling, he reached for a yellow legal pad, uncapped a fountain pen and said, "So how would you like to carve it up?"

"I wanta keep two-fifths of everything for myself. I want my wife, Marie Elena Contraire Jimson, to get a fifth and I want my two kids to have a fifth each. When I die, I want my two-fifths to go to the kids since they're blood kin and I've known them a hell of a lot longer than I have old Contrary Mary. And that's about it except for one or two other things."

After completing his notes, Parmenter looked up and said, "I'll need some additional details, documents and—"

Jimson didn't let him finish. "Got everything right here," he said, bent over, picked up a Wal-Mart shopping bag from the floor and slid it across the lawyer's desk. Parmenter quickly examined the papers inside and smiled for the second time.

"It seems you've brought exactly what I need. *Money* magazine again?"

Jimson nodded. "It's plumb full of useful tips."

"I'll have to buy a copy one of these days," Parmenter said.

Jimson finally accepted an offer from one of the major oil companies and flew Parmenter up from New Orleans to handle the negotiations. A little less than six months later, Obie and his son, Jack, were out quail hunting when Jill tracked them down in her old Volkswagen.

"He just called!" she said.

"Who?" her father asked.

"That guy from the oil company."

"What about?"

"He said we've got production."

"Didn't say how much, did he?"

"He said to tell you it's a barnburner. What's a barnburner, Daddy?"

"It means we're stinking rich," Obie Jimson said, gave out a rebel yell, threw his hat to the ground and did a credible jig around it.

That night the four Jimsons celebrated at the Stack Boys Ranch Inn with what Roy Stack later testified were "great big porterhouses, lots of eighteen-dollar-a-bottle California champagne and maybe a glass or two of whiskey apiece."

Then all four Jimsons—Obie, Contrary Mary, Jack and Jill—went home and went to bed. At some time between midnight and 3 A.M., Obie Jimson rose and went to his office in the old ranch house. A loaded shotgun, one of the same guns he and Jack had used to hunt quail that afternoon, was taken from the locked gun rack. Its muzzle was inserted into Obie's mouth and the trigger pulled. He was found by his wife, the former Marie Contraire, who screamed and rushed off, still screaming, to find Jack and Jill.

When the deputy sheriff who responded to Marie Jimson's frantic telephone call finally thought to ask where she had found her two stepchildren, she said she'd found them where they always were at night, in bed with each other.

The only fingerprints found on the shotgun that ended Obie Jimson's life belonged to his son, Jack. He and his sister, Jill, by then 21 and 19 respectively, were arrested and indicted for first-degree murder. Bail was set at $1 million each and posted by the president of the bank where Obie Jimson had done business. The bank president demanded and got an 18.9 percent fee on the pledged $2 million, explaining to Jack Jimson it was the same rate he'd pay if he'd put it on his Visa card.

Barred from the ranch by their stepmother, who announced—through a recently hired media consultant—that she would not "sleep under the same roof with the incestuous fornicators who murdered my dear husband," Jack and Jill Jimson checked into a suite at the county seat's Ramada Inn, fired their local attorney and called Randolph Parmenter in New Orleans, who strongly recommended that they retain as defense attorney Combine Wilson of Austin, Texas, who was notorious for his brilliance, flamboyance and enormous fees.

"Well, I reckon we can afford him, can't we?" Jack Jimson said.

"Jill still on the phone?" Parmenter asked.

Assured that she was, Parmenter reminded the brother and sister of the legal documents he had drawn up for Obie Jimson, which they had both signed, as had their stepmother, Marie Contraire Jimson.

"If Obie were to die, which, unfortunately, he has," Parmenter said, "you two were to inherit his forty percent of the gas revenue. This means the two of you together will now receive eighty percent of all revenue and your stepmother, twenty percent. If you die, she gets your share. If she dies, you get hers."

"What kind of money are we talking about?" Jack Jimson asked.

"Well, you've got five producing wells now and so we're talking about twelve million cubic feet of gas a day. With your three-sixteenths royalty on the five wells, that amounts to a little over twenty thousand dollars a day per well, or about three million a month. Of course, the production tax on that'll be two hundred and twenty-eight thousand a month, but that still leaves you two with eighty percent of two point seven-seven million a month."

"About twenty-five million a year, huh? For Jill and me?"

"Yes."

"That's kind of interesting."

"I'm sure Combine Wilson will find it so," Parmenter said.

Wilson found it so interesting that, instead of setting a fee, he agreed to represent his two young clients—or orphans, as he liked to call them—on a contingency basis, virtually unheard-of in a murder case. He explained that if he got them off and out the courtroom's front door, they would pay him 10 percent of their gross incomes for the next three years.

"But if I don't get you two little darlin's off," Combine Wilson had said, "you don't pay me a dime."

Jack Adair paused in his recitation, reached for his glass and drank some more beer, which had grown almost warm. "Now ten percent of the override from that much natural gas was, as Combine himself liked to admit, 'a tidy sum.' And to earn it, he put on a brilliant show. Most say his finest."

"An orator, I take it," Parvis Mansur said.

"Spellbinder," said Adair. "He wept and raved about

unloved children driven by loneliness, despair and criminal neglect into each other's arms, thus giving incest a nice warm glow. He railed against an aging, indifferent and philandering father who brought home as stepmother to his children a woman who had been arrested sixteen times in Houston for prostitution. He produced expert witnesses from Detroit and Los Angeles who went after the prosecution's physical evidence, such as it was, and ripped it to shreds. He put the sheriff's deputy on the stand and got him so rattled he shook, and then reduced at least three other prosecution witnesses to tears. But what Combine did best was to provoke a mediocre county judge into making some awfully bad law. And finally, there was Combine's summation that was demagoguery at its finest and most effective."

Adair paused to finish his beer and continued. "I'm told it was a kind of half-whispered, half-shouted demagoguery. Lawyers flew in from all over, a few for the entire trial, but most just to hear Combine's summation. And it must've sounded like implacable, irresistible logic— unless you studied it closely, as I eventually did, and found it not much more than visceral rhetoric, but brilliantly organized and beautifully told. Kelly was there. He can tell you."

The two half sisters and the Iranian looked at Kelly Vines. But it was B. D. Huckins who asked the question all three were thinking. "What were you doing there?"

"Representing a client—the same Short Mex and Big Mick outfit Jack mentioned earlier. They'd sent me down because they thought they might be able to nibble around the edges, or at least catch a few crumbs that might fall from the table, if the verdict went the way they hoped."

"And did it?" Huckins asked.

"No."

She looked at Adair. "Well?"

"After the prosecutor was all done, and after Combine

had finally closed his mouth, and after the judge's dubious instructions, the jury went out and stayed out for an hour and fifteen minutes, just long enough to make it look halfway decent, then came back in and found both Jack and Jill Jimson guilty of first-degree murder."

Nineteen

Dessert was a sin-rich flan and after Merriman Dorr himself served it to everyone except Kelly Vines, who said he didn't care for any, Dorr asked whether the two of them could speak privately.

Vines rose from the table and followed him out into the hall, where Dorr looked left, right and left again, the way he might look if he had come to a stop sign.

"Enjoy your lunch?" he asked Vines.

"The trout was good."

"Think the salad had a smidgeon too much tarragon?"

"The salad was fine, too. How much?"

"One thousand cash," Dorr said. "No checks. No plastic."

"The trout wasn't all that good."

"You're paying for what it costs to bring the help in on a Saturday. Then there's the liquor and the room. But what really jacks up the price is the privacy and that's sort of hard to cost out because there's none better anywhere."

"Cash only must simplify your bookkeeping," Vines said, took a none-too-plump roll of one-hundred-dollar bills from his pants pocket, peeled off ten of the hundreds slowly enough for Dorr to keep up with the count and handed them over. Dorr counted them again, even more slowly, and said, "I don't know what you and B. D.'ve got going, but—"

"Let's keep it like that."

Dorr ignored the interruption. "But whatever it is, if she or maybe even you ever need to go some place quick, I know where I can get me a Cessna."

"What do you charge—two hundred dollars per mile?"

"You might practice up on your listening," Dorr said, shoving the now folded $1,000 into a hip pocket. "I'm offering you a service through her. I mean, if she tells me you've got to go someplace in a hurry, that's fine, I'll fly you there although it's got to have her okay because I don't know you or your partner, if that's what he is. But if there's anything at all I can do for B. D., I'll do it for free gratis because to me she's the case ace."

"Why?" Vines said.

"Why what?"

"Why's everyone so willing to jump off tall buildings for her?"

"Because if you offer to jump today, you might not get pushed off tomorrow."

When Kelly Vines returned to his seat at the round table, Jack Adair was already well launched into his account of the million-dollar bribe: ". . . so when the state court of appeals upheld their convictions, it also revoked their bail. The boy was sent to the state penitentiary at Goldstone and the girl to the Female Correctional Institution, which is what they'd named the state prison for women when they built it back in nineteen eleven."

"And the sentence?" Parvis Mansur asked. "You never said."

"Death by lethal injection."

"Really. Both of them?"

"Both."

"Who would administer it—a doctor?"

"A medical technician."

Suspecting that her brother-in-law had a long list of other questions to ask about the mechanics of the execution, B. D. Huckins broke in with: "Let's get to the bribe."

With an agreeable nod, Adair said, "The attorney general himself appeared before us for the state. He isn't much of a lawyer but he is a damned fine politician, which is why he's now governor. Then came Combine Wilson and that's when all of us on the court sat up and took notice because this was Combine the legal scholar, not Combine the crowd pleaser. And if some of us hadn't been careful, we'd've found ourselves nodding along with him and maybe even amening now and again as he told us what the law really was and not what some semi-literate county judge down in Little Dixie thought it ought to be."

"Little Dixie?" Dixie Mansur asked.

"That's what they call the section of my state where the Jimson kids were first tried."

"Is it meant to be a compliment or a slam?"

"It started out one way but ended up the other."

"That's what I figured," she said.

Adair looked at each member of his audience. "Any other questions?" When no one had any, Adair continued. "But despite Combine's brilliance, I could sense that at least four of the brethren weren't buying his argument. It could've been because three of them were up for reelection and figured that voting to put two rich kids to death wouldn't do them any harm with the voters in my state, who, on the whole, are rather partial to executions. The fourth vote belonged to the lone weirdo on the court, who got and, I guess, still gets a kind of kinky pleasure from upholding death sentences. At least he's never yet voted to overturn one. But then I have to admit I got plenty of satisfaction—of a different kind, I hope—from voting just the opposite."

"You're opposed to the death penalty then?" Mansur asked.

"Yes, sir, I am. Unalterably."

"How peculiar."

"Ever see one carried out, Mr. Mansur?"

Before Mansur could reply, which he obviously wanted to do, B. D. Huckins again interrupted with an impatient, "Let's get on with it."

Adair smiled at her. "With my account rather than my philosophy, I take it?" Not waiting for an answer, he said, "After I did my vote-counting, I came up with what appeared to be a four-to-four tie with old Justice Fuller holding the swing vote."

Parvis Mansur couldn't resist another interruption. "When you say old, is that a colloquialism or a statement of fact?"

"Justice Fuller was then eighty-one, which made him not only old but aged. His full name was Mark Tyson Fuller and he'd served on the court for thirty-six years and liked to call himself its institutional memory, although for a quarter of a century the clerks had been calling him The Weathervane because of his voting with the majority eighty-nine percent of the time."

"Was he competent?" Mansur asked.

"He wasn't much of a legal scholar and he was lazy, but he had a facile mind, all of his marbles, and he was the best vote-counter on the court—even better than I was and I was more than a fair hand. But he was also determined to stay on the court till he died because his wife had Alzheimer's and the constant care she required had almost ruined him financially."

"How much does a supreme court justice make in your state?" Dixie Mansur asked.

"Sixty-five thousand," Adair said. "The chief justice gets seventy."

"Huh," she said. "Law clerks down in L. A. make almost that much."

"I'm sure they do," he said. "But some of us could afford to serve on the court. Others thought a term or two would help them politically or when they returned to private practice. And some of us enjoyed the prestige. There's an old saw about how a state judge is a lawyer who knows a governor. But in my state, being *elected* a supreme court justice means you're a political animal who ranks just above the lieutenant governor and only a rung or two below a U. S. senator."

B.D. Huckins glanced at her watch and said, "Could we—"

"Yes, ma'am," Adair said. "No more digressions." He leaned forward, resting his elbows on the dining table, and stared at Parvis Mansur, who stared back with brown-velvet eyes that would have looked as mild as a doe's had it not been for a slight cast in the right eye, which managed to give the Iranian's entire countenance a look of profound skepticism. The rest of Mansur's face was also slightly out of kilter, Adair decided. The eyes themselves were set too far apart in the thin-nosed and big-jawed face that seemed to be missing some essential component, possibly a mustache, and Adair found himself wondering how many times Mansur had grown one only to shave it off.

"To continue," Adair said. "Justice Fuller made his approach a few days after we'd finished hearing the Jimson case. He dropped by my chambers and hinted how he was kind of leaning toward overturning the two kids' conviction and ordering a new trial. So I told him fine, I was leaning that way myself. Then he switched to what a tough reelection he had coming up, which was utter nonsense, but I let him prattle on till he came to what was really on his mind."

"Which was what?" Mansur asked.

"He asked me to let him write the majority opinion because he said he had a real feel for the case, and also because he thought it might give him a little political boost, which was more nonsense. But I'd counted the votes by then and couldn't see any harm in it, so I said, 'Okay, Mark, you write it.' So he eventually did and the court voted five to four to overturn the verdict and order a new trial for the Jimsons."

Adair paused to look at Kelly Vines. "Okay so far, Kelly?"

"So far."

"About a month after that an investigator for the state attorney general's office got an anonymous phone call from some guy with an obviously disguised voice who claimed Justice Fuller and I had split a million-dollar bribe to make sure the Jimson appeal went the way it did."

"Just like that?" B. D. Huckins said. "Out of the blue."

"Just like that," Adair said. "Thirty minutes after the call came in, the attorney general himself was in my chambers, playing me a tape cassette of the call, which was a damn fool thing for him to do. But with the primary just a few months away, I expect he was thinking more about his gubernatorial campaign and political fallout than he was about the law. So I listened, thanked him kindly and asked whether somebody else was playing a copy of the tape for Justice Fuller."

"And were they?" Mansur asked.

"I don't think it'd even occurred to the A.G. because he looked surprised, maybe even shocked, and said no, of course not, because he'd wanted to talk to me first. I had to point out that I didn't think the two of us should discuss the matter any further. He remembered his law then and left. It was about ten-thirty in the morning and he left all hunched over like the sky was falling, which, in a sense, I suppose it was. It was then I decided I'd better get myself a good cheap lawyer. So I called my son-in-law."

Mansur looked at Kelly Vines. "You, of course."

"Me," Vines said.

Jack Adair, looking suddenly tired, leaned back in his chair and said, "I think Kelly should tell you what happened next."

After talking to Adair, Vines had telephoned the home of Justice Fuller only to get a busy signal. He kept redialing for fifteen minutes, then called the operator, claimed it was an emergency, and asked her to find out whether the Fuller phone was in use or off the hook. She checked and said it was off the hook.

The Fuller house was a large old two-story frame monster, painted white, with a deep covered porch that advertised it had been built back in the 1920s before air-conditioning. It was also in the heart of a steadily deteriorating neighborhood that had been designated a "Historical Section" by the city in a vain attempt to maintain property values.

Kelly Vines rang the doorbell repeatedly. When no one responded, he tried the door itself and found it unlocked. His first impulse was to get back in his car and return to his office. Instead, he entered the house out of what he described as "curiosity and an ill-defined sense of obligation."

A wide center hall led to the stairs. To the right was the living room. To the left, the dining room, which adjoined the kitchen. Vines walked into the living room and found Mrs. Mark Fuller, the Alzheimer's victim, sitting in a rocking chair much like the one John Kennedy had popularized, dressed in a long pink flannel nightgown and dead from what seemed to be a gunshot wound in her chest. Her hands, folded in her lap, still held a pair of silver-rimmed eyeglasses.

Vines left the living room, crossed the hall and entered the dining room. Justice Fuller sat in an armchair. It matched the dining table that was made from some very dark, almost black wood, possibly Philippine mahogany. The table was part of a suite composed of eight matching chairs, a carved sideboard and a glass-fronted china cabinet.

Seven of the eight chairs were drawn up to the long table. The one Justice Fuller sat in had been shoved back three feet from the head of the table, almost to the wall, apparently to keep blood from splattering the one-page handwritten letter that lay on the table just in front of two open shoeboxes that were filled with packets of one-hundred-dollar bills, each packet bound by a red rubber band.

Justice Fuller sat sprawled in the armchair, his head thrown back. An inch or so above the bridge of his nose was a black hole whose diameter was about that of a pencil. On the floor beside the chair was a small semiautomatic pistol.

Vines stared at the dead supreme court justice for either seconds or minutes, he could never remember which, then turned to read the handwritten letter. It lay centered on the table and anchored by a full lower set of dentures that served as a paperweight.

Using a ballpoint pen to push the false teeth aside, Vines read the looping handwriting of the to-whom-it-may-concern letter:

> After receiving a disturbing call this morning from the state attorney general's office, I have decided to end my life and also that of my incurably ill and much beloved Martha.
>
> The reason for these drastic measures is that

Chief Justice Jack Adair and I each accepted a $500,000 (five hundred thousand dollars) bribe from a party or parties unknown to vote as we did on the Jack and Jill Jimson appeal. It was Chief Justice Adair, heretofore one of the most honorable men I have ever known, who, fully cognizant of my precarious financial condition, approached me with the offer to divide $1,000,000 (one million dollars) in bribe money evenly. But now the burden has simply grown too great and Martha and I have grown too old. I am dreadfully sorry.

The letter was signed, "Sincerely, Mark Tyson Fuller."

Kelly Vines used his ballpoint pen to push the false teeth back to where they had been, went to the phone in the living room and called a newspaper reporter he knew. He then waited exactly five minutes and called the police. The reporter, accompanied by a photographer, arrived first. The photographer, having quickly taken pictures of the dead justice, his murdered wife and the suicide note, was taking pictures of the two shoeboxes full of one-hundred-dollar bills when the police arrived.

"There were four of them," Vines said. "Two homicide detectives and two uniforms. First, they threw out the reporter and the photographer. Next they yelled at me for a while. Then they made sure that both Justice and Mrs. Fuller were really dead. After that, they read the suicide note. And finally, they counted the money. But no matter how many times they counted it—and it was at least six or seven times—the total still came to only four hundred and ninety-seven thousand dollars."

Twenty

As Vines expected, it was Parvis Mansur who asked the first and most pertinent question. "Were two enough?"

"Two shoeboxes? Yes."

"Is that an estimate—a guess?"

"Neither."

"May I ask how you knew?"

"From some ex-clients who carried large chunks of cash around in shoeboxes."

"How much American money will fit into one?"

"In hundreds?"

"Yes. In hundreds."

"The average shoebox is twelve inches long, six inches wide, three and a quarter inches deep and can hold up to three thousand U.S. bills, if they're tightly packed. But the people I knew didn't pack more than twenty-five hundred bills into one. By using hundred-dollar bills, they had a convenient, portable container that held a quarter of a million dollars and weighed only five point one pounds."

"How do you know how much it weighed?" B.D. Huckins asked.

"Because there are four hundred and ninety U.S. bills to the pound."

"You also learned this from your former clients?" Mansur said.

"Where else?"

"They must've been exceedingly prosperous."

"They were pot smokers who became dealers, grew into major wholesalers and eventually took in so much cash they had to weigh it to count it."

"What happened to them?" Dixie Mansur asked.

"Who cares?"

"Let's return to the reporter and the photographer," Mansur said. "As soon as you read the suicide note and looked at the two shoeboxes, you realized they could, in fact, contain no more than half a million dollars, right?"

"Right."

"So to preserve everything on film before the police arrived, you called the reporter and urged him to bring a photographer along. Also true?"

Vines nodded and Mansur nodded back contentedly. The silence that followed was finally broken by B.D. Huckins with an exasperated sigh. "I don't understand."

"Don't understand what?" Vines said.

"Any of it. Especially the money thing. Was there a million or only five hundred thousand? Did the judge, what's his name, Fuller, kill himself and his wife, or did somebody else do it? And finally," she said, turning to stare at Jack Adair, "did you take the half million or not and, if so, who from?"

Vines also looked at Adair and said, "Well?"

Adair decided to examine the ceiling. He was still examining it when he came to his decision and said, "Tell 'em, Kelly."

"Everything?"

"Everything."

After infuriating the two homicide detectives by refusing to answer any of their questions unless he had legal counsel present, Kelly Vines enraged them even more when he handed each a business card and suggested in his most imperious tone that if they wished to question him further, they should call his secretary and arrange an appointment.

The two detectives were still sputtering when Vines walked out of the Fuller house, got into his car and drove immediately to a three-year-old, seven-story condominium building that now occupied the site of the demolished grade school he had attended for seven years. The apartment building, advertised as offering "the ultimate in luxury and prestige," overlooked the twenty-acre park that Vines had crossed daily to classes that had begun with kindergarten and ended with the sixth grade.

A drive now looped up through ten acres of expensively landscaped grounds to the condominium's entrance. Vines got out of the Mercedes sedan, the same sedan he would later drive to California, and turned the car over to the doorman, who, Vines remembered, had dropped out of high school halfway through the eleventh grade in 1965 to enlist in the Marines. The doorman never seemed to remember Kelly Vines.

After taking the elevator up to the top floor, the seventh, Vines used a key to let himself into his father-in-law's apartment that occupied 2,600 square feet. He crossed the living room, went down a hall and entered what the architect had decreed to be the master bedroom, which featured an enormous walk-in closet next to the bath. The closet's twin sliding doors had been covered by full-length mirrors until Jack Adair had had them removed, explaining that the last thing he wanted to see first thing in the morning was a naked or half-naked fat man.

Vines entered the closet, turned on its light, knelt down and found twelve of them stacked in a corner, hidden—or at least concealed—by two old Burberry topcoats that were then too small for Adair but far too good to throw away.

The twelve shoeboxes were divided into twin stacks of six each. The boxes bore the brand names of Ferragamo, Johnston & Murphy, Bass, Allen-Edmonds and Gucci. One of the Gucci boxes was at the bottom of the near stack. The other Gucci box was second from the top of the far stack. Vines automatically removed both of them, certain that Adair would go barefoot before wearing anything made by Gucci. He carried the two shoeboxes out of the closet and placed them on the king-size bed. When he lifted off their tops he discovered that again someone had used red rubber bands to bind the one-hundred-dollar bills into packets.

Vines called down for his car. When he came out of the condominium building, he opened the Mercedes's trunk and carelessly tossed in a green plastic garbage bag. After that, he drove around aimlessly for fifteen minutes until he was reasonably sure he wasn't being followed. From a phone booth he called a client who was a senior partner in the wholesale marijuana concern.

They met an hour later in the State Historical Museum, which was only two blocks from the state capitol. They met in the museum's basement where the century-old stagecoaches, buggies and covered wagons were kept on display. The client was a lanky 32-year-old who wore jeans, scuffed cowboy boots and a white oxford cloth button-down shirt with its sleeves rolled just above his elbows. The client had quit smoking both tobacco and marijuana six months before and now kept a toothpick in his mouth. Four or five times a day he dipped the tooth-pick into a small vial of cinnamon oil.

"What's up?" the client asked.

"I need to use one of your laundries."

"No shit?"

"Which one do you suggest?"

The client dug a forefinger into his right ear, which always seemed to help him think, and said, "Well, Panama's not bad, but you can't be sure everybody down there'll speak English, although most of 'em do, but I still sorta like the Bahamas because all of 'em speak English there, even if you've got to work at it sometimes to understand what the fuck they're saying. How much we talking about?"

"Five hundred thousand."

"Oh," the client said, as if the amount were scarcely enough to fool with. "Well, it'll cost you."

"How much?"

"First off, we'll take ten percent and our pet bank down in Houston's gonna take another ten, so what you'll have left by the time it gets where it's going is about four hundred K."

"Then let's do it," Vines said.

"When?"

"Today. Right now."

When Kelly Vines walked into the reception room of the chambers of the chief justice of the state supreme court on the third floor of the state capitol building, the 54-year-old secretary looked up with an apprehensive expression that dissolved into relief when she saw that her visitor was the boss's son-in-law and not the police.

"He's been asking for you," said Eunice Warr, who had been Adair's secretary for thirteen years.

"How's he doing?"

She shrugged. "About like you'd expect."

Vines smiled slightly. "You think he took it, Eunice?"

She shrugged again. "Says he didn't."

The chief justice's large chamber was panelled in pecan and carpeted with woven wool and filled with a huge teak desk, two brown leather couches and at least six brown leather easy chairs. Maroon velvet curtains decorated three wide ceiling-high windows that looked out on the Japanese-designed executive office building across the street where the governor worked.

Adair sat in a high-backed leather swivel chair, his feet up on the massive desk, listening through an earphone to a small gray multiband Sony radio, the ICF-2002 short-wave model.

Adair took the earphone off and said, "Well, at least it didn't make the BBC yet."

"What else have you heard?" Vines said as he sat down in one of the leather easy chairs.

"Just what's on the local all-news station," Adair said, reaching for his black cane. After removing its handle and cork, he poured two drinks into a pair of glasses that he took from a desk drawer.

"I was holding out till you got here," he said as he rose and handed Vines one of the glasses. "Didn't quite seem like the time to be drinking alone."

Vines tasted his whiskey and said, "Anyone call you?"

"Not a soul."

"Or drop by to commiserate?"

"Be like commiserating with an ax-murderer."

"Paul didn't call—or Dannie?"

"Paul's off doing the Lord's work in Cyprus, I think, and as for Dannie, well, your wife and my daughter doesn't seem to be paying much attention to current events these days, which, I assume, you must've noticed."

"But you did hear about the Fullers and the suicide note?" Vines said.

Adair nodded and sipped some of his whiskey. "They say you found the bodies."

"I also went to your apartment."

"Well, you've got a key."

"I looked around."

"Get to it, Kelly."

"I looked in that big walk-in closet—the one in your bedroom."

"You're saying, for some reason, that you looked there first, right?"

Vines nodded.

"And found what?"

"Two Gucci shoeboxes. The first one contained two hundred and fifty thousand dollars in one-hundred-dollar bills. The second one contained the same fucking thing."

Vines knew that no one, not even a great actor, could feign the shock that widened Adair's kitten blue eyes, dropped open his mouth and produced the violent sneeze, a powerful hay fever-type blast that made him fumble for his handkerchief and blow his nose. After he was done with that, he remembered his drink, gulped it down and, in an almost conversational tone, said, "Son of a bitch."

After that, Adair stared down between his knees at the wool carpet, looked up at Vines and said, "I never bought a pair of Guccis in my life."

The anger came then—a slow cold rage that narrowed Adair's eyes, drained his plump cheeks of all color and caused the three chins to quiver angrily when he again spoke. "It still there?" he demanded. "In my closet? In a pair of fucking Gucci shoeboxes?"

Vines looked at his watch and said, "It should be on its way down to the Bahamas right about now."

Adair's anger evaporated. Color returned to his cheeks and curiosity to his expression. "I thank you, Kelly," he said with careful formality. "But I've got to say it was a goddamned dumb thing for you to do."

"It's also a felony. You were set up, Jack. But without the money, they have no case. At least not one they can win."

Adair swivelled around in his chair so he could look across the street at the almost new building where the governor worked. "They'll try, though, won't they?"

"Yes."

"And what d'you suppose they'll poke around in first?"

"The usual: your bank accounts, safety-deposit boxes, assets, investments, tax returns."

"Tax returns," Adair said to the building across the street.

The silence began then. It was one of those ominous silences that seldom lasts very long because somebody coughs or clears his throat before somebody else screams. Kelly Vines ended the silence in the chambers of the chief justice with a murmured question. "What's the problem, Jack?"

Adair swivelled around to face him and spoke in a voice without inflection. It was a tone Vines instantly recognized because he had heard it often from clients who, when all hope was gone, used it to describe their transgressions without emotion or embellishment. It was, Vines had learned, the voice of truth.

"Four years ago," Adair said, "I told the payroll folks to start taking double state and Federal withholding out of my salary. I figured the additional withholding would make me come out about even with the tax people at the end of the year and take care of whatever tax I might owe on interest, dividends and other outside income."

"Very prudent," Vines said.

"The thing is," Adair said, "I forgot to file my state and Federal returns that first year. When I finally remembered, I just kept putting it off. And when nothing happened, I just kept on putting it off."

"For how long?"

"As I said, four years now."

143

"They've got you, Jack."

"I know."

"You could've gone to H and R Block, for Christsake. You could've let Eunice handle it for you. You could've— aw, shit—it just doesn't make sense."

"Procrastination rarely does."

There was nothing ominous or threatening about the new silence that developed. Rather it was the sad kind sometimes experienced at graveside services when no one can think of anything to say, good or bad, about the dead. Finally, Kelly Vines said, "Maybe I can make a fancy move or two and rig up some kind of a trust that'll salvage something, if we're lucky."

"Can you keep me out of jail?"

"I can try."

"That's not what I asked."

"I'm not in the miracle business, Jack."

"Would it take a miracle to find out who stuck those shoeboxes in my closet?"

"No," Vines said. "That won't take a miracle."

Twenty-one

After Parvis Mansur had listened to what Adair and Vines had to say about disbarment, Lompoc penitentiary life, the death of Blessing Nelson and murder in the Blue Eagle Bar, the Iranian took over the discussion and aimed it right at what obviously disturbed him most.

Making no effort to disguise his skepticism, he said, "In effect, Mr. Adair, you're saying that nobody really wants to kill you—at least not yet. If they did, they could easily have done when they photographed you from the rear of that pink van. After all, an Uzi's as simple to operate as a Minolta. Some say simpler."

"Or they could've had me killed in prison."

"But since they didn't, you believe you're still alive because of what you know, correct?"

"Because of what they *think* I know."

"Is there a possibility that your memory might improve at some propitious moment?"

"If there really is something to remember, it could come to me one of these days. Or nights."

"What if someone were to put a gun to your head and say, 'Reveal or die'?"

"That might jog the memory. Then again, it might not."

After permitting himself a fleeting look of utter disbelief, Mansur turned to Vines. "I assume Mr. Adair's enemies are also yours?"

"That's a safe assumption."

"Not exactly pussycats, are they?"

"Apparently not."

Mansur grimaced and closed his eyes, as if at some sudden pain, which Vines thought was probably mental. When he opened them to look at Vines again, they still appeared as skeptical as ever. "If I understand my sister-in-law correctly," Mansur said, sounding almost bored or possibly resigned, "you want me to winkle these enemies of yours out of their concealment. And to do this I'm to spread the word that the pair of you can be purchased from your putative protectors, Mayor Huckins and Chief Fork, for one million dollars in cash. Correct so far?"

"So far," Vines said.

"May I ask how you arrived at that nice round sum?"

Adair said, "I decided a million's just small change to them. Respectable change, of course, but still small."

"One other item," Vines said. "We also want you to make it look like a setup—as if you'd tricked us into it."

"Well, now," Mansur said, sounding interested and pleased for the first time. "A touch of humbug. Marvelous. It could work nicely, providing . . ." The sentence died as he gave Huckins an amused look. "Well, B.D.?"

"Sid and I want a straight switch, Parvis," she said. "You pass the word and Mr. Mysterious makes his approach. When the time and place are agreed to, you trade Adair and Vines for the million any way you can. After that, they're on their own."

Mansur cocked a questioning eyebrow at Adair. "Satisfactory?"

"Sounds fine."

Mansur leaned back in his chair to study Adair. "For some reason, neither you nor Mr. Vines look like a couple of guys who'd willingly walk through death's front door."

"We're not," Adair said.

"So you have some . . . contingency plan"

Adair only stared at him.

"Which is none of my affair, of course. My only task is to establish contact and make sure no one is cheated or harmed—at least until the money is safely in my hands."

"That's what you're good at, isn't it?" Vines asked.

"Arranging things?" Mansur said. "Yes. That's what I'm very good at." He looked around the table, wearing a bright smile, and said, "Any other questions, comments?"

"Only one," Adair said. "I'm always curious why a man takes on a lousy job. Since we're not paying you anything and, as far as I know, the mayor and the chief aren't either, my question's the usual crude one: what's in it for you?"

Mansur turned to his wife with a fond smile and covered her hand with his. "Continued domestic bliss," he said.

"Which we all know is beyond price," said Adair.

"Precisely."

Dixie Mansur withdrew her hand from her husband's, looked at Kelly Vines and said, "You forgot something."

"What?"

"You told the judge—or said you told him anyway—that you thought you could find out who put those two shoeboxes full of money in his closet. Well. Did you? Find out?"

"Yes."

"How?"

"I asked the doorman at Jack's condo building."

"The one you went to high school with who didn't remember you?"

"He remembered me," Kelly Vines said.

* * *

The doorman looked down at the fifty-dollar bill in his right hand, then up at Vines. "What's this for, Kelly, old times' sake?"

"Some friends played a joke on Judge Adair and he'd like to find out how."

"What kind of joke?" the doorman asked. "Sick? Funny? Practical? What?"

"Practical."

"Tell me about it. I could use a giggle."

"They put something in his apartment—or had somebody put it there."

"What?"

Vines used his hands to indicate something about the size of a breadbox. "About this big—maybe a package."

"You're a lawyer now, right? I remember in school how you were always on the debate team. I even remember how you got to go to Washington, D.C. one time and debate some other team from Wisconsin. I think it was Wisconsin. Is that how come you decided to be a lawyer— because you like to get up in front of everybody and argue about stuff?"

"Probably," Vines said.

"Something about yea-big, huh?" the doorman said, using his hands to shape his own breadbox. "What was in it that was so funny?"

"Dead fish."

"I don't get it."

"It had to do with a fishing trip the judge had to cancel at the last minute."

The doorman frowned, as if he still couldn't quite appreciate the humor. "So the guys who went on the trip dropped off some of their catch to show him what he missed, right? But by now the fish're kind of old and beginning to stink." He thought about it some more, nodded grudgingly and said, "Yeah, well, I guess some people'd think that was funny."

The doorman's gray-blue eyes widened, then narrowed, as if he suddenly remembered something—or wanted it to appear that way. "Hey, is that what you brought down from his apartment this afternoon in that Hefty bag you tossed into your Mercedes trunk—the fish?"

"We had a good laugh," Vines said.

"You and the judge, huh?"

"Right. And now we'd like to play one back on whoever dumped the fish on him."

The doorman took off his Ruritania guards cap with the shiny black visor, examined the fifty-dollar bill he still held in his right hand and tucked it behind the cap's sweatband. But instead of putting the cap back on, he held it waist-high and upside down, as if waiting for alms. When none was dropped in, he said, "You know, I seem to remember somebody that had a key to the judge's place."

Vines sighed, reached into a pocket, brought out another fifty and dropped it into the cap.

"I'm trying to remember if it was a real big package or a real little one."

Vines put another fifty in the cap.

"Or if it was a man or a woman."

When Vines's hand came out of his pocket this time, it held three fifty-dollar bills. "You just bumped the ceiling," he said, dropping them into the cap.

The doorman immediately covered his head with the cap and its treasure of $300 in fifty-dollar bills. "A short guy," he said. "With what looked like a sack full of groceries. He had a key to the judge's place and said the sack had legal documents the judge wanted dropped off. Funny-looking guy. Short—like I said. Five-two and chunky fat. He was also mud-ugly and had this funny nose with one hole twice as big as the other. That nose was something you couldn't help noticing because it sort of turned up and took aim at you. Well, anyway, he had a key and slipped me a twenty, so I told him to go on up."

"You didn't ask for some I.D.?"

"Well, shit, Kelly, you don't ask a priest for I.D."

Twenty-two

Sid Fork finally found what he had been searching for in the larger bedroom of his measle-white two-bedroom house up on Don Domingo Drive. The bedroom contained what he regarded as the Fork Collection of American Artifacts. Some of them—his sixty-two pre-1941 Coca-Cola bottles, for example—were preserved inside glass-door cabinets. Less fragile treasures, such as his 131 varieties of barbed wire, were neatly displayed on fiberboard panels that took up a third of one wall.

Among the other displays was a nicely mounted collection of the ninety-four varieties of "I Like Ike" buttons that were handed out during the presidential campaigns of 1952 and 1956. The political buttons, carefully arranged by size, were next to a dramatic display of the last copies ever printed of *Collier's, Look, Liberty, Flair,* the old *Saturday Evening Post,* the old *Vanity Fair, McClure's* and a half dozen other extinct magazines.

Much of the stuff Fork had collected over the years had yet to be sorted and catalogued and was stored in splintery wooden crates and stained cardboard boxes that were stacked to the ceiling in one corner of the bedless bedroom. But Fork's special pride was his collection of glass insulators that once had graced electric powerlines, both rural and urban, from Florida to Alaska. The green, purple, brown and gray spool-like insulators were lined up on two long high shelves and illuminated by track lighting. It was behind the insulators on the top shelf that Fork finally found the snapshot album.

He took it over to his eighty-one-year-old rolltop oak desk, switched on the fifty-two-year-old gooseneck lamp, dusted the album's black leatherette cover with a woman's lace handkerchief, whose provenance escaped him, and went through the album page by page until he came to a large color photograph—a jumbo print—of two young men and two young girls, one of the girls scarcely more than a child.

Fork stared at the photograph for seconds before he removed it from the album and rummaged through the junk mail on his desk for the X-acto knife. He used the knife and a ruler to cut out the head and shoulders of one of the young men in the snapshot. After another brief search, he located the bottle of rubber cement and carefully mounted the cut-out head and shoulders on a plain three-by-five-inch index card. From the right pocket of his old tweed jacket, Fork took nine other index cards and slipped the new one among them. After shuffling all ten cards, he dealt them out on the desk.

The cards displayed full-face color photographs of ten men whose ages ranged from 20 to 40. None of the men was handsome or even good-looking and a few were actually ugly. All stared straight at the camera. None was smiling.

Fork gathered up the ten cards, stuck them back into his jacket pocket and left the room, pausing only to admire a framed four-color magazine advertisement, at least fifty-five years old, that portrayed a pretty young woman in a big shiny roadster somewhere west of Laramie. The ad's illustration was Sid Fork's favorite folk art; its copy his most beloved poem.

The chief of police found the whiskey priest at 3:13 P.M. on that last Saturday in June. He found Father Frank Riggins sitting on a bench under a eucalyptus tree not far from the bandstand in Handshaw Park. The priest wore old blue jeans, some new Nike walking shoes without socks and a green T-shirt with a line of yellow type that proclaimed: "There Are No *Small* Miracles."

"Thought you might be here," Fork said as he sat down on the bench, took a small white paper sack from his jacket pocket and offered it to Riggins. "Joe Huff's wife made it. Calls it her Vassar recipe."

Father Riggins stared at the paper sack, shook his head sadly and said, "I shouldn't."

"Got pecans in it."

"Don't tempt me, Sid."

"One piece won't hurt."

"Substitutions are a cop-out," Riggins said as his right hand dived into the sack and came up with an inch-thick, two-inch square of pecan-studded fudge. He took a large bite, chewed slowly, smiled gloriously and said, "It hurts my teeth more than my conscience."

"Take the sack," Fork said, offering it to Riggins.

"Aren't you having any?"

"Never much cared for fudge."

The priest took the sack, peered inside to count the remaining pieces and looked up at Fork with a faint smile. "Now that you've compromised me, what d'you want to know—more about what I told Joe Huff and Wade Bryant this morning?"

Fork nodded.

"I didn't get a good look at him."

"Why not? You don't wear glasses."

153

"It was dark."

"Felipe keeps that pet shop window pretty well lit and there's a streetlamp right out in front of the Blue Eagle."

"He was dressed like a priest—or the way we all used to dress."

"Can't swear he wasn't one though, can you?"

"Of course I can't. There've been all kinds of priests—crazy ones, rapists, embezzlers, thieves, deviates and, of course, drunks. Lots and lots of drunks. So why not a killer?"

"We both know he wasn't any priest, Frank."

Riggins sighed. "I suppose we do."

"Could you recognize him again?"

"Probably."

"What'd he look like?"

"I can only tell you what I told Joe and Wade this morning."

"That'll do fine."

Riggins thought about what he was going to say, then nodded, as if reassuring himself, and said, "Well, he was short. That's what you noticed first. No more than five-one, if that. And very heavy—you know, almost round. And he had those very stubby legs and gray hair cut short. Not just a crew cut, but as if somebody'd grabbed a pair of scissors and just whacked it off. I was too far away to see the color of his eyes, but he was no beauty."

"Why?"

"Well, he had this strange nose that looked a little like a pig's snout with its bottom all turned up so you could see his nostrils even from across the street."

"I brought some pictures I'd like you to look at."

"A rogues' gallery?"

"Something like that," Fork said, removed the ten index cards from his jacket pocket and handed them to Riggins, who went through them slowly, stopped at the seventh one and said, "Well . . . I don't quite know."

"Don't quite know what?"

"He looks so much younger here."

The chief of police took the index card from the priest and glanced at the face of the man he had cut out of the jumbo print with the X-acto knife.

"That's because he was younger then," Fork said, still looking at the photograph. "Twenty years younger."

Seated in the chocolate-brown leather chair in her living room, B.D. Huckins put down the glass of wine so she could go through the ten index cards Sid Fork had handed her.

"How am I supposed to know which one Frank Riggins picked?" she said.

"You'll know," Fork said, drank some of his beer and watched as the mayor glanced at seven of the index cards without expression. She stopped at the eighth, narrowed her eyes and clamped her lips into the thin grim line that helped form her pothole complaint look. Her expression remained grim when she looked up from the photograph and said, "It can't be."

"You know better'n that, B.D."

She tapped the man's face on the index card with a forefinger. "Where'd you get a picture of Teddy?"

"Remember the day we all moved into that shack he'd rented out on Boatright?"

The mayor nodded reluctantly, as if she found the memory disturbing.

"And the landlord, old man Nevers, came by to see if he could bum a drink and Teddy lined all four of us up—you, me, him and Dixie—and made Nevers take our picture with your Instamatic before he'd give him a drink?"

"I don't remember any of that," she said.

"Well, I do. And I also remember getting jumbo prints made of that roll and pasting them in my album."

"I don't understand why."

"Why what?"

"Why you'd even think of Teddy or show his picture to Frank Riggins." She grimaced, as if at some bad taste. "Teddy. Jesus."

"What'd I use to call him?"

"Teddy? Snout."

"And if I didn't call him Snout, I called him Porky. So this morning, those two ace homicide detectives of mine came up with an eyewitness—Father Frank—who claimed he saw some real short guy of around forty who looked like Porky Pig go into the Blue Eagle and come out just about the time poor old Norm got shot. So I started thinking about whether I knew any short mean guys with piggy noses who might go around shooting people for money or just for the hell of it and I came up with Teddy. I mean, he just popped into my mind."

"After twenty years?" she said.

"Teddy sort of sticks in the mind—even after twenty years."

The mayor closed her eyes and leaned back in the leather easy chair. "We should've drowned him." When she spoke again several seconds later her eyes were still closed and her voice sounded weary. "Was Teddy dressed up like a priest?"

"I just told you that."

"No, you didn't."

Fork replayed the last few minutes of conversation in his mind. "You're right. I didn't. So who did?"

"Kelly Vines—indirectly."

"When?"

"Today. Out at Cousin Mary's."

"Let's hear it," Fork said. "All of it."

Huckins's account of the lunch was condensed yet comprehensive and included Kelly Vines's recollection of his conversation with the doorman who was reluctant to ask a priest for identification. When she had finished, Sid Fork's first question was, "What'd you all have for lunch?"

"Trout," Huckins said and quickly recited the rest of the menu, knowing Fork would ask if she didn't.

"How was it—the trout?"

"Very good."

"Who paid?"

"Vines, I think."

"Tell me again what Vines said the doorman said about the short guy in the priest suit."

"You mean what he looked like?"

Fork nodded impatiently.

"Let me think." Huckins closed her eyes again, kept them closed for at least ten seconds, opened them and said, "The doorman told Vines the priest was short and mud-ugly and had one nostril twice as big as the other one. He said the nose turned up and aimed what he called the two holes right at you."

"And that didn't make you think of Teddy right off?"

"No."

The nod that Fork had intended to be sympathetic was betrayed by its condescension. "Well, you're not a cop."

"But since you are, tell me this. What'll the cops do about Teddy?"

"Whatever's within the law."

"And Sid Fork? What'll he do?"

"Whatever's necessary."

Twenty-three

The 51-year-old Durango detective, who had once worked bunco and fraud in Dallas, looked up from his copy of *People* magazine when the tall elderly white-haired man with the neat tar-black mustache strode into the lobby of the Holiday Inn and headed for the shallow alcove where the house phones were.

Marking his place in *People* by turning down a page corner, Ivy Settles placed the magazine on the table next to the couch and rose, not taking his eyes off the man who stood, pine-tree straight, the phone to his ear, waiting for his call to be answered.

Settles studied the man's muted brown plaid jacket, deciding it was a silk and wool blend that had cost at least $650—maybe even $700. The deeply pleated fawn gabardine slacks, he guessed, would go for $400, even $425. And those two-tone brown and white lace-up shoes with the moccasin toes—a style Settles hadn't seen in twenty years—were probably handmade and cost as much as the jacket. Including socks, shirt and underwear, Settles figured the man was wearing close to a couple of thousand dollars on his back and feet.

The detective stuck his hands down into the slash pockets of the Taiwanese-made windbreaker he had paid $16.83 for, including tax, at Figgs' department store and crossed the lobby on feet shod in penny loafers from Land's End. The rest of him was clad in chinos by Sears, a white short-sleeved shirt by Arrow and underwear by Fruit of the Loom. Settles liked cheap clothes and guessed that everything he wore, including his white drugstore socks, hadn't cost as much as the black lizard strap that bound the thin gold watch to the white-haired man's left wrist.

With his hands still stuck down into the windbreaker's pockets, Settles stopped just behind the man, as if the pair of them were forming a line. The man was now talking into a house phone in a crisp and pleasant voice that sounded far too young for his age. Settles thought of it as the man's up-North voice and remembered how easily it could slide into soft southern tones that sounded remarkably like Charleston.

"Yes, in the lobby," the man said into the phone. "I thought I might pop up for a minute or two with something that should interest you."

Finally sensing someone behind him, the man turned to face Settles, who stood, hands still inside the slash pockets, rocking back and forth on his heels. The man frowned and pointed to the other house phones. Settles smiled slightly, shaking his head.

The man turned his back on the detective and again spoke into the phone. "Let's make that five minutes instead of right away. I have another call to make."

The man hung up, turned to face Settles again and said, "You queer for this particular phone, friend?"

"It's been a while, Soldier," Settles said.

The man frowned again, this time trying to look puzzled. He might have succeeded were it not for the glittering green eyes that could never quite conceal their slyness. "Don't believe I've had the pleasure," he said in the nicely chilled up-North voice.

"Dallas," Ivy Settles said. "February of seventy-three. I took you down and put you on the Greyhound to Houston after the stockbroker's widow refused to press charges."

"My fiancée," the man said. "Edwina Wickersham."

"Who you gave the money back to."

"Repaid the loan, you mean." The white-haired man studied Settles carefully, taking his time, starting with the penny loafers and working his way up to the round face, where a delicate nose and a hesitant chin clashed with a pair of know-it-all gray eyes and a thin wiseacre mouth.

"You got fat, Ivy," the man said. "And you appear to have fallen on hard times—although with you it's always been kind of hard to tell. What are you now—a Holiday Inn house dick?"

"Who was the call to, Soldier?" Settles asked.

"That's really none of your fucking business, is it?"

Settles nodded, as if in agreement, picked up one of the house phones and tapped three numbers. When the call was answered he said, "This is Settles down in the lobby. You just get a call from Soldier Sloan?" He listened, glanced back at Sloan and said, "No, no trouble. Just checking. I'll send him on up."

After Settles hung up, Soldier Sloan smiled a warm, almost cozy smile and asked, "How d'you like working for Sid Fork, Ivy?"

"It's nice and quiet and that's how Sid and I like it."

Sloan looked around the almost empty lobby. "Graves aren't this quiet."

"Well, we got the Fourth of July parade coming up next week."

"Doubtless a day of revelry and madness."

"I'll see you to the elevator, Soldier. Make sure you punch the right button and all."

As they waited for an elevator, Settles said, "Hear you promoted yourself to brigadier general."

"And high time, too, don't you think?"

Settles smiled and nodded happily, not in response to Sloan's question, but as if he had just arrived at some welcome conclusion. "I sure like that new mustache, Soldier. Reminds me of the one Cesar Romero used to wear before his went white. Now there was a mustache—not like those floppy cookie-dusters Selleck and all the Highway Patrol kids wear nowadays. I bet yours grew in coal-black. Bet you don't even have to dye it. All that white hair. Black eyebrows. Matching mustache. I've gotta say it sure makes you distinguished-looking, Soldier, and how long do I tell Sid you're gonna be with us this time?"

"Leaving on the evening tide."

"Sid'll be sorry he missed you," Settles said as the elevator doors opened. He watcher Sloan enter the elevator, turn and press the 4 button. " Good seeing you again, Soldier."

"Always a pleasure," the old man said just before the doors closed.

After half a lifetime in bunco and fraud, Ivy Settles watched the lighted floor indicator of the elevator Soldier Sloan was taking to the fourth floor—just to make sure, he told himself, it didn't go sideways. The elevator had paused at three and continued on to four, where it now seemed stuck.

The other elevator, to Settles' right, was on its way down. It, too, had paused at three and Settles decided to ask its passenger or passengers if they knew what the trouble was on the fourth floor.

The doors of the right-hand elevator opened and a very short, very heavy man came out. He wore a giveaway cap advertising Copenhagen snuff, thick tinted glasses and dark blue coveralls that had "Francis" stitched in red above the left breast pocket. In his right hand he carried a large black toolbox that looked old and battered.

"What happened to the other elevator?" Settles asked.

The man stopped, looked up at Settles, then up at the floor indicator numbers and back at Settles. "Beats me."

"Where'd you get on?"

"Three."

"You're not the elevator repair guy, are you?"

The short man turned his back on Settles. An arc of two-inch-high red letters spelled out "Francis the Plumber" across the coveralls. Below the name was a phone number. The man turned to face Settles again.

"I'm Francis and there was a backed-up toilet in three twenty-two and it's Saturday and I'm on double time. So if somebody wants me to stand around talking about busted elevators, somebody's gonna get charged for it."

"Wait here," Settles said.

"Why?"

Settles brought out his badge and showed it to the plumber. "Because I said to."

After hurrying to the shallow alcove where the house phones were, Settles snatched one up and tapped three numbers. After two rings a man's voice answered with a hello.

"Mr. Adair?" Settles said.

"This is Vines."

"Settles again—down in the lobby. Has Soldier Sloan showed up yet?"

"Not yet."

"Would you go take a look at the elevator on the fourth floor—the car on your right—and then come down and tell me what's wrong with it?"

"Come down to the lobby and tell you?"

"Please."

"All right," Vines said and hung up.

Settles hurried back to the elevators, where Francis the Plumber had failed to wait. The detective turned and trotted across the lobby to the hotel entrance. He went through it just in time to see a pink Ford van make a right turn out of the parking lot. On the side of the van was a large magnetic stick-on sign that advertised "Francis the Plumber" in big black letters. Beneath them, in smaller ones, was the slogan "Nite or Day."

Embarrassed and irritated by his own vanity, Ivy Settles fumbled his glasses from his shirt pocket and put them on. But by then, even with the glasses, it was impossible to read the license plate of the pink Ford van.

Twenty-four

The elevators were down the corridor and around a corner from Kelly Vines's fourth-floor room. When he reached them he found Soldier Sloan lying face up and half out of the right elevator, whose two automatic doors were gently nudging the old man's waist every three or four seconds.

It was obvious to Vines that Sloan was dead. Those too-green eyes had lost their glitter and stared up without blinking at the corridor's vanilla ceiling. Vines knelt to put a hand to the old man's neck, feeling for the pulse he knew he wouldn't find.

If there was a cause of death, Vines couldn't see it. There were no visible wounds or blood, but he did find Sloan's position peculiar. It was as if the old man had turned to face the rear of the elevator, then fell backward, sprawling halfway through the open doors.

Vines explored the dead man's pockets almost without thinking of the consequences other than to remind himself he was no longer an officer of the court. He left the watch pocket until last because he was confident of what he would find there.

In the other pockets he found a comb, a Montblanc fountain pen and an ostrichskin wallet, well worn, that contained $550 in fifty-dollar bills. In the other pockets he found a car's ignition key attached to a Mercedes emblem that didn't necessarily mean anything; a small pocket knife with a gold case that Vines thought was probably 14 carat; a handkerchief of Irish linen; and a small combination address book and pocket diary. The address section was almost filled with names and phone numbers, but very few addresses. The diary section was blank and the page for that June Saturday, the twenty-fifth, had been torn out.

In Sloan's watch pocket, as expected, Vines found a folded-up thousand-dollar bill, issued in 1934 and bearing the engraved portrait of Grover Cleveland and the signature of Henry Morgenthau, Jr., Secretary of the Treasury. On the back of the old bill was some fancy engraving to discourage counterfeiters.

The torn-out diary page was also in the watch pocket, folded up, like the thousand-dollar bill, into the size of a postage stamp. Vines carefully unfolded it, noticing that most of it was for a diary and about an inch at the bottom for a "memo." At the top of the page were initials and numbers reading, "KV 431" and "JA 433," which Vines immediately deciphered as being his and Jack Adair's initials and room numbers.

At the bottom of the page in the space reserved for the memo was another entry that read: "C JA O RE DV." Vines could make nothing out of this and put everything back where he had found it, including the torn-out diary page and the thousand-dollar bill, both of them carefully refolded. After that he rose and went to tell Ivy Settles that Soldier Sloan was dead.

* * *

Settles, the first policeman to reach Soldier Sloan's body, watched as the Holiday Inn's young assistant manager used a key to turn off the elevator so its two doors would stay open and stop nudging the dead man's waist. Settles knelt beside Sloan, checked for vital signs and looked up at Vines, who, like Adair, was now leaning against the wall opposite the elevators. "He's dead," Settles said. "Just like you said."

Because Vines could think of nothing to add to this, he said nothing. Chief Sid Fork arrived a few minutes later, nodded at Vines and Adair, glanced at the dead Soldier Sloan and began questioning Settles. He was still questioning him when the two homicide specialists, Wade Bryant and Joe Huff, arrived and joined the interrogation of Ivy Settles.

The bald, black and professorial Huff asked an occasional question as he used his Minolta to take photographs of the dead man. When he had taken enough, he interrupted Wade Bryant and said, "Let's turn him over."

Once Soldier Sloan lay on his stomach, the saucer-sized bloodstain on the back of his muted plaid jacket was visible. With the help of Bryant, Huff removed the jacket and took some pictures of a bloodstain the size of a dinner plate on the back of Sloan's pale yellow shirt.

Out of curiosity, Kelly Vines asked, "What d'you guys do for a coroner?"

"Because we're ninety-two miles from the county seat, they named Dr. Joe Emory assistant deputy coroner," Huff said, pulling out Sloan's shirttails and pushing the shirt itself up toward the dead man's armpits. "The fancy title doesn't mean much because the county pays Joe on a piecework basis."

"He likes doing autopsies?"

"He likes the money," Huff said.

Once the shirt was up around Sloan's armpits, the small

puncture wound was visible. The wound itself hadn't really bled much and had the diameter, in Huff's words, "of a fat ice pick."

As he rose, Huff added, "He died quick anyway," and aimed his Minolta at Sloan's bare back.

"If the angle was right and the guy knew what he was doing," the still kneeling Wade Bryant said, "then he probably didn't feel much of anything."

"He felt it," Huff said. "He felt it enough to turn around, see who'd done it and keel over backward."

The assistant hotel manager edged over to Fork. "Couldn't you guys at least pull him out of the elevator, Sid? We're going to need it."

"No, you're not," Fork said.

"So when can we start using it?"

"In an hour or two."

"Well, shit," said the assistant manager and headed for the stairs.

Bryant gave the dead Sloan a final close look and rose. "While we're waiting for Doc Emory, Chief, I thought maybe Ivy here could tell us some more about his new pal, Francis the Plumber."

"I already told you," Settles said.

"We'd like to hear it again," Bryant said, looking for support to Huff, who was adjusting his Minolta. The black detective looked up just long enough to nod and went back to his camera.

"One more time, Ivy," the chief of police said.

Settles gave Fork a reproachful look and said, "He was about forty and short and fat—five-one and maybe two hundred and ten. Wore dark blue coveralls with Francis the Plumber across the back in red letters—and a phone number I don't remember. He carried an old beat-up black toolbox. Had tinted prescription glasses, the kind that go from real light gray to real dark gray depending on the light. Had a gimme cap from Copenhagen snuff. Had a thin nasty mouth. Drove a pink Ford van with a stick-on 'Francis the Plumber' magnet sign on one side—maybe both sides, but I don't know that for a fact. And no, I didn't get the license number this time either."

"You forgot his nose," Huff said, still working on his camera.

"Yeah. Right. The nose. Well, it was kind of squashed up, like I told you, and had this one big nostril and this regular size one and they both looked about a mile deep. They were also hairy. He had a regular forest growing in there and most of it was gray."

"Tell us again why you let him skip, Ivy," said Wade Bryant, whose increasingly sly tone matched his too-tall-elf looks.

"I didn't let him. I showed him my shield and told him to stay put while I went and called Vines here. The guy was a plumber and possibly—just possibly—a solid citizen. What you two guys would've done, of course, is make him kiss the floor right off. With all your experience you know for a fact that plumbers are automatic suspects." Settles paused, glared at Bryant, and added, "Oh, yeah. One more thing."

"What?" Bryant said.

"I watched Soldier's elevator all the way up. I mean I watched its numbers light up. It stopped at three on the way up and the other elevator, the one the plumber rode, stopped at three on the way down. So I'd say the plumber got on Soldier's elevator at three, killed him on the way up to four, got out, took the stairs back down to three and rode the other elevator from there to the lobby, where, for some reason, I neglected to beat the shit out of him."

Twenty-five

After a grateful swallow of the bourbon and water Kelly Vines had handed him, the chief of police looked at Jack Adair and said, "Tell me something. Was Soldier ever a soldier?"

"In two wars," Adair said, turning from the window in Vines's room where he had been inspecting the ocean. "And Soldier, incidentally, was his real name."

"Couldn't be," Fork said.

"Years ago I saw his birth certificate. It was back in the early fifties when a certain Mrs. Shipley in the State Department was suspicious of almost anyone who applied for a passport, but particulary suspicious of applicants who'd served in the Lincoln Battalion in Spain and later with the OSS, which is why Soldier'd come to me."

Fork made no effort to hide his surprise and disbelief. "What the hell was he doing in Spain?"

"Purely by chance Soldier'd landed a job to shepherd nine Dodge ambulances from Detroit down to Mexico and over to Spain. They'd been bought for the Loyalists by some folks who, I think, were later called premature anti-Fascists." Adair smiled. "Soldier always said his old pal Hemingway helped raise some of the money."

"How old was Soldier then?"

"When he went to Spain? He'd have been just twenty. He was born April sixth, nineteen seventeen, and I remember the date because it was the day we declared war on Germany." Adair smiled again, rather gently, and added, "World War One."

Sid Fork's impatient nod indicated he knew all about World War One. "And that's why his folks named him Soldier?"

Adair nodded. "His full name was Soldier P. Sloan. The 'P' was for Pershing. A general—in World War One."

"And he joined up after he got the ambulances over to Spain?"

"So he claimed. Anyway, it was his experience there that got him commissioned a second lieutenant in the OSS just after the war started." Adair gave Fork another almost apologetic smile. "World War Two."

"So what'd he do—or claim he did?"

"In the OSS? Engaged in all sorts of hugger-mugger—at least when it didn't interfere with his black market operations." This time Adair's smile was more knowing than apologetic. "Black markets and wars always seem to go hand in hand."

Fork neatly cut off any further discussion of black markets by asking, "Why'd he want a passport in the fifties?"

"Debts," Adair said.

"Wanted to skip out on 'em probably."

"Something like that. So I called in a favor that a certain Republican congressman owed me and Soldier got his passport. When he came back from Europe four years later in fifty-five he was thirty-eight years old and suddenly a retired lieutenant colonel. He promoted himself two more times after that, impressing a never-ending series of gullible but wealthy widows who provided him with clothes, cars, cash and whatever remaining charms they had to offer."

"I sort of inherited Soldier from Jack," Kelly Vines said, putting his drink down carefully on the coffee table and leaning forward to stare at Fork. "Where'd you run across him, Chief?"

"He was our first hideout customer," Fork said. "And afterwards he sent us about a third of our other clients, including you two. He sort of adopted the three of us—B. D., me and Dixie—and liked to take us out for Sunday dinner. Well, that got old pretty quick for me and B. D., but Dixie always went until she married Parvis. She said she liked Soldier's manners." He looked at Vines coldly. "Satisfied?"

After Vines replied with a shrug, Fork asked, "So what do we do with him after the autopsy—bury him, cremate him, donate him—what? He have any kids, ex-wives, brothers, sisters, anybody?"

Adair sighed. "He had a thousand acquaintances and Kelly and me. But from what you say, he also had you, the mayor and Dixie. So I suppose we should bury him with a headstone and all."

"'Soldier P. Sloan,'" Vines said. "'1917–1988.' Then a line or two after that."

"We'll leave the wording up to you, Kelly," Adair said and turned to Fork. "So what'll it cost, Chief—the plot, the stone, a cheap casket and a few words by a not overly sanctimonious priest?"

"Soldier a Catholic?"

"Fallen away, I'm afraid."

"Then I know just the priest. As for how much, well, he had about five hundred and fifty in his wallet, but that won't quite cover what we're talking about." When he felt Kelly Vines's hard stare, he hurried on. "He also had a thousand-dollar bill in his watch pocket, but I'm not sure you can spend that."

"It's perfectly legal tender," Adair said. "And since you're the chief of police, the bank shouldn't ask any questions."

"There was something else in Soldier's watch pocket," Fork said. He fished the folded-up diary page from his shirt pocket and handed it to Vines. "Except it doesn't make sense."

Vines unfolded the page and studied the numbers and capital letters, as if for the first time. "I was never any good at crossword puzzles," he said, "but this first notation, 'KV 431' and 'JA 433' is pretty obvious. It's Jack's room number and mine." He looked up and handed the page to Adair. "The rest is gibberish."

Adair read the other line of capital letters silently, then aloud, "C JA O RE DV." He read it aloud again, rose, walked to the window, as if its light might help, silently read the letters yet again, stared out at the ocean for a few moments and turned to Vines. "Maybe it's simpler than it looks."

"Maybe it's an old OSS code," Fork said.

"More likely it's just the crude shorthand of an old man who didn't trust his memory," Adair said. "'C JA' could mean, 'See Jack Adair.' The next thing could be either a zero or a capital O. If it's a zero, it could read, 'See Jack Adair zero,' which doesn't make sense unless you translate zero into 'alone' or 'by himself.' RE probably means just what it looks like: 'in regard to.' The last initials are DV and the only DV I know is my daughter and Kelly's wife, Danielle Vines."

Vines asked, " See Jack Adair alone in regard to Danielle Vines?"

"Maybe. Maybe not. But I'd best go see Dannie."

Sid Fork shook his head and said, "Dumb idea, Judge."

"Why?"

"You plan to drive?"

Adair nodded.

"Where to?"

"Agoura, isn't it?" Adair said, looking at Vines, who also nodded.

"Somebody could pull up alongside you on the freeway with a shotgun loaded with double ought and no more Jack Adair."

"They could walk through that door and do the same thing," Adair said.

Fork turned to examine the hotel room door, then turned back. "That's why I'm moving you both in about thirty minutes."

"Where to?"

"To a place with the tightest security in town."

"No jail cell, thanks," Adair said.

"I'm not talking jail cell," Fork said, "I'm talking about nice clean rooms, semi-private bath, guaranteed privacy, phone, bed and breakfast, and all for only a thousand a week. Each."

"Must be some breakfast," Vines said. "Does she really need the money?"

"Yes, sir. She does."

"Who?" Adair said.

"The wife of the late Norm Trice, who owned the Blue Eagle," Vines said. "She lives in this huge old Victorian place where the security looks fairly good from what I saw." Vines took in the hotel room with a small gesture. "Better than this anyhow."

Adair looked at Fork. "And you're recommending it?"

"Strongly."

"I'm still going to go see my daughter."

"It's still a dumb idea."

"He could fly down," Vines said.

"From where?"

"You told me there used to be a field here."

"I also told you the Feds closed it down."

"That wouldn't stop some pilots."

"Who you got in mind?"

"That guy who owns Cousin Mary's," Vines said. "Merriman Dorr. He told me he could get himself a Cessna and fly us anywhere—providing the mayor said it was okay."

After several seconds of frowning thought, Fork reluctantly agreed. "Well, at least it makes more sense than driving."

Vines rose, walked over to Fork and stood, staring down at him. "I don't quite understand all this sudden concern for our safety, Chief."

"It's not all that sudden," Fork said. "I've been worried ever since Norm Trice got killed and those photos turned up. Soldier getting killed doesn't make me worry any less. But what got me really bothered was when the mayor and I compared notes."

Fork looked from Vines to Adair and back to Vines to make sure he had their attention. "Remember your telling everybody out at Cousin Mary's about that doorman who gave you a description of a short fat priest with a snout who stuck those two shoeboxes full of money in the judge here's closet?"

Vines said yes, he remembered.

"Well, if what B.D. says you said is right, then that doorman's description of a short fat priest is a perfect fit to the description I got from an eyewitness who claims he saw the same guy go in and come out of the Blue Eagle the night poor old Norm Trice got shot."

"Also a priest?" Vines asked.

"Dressed up like one. Now this same description, except for the priest suit, fits what one of my best detectives says the plumber who shot Soldier looks like. You both heard Ivy. And what all this means is that I'm damn near positive that the guy with the two shoeboxes full of money

174

and the guy who killed Norm Trice and Soldier Sloan are all one and the same."

"You're also beginning to sound as if you know who he is," Vines said, some reluctant admiration creeping into his tone.

"I know all right. He's Teddy Smith—or Teddy Jones—depending on which one he feels like that day. The mayor and Dixie and I knew the little shit twenty years ago when I ran him out of town after he—well, it doesn't matter now."

"Smith," Adair said, looking at Vines. "Wasn't that the name of the man Paul told you he was going to see in Tijuana, the one—"

Three quick hard raps on the hotel room door interrupted Adair, who, now wearing a thoughtful expression, went over to open it. B. D. Huckins nodded at him as she strode in, ignored Kelly Vines and crossed the room to where the chief of police sat. She stood with her fists on her hips, glaring down at Sid Fork and impressing Adair with the way she managed to dominate the room without saying a word.

She was still glaring down at the chief of police when she said, "Cancel it, Sid."

"Cancel what?"

She used a small, almost savage clenched-fist gesture to indicate and cancel Vines and Adair. "Them," she said. "Everything. It's all off."

"Goddamnit, B.D., you can't do that."

"Watch me," she said.

Twenty-six

Sipping occasionally from the glass of straight bourbon she had demanded and Kelly Vines had served her, Mayor B.D. Huckins paced the ocean-view Holiday Inn room, describing with curious relish how she first had learned of the death of Soldier Sloan.

"Was it from the chief of police or the city attorney or even from those two dopers who drive the meat wagon for Bruner Mortuary?" she asked, obviously not expecting an answer. "No, it was from Lenore Poole who strings for that flaky west coast radio network. And guess what Lenore wants to know?"

Since this wasn't a real question either, none of the three men answered. The mayor took another small sip of her bourbon, turned to the window, inspected the Pacific and said, "Lenore wants to know my reaction to the serial killer who's terrorizing Durango."

She turned quickly from the window to fasten the cold gray stare on Sid Fork. "So here's Lenore, who teaches English and a course in journalism at the high school—and who's convinced she's going to be a TV reporter in

Santa Barbara, or maybe even down in L.A., once she saves up enough to have a little corrective surgery done on that chin of hers—telling me about how some plumber stabbed Soldier Sloan to death in an elevator."

"I thought she was saving up for a Harley," Sid Fork said. "That's what she told me."

B.D. Huckins ignored him and turned to Jack Adair, who sat in one of the room's three easy chairs and appeared to be the most sympathetic member of her audience.

"Lenore says, Hey, there's this old Sloan guy today and poor Norm Trice last night, so don't you think it looks like we've got a serial killer on the loose? But all I can tell her is that I can't comment on an ongoing investigation and she'd better talk to the chief of police, who, Lenore tells me, she's been trying 'to get ahold of'—this is an English teacher now—except he can't be found." Huckins switched the cold gray eyes back to Fork. "So where the fuck were you, Sid?"

"Right here."

"Then why didn't you call me—or have somebody call me?"

"I thought somebody did."

The mayor responded to this admission of obvious incompetence with a resigned headshake and turned again to Jack Adair, the ex-politician, who remained her most sympathetic listener. "So now Lenore takes off in another direction and says if I won't agree they're serial murders by a crazed killer, maybe I'll at least admit it's a crime wave. And I tell her, Sorry, Lenore, no crime wave either, and hang up."

She turned to Fork again. "That's when I start calling around, Sid, trying to find you. But by then *my* phone starts ringing—so much for unlisted numbers—and it must be one hell of a slow news day because papers, TV and radio stations from all over are calling me and—"

"Where's all over?" Fork asked.

"San Francisco. Vegas. L.A. Santa Barbara. San Diego. San Jose. Even Oakland. To me, that's all over. And they all want to know about the, quote, hysteria that's gripping a small sleepy California coastal town, unquote. A couple of them even played me parts of Lenore's nutty radio story that adds two years to my age and says Durango's thirty-eight-year-old mayor, quote, hotly denied, unquote, that two murders in two days are either a crime wave or the work of a serial killer. But check this, Sid. Lenore must've talked to some of your people because she said Soldier's name is S. Pershing Sloan and that he's a retired major general." She paused, wrinkled her forehead into a puzzled frown and said, "Pershing?"

"His middle name," Fork said, leaning forward in his chair and looking interested for the first time. "What'd Lenore say about Norm Trice?"

"She called him the owner of Durango's most fashionable night spot."

"Sounds like Lenore," Fork said with a grin and asked, "So what'd you tell 'em, B.D.—all those reporters?"

"I told them to call the chief of police, who'd informed me that an arrest is imminent."

"Good."

"You know what all this will do, don't you?"

"Sure," Fork said. "It'll create a slowdown in the hideout business."

The mayor used three slow headshakes to disagree. "It'll kill it, not slow it down."

"It'll come back."

"Like hell."

Sid Fork rose from his chair and walked slowly toward the window. "All right," he agreed. "Let's say it's finished. Done with. But what about our deal with Vines and Adair here?"

"Unless you can change my mind," she said, "that's dead. Let 'em go hide out somewhere else."

When he reached the window, Fork gave the ocean a quick just-checking glance, turned, leaned against the sill, folded his arms across his chest and regarded the mayor with the detached gaze of a man who already knows the answers he'll get to his questions.

"Tell me something, B.D. Tell me how you're going to scrape up the money to keep the library open after our fiscal year ends next month? Or start up that summer-in-the-park program you promised for June and here it is damn near July? Or keep the clap clinic open? Or even, for God's sake, find enough money to clean up the horseshit after the parade on the Fourth?" Pausing to indicate both Vines and Adair with a nod, Fork said, "There's a million bucks sitting right here in this room on two chairs. So before you walk away from it, think about what I just said."

Huckins was already looking appropriately thoughtful when she turned and sank slowly into the chair Fork had just vacated. She rested her drink on the chair's arm and thrust out her long bare tanned legs, crossing them at the ankles. She wore a bright yellow cotton blouse and a tan cotton twill skirt that ended at her knees. On her feet were a pair of Mexican sandals. Jack Adair stared at her legs until she asked, "Never seen a pair before?"

"Not recently," he said.

Huckins once again looked at Sid Fork, who, arms still folded, leaned against the windowsill. "What I've been thinking about most, Sid, is the eighth of November—not the fourth of July."

Mention of the election date transformed Adair's sympathy into deep interest. "How's it look?" he asked.

Still staring at Fork, she said, "What about it, Sid? What's your guess on how many votes there'll be in two unsolved murders with maybe more to come between now and November?"

"There'd be just one hell of a lot of votes in catching the killer, B.D."

"But when're you going to catch him? After Adair and Vines are dead?"

Before Fork could reply, Kelly Vines said, "We might as well get this straight. Jack and I aren't going to sit around indefinitely, waiting for negotiations to start, while some guy dressed up like a priest or the United Parcel man is figuring out how to shoot, stab or garotte us. There comes a time when patience runs out and common sense takes over."

"Which brings us to Sid's Teddy theory," the mayor said.

Fork made a noise far down in his throat that got the room's attention. "It's more than a theory," he said.

The mayor gave him a dubious look. "You really think it was Teddy who killed Soldier Sloan?"

"Know it was. Killed him in the elevator all decked out like a plumber. Toolbox and everything."

"So when you find Teddy and arrest him," she said, "he'll stand trial, right?"

Fork's answering shrug could have meant yes, no or maybe.

"And if he stands trial," the mayor continued, "a lot of funny stuff could come out about you, me, Teddy and Dixie from the old days—funny-peculiar stuff that most people don't know or have forgotten. Stuff that wouldn't do me any good on November eighth."

"If there is a trial," Fork said.

"You mean, of course, a trial that soon," Adair said. "Before November eighth."

"Ever," Fork said.

"The chief's talking about something else, Jack," Vines said.

"I'm well aware of that."

"I'm pretty sure I'm going to find Teddy," Fork said,

almost musing aloud. "Or maybe he'll find me. But either way I'm pretty sure he'll resist being arrested."

"Which means you're pretty sure you're going to kill him," Adair said in a mild and almost indifferent tone he might have used to remark upon the weather.

The tone made Fork suspicious. "That bother you just a whole lot, Judge?"

All mildness left Adair's voice. It now sounded sternly judicial and, in his opinion, terribly pompous. "I've never been convinced that premeditated homicide is ever justified, whether committed by the individual or the state."

"That's bullshit if I ever heard it," B.D. Huckins said.

"Is it now?"

"Sure it is. Look. You and Vines dreamed this thing up, this plan of yours, set it in motion and it's already got two people killed. Maybe three, counting that friend of yours in Lompoc. So it's time to switch off the sermonette. But if you guys want to walk away, fine. That's your business. Of course, Sid and I'll have to finish what you started because now there's just no way to stop it."

"None at all," Fork said.

"I could be off base," she continued, "but I think the only way you two can come out of this thing about even or a little ahead—and I'm not talking about money—is to finish what you started. Otherwise, you've wasted three lives for nothing—although maybe you can justify that but somehow I don't think so. And that, Mr. Adair, is why I said you were talking bullshit."

Adair, his cheeks a bright pink, stared down between his knees at the hotel room carpet while the woman and the two men stared at him. Finally, he looked up at Huckins and said, "After careful reconsideration, Mayor, you're not altogether wrong."

She looked at Vines. "What's that mean?"

"It means we're still in business."

"Good," B.D. Huckins said.

Twenty-seven

By five o'clock that same Saturday afternoon, Jack Adair and Kelly Vines had checked out of the Holiday Inn and were dutifully following Virginia Trice into the large old bathroom on the second floor of her fourteen-room Victorian house.

The bathroom, at least ten by thirteen feet, separated their two bedrooms and contained a very old six-foot-long tub that stood on cast-iron claws; a fairly new tiled shower; a sink with separate faucets; a chain-flush toilet; and more towels than Adair could ever remember seeing even in the finest hotels.

"Towels," Virginia Trice said, indicating two large stacks of them.

"Very nice," Adair said.

They left the bathroom and regrouped in the hall. "What d'you guys like for breakfast?" she asked.

Adair looked at Vines, who said, "Anything."

"Bacon and eggs?" she said. "Coffee? Juice? Home fries? Biscuits or toast? Cantaloupe maybe?"

"Coffee, toast and juice would be fine for me," Adair said.

"Me, too," said Vines.

"You can have anything you want," she said. "After all, for what you're paying . . ." The sentence died of acute embarrassment.

"Speaking of the rent," Vines said, removed an unsealed Holiday Inn envelope from his hip pocket and handed it to Virginia Trice.

She looked inside the envelope, but didn't count the twenty one-hundred-dollar bills. "It's way too much, isn't it?"

"Not considering the inconvenience we're putting you to," Adair said.

"Okay. If you say so. And it sure comes when I can use it."

"I was very sorry to hear about your husband," Adair said.

"That's nice of you. Funeral's Monday. If you like funerals, you're welcome. It'll be at Bruner's Mortuary because Norm wasn't much of a churchgoer. The Eagle'll be closed all day Monday out of respect. Sid Fork says I oughta keep it open. But I don't know. It just doesn't seem right. What d'you think?"

Adair said he was certain she knew best.

Obviously grateful for the reassurance, Virginia Trice said, "Well, the phone's down at the end of the hall near the stairs on a small stand. I put radios in both your rooms—cheap little jobs—but they'll bring in our local FM station, which sucks, and for some reason an all-news CBS station down in L.A. that's AM. No TV though. Norm wouldn't have one in the house because he had to buy a dish for the set in the Eagle and they'd never let him turn it off. Norm really hated TV. Let's see. What else? Oh. I almost forgot the keys to the front door. They're in your rooms on the bedside tables. Come and go as you like. If you wanta have a friend spend the night, fine. I don't get home till around one on week nights and around two-thirty on Saturday nights like tonight. And I guess that's about all the rules there are."

Adair smiled and said there didn't seem to be any so far.

"Probably because I'm not much of a landlady," she said.

Vines said he thought she was the ideal landlady.

Virginia Trice nodded at the compliment, tried to smile, didn't quite succeed and suddenly remembered something. "Jesus. There is one rule. This place is all wired up. But as long as you use your front door key to go out and come in, you're okay. And don't open any windows either because they're wired up, too. I don't know if you noticed, but the whole place is air-conditioned—except the attic. So if you don't use your front door key going out and coming in, or if you forget and open a window by mistake, the cops'll be here in three minutes, maybe four."

"That's very reassuring," Adair said.

"Can I ask you guys something?"

Vines nodded.

"How bad is it—your trouble?"

"Moderate," Vines said.

"Sid said you might help him catch Norm's killer. Is that straight or was Sid just shining me on like he does sometimes?"

"He wasn't shining you on," Vines said.

"Good," Virginia Trice said, nodded to herself and, a moment later, said "Good" yet again.

By 5:35 that same Saturday evening, Adair and Vines stood beside the Mercedes sedan and watched the four-seat Cessna taxi toward them along the cracked and broken runway of what once had been the Durango Municipal Airport. All that was left of the airport was its disintegrating runway, two roofless corrugated aluminum hangars, a couple of rusting gasoline pumps, from which somebody had stolen the hoses, and the airport "terminal"—a one-story building about the size of a gasoline station office, which had long since been vandalized.

"All part of the trend, I guess," Adair said as he watched Merriman Dorr cut the engine and climb down from the Cessna. "The small-town train depots were the first to go, then the bus stations and now we're getting ghost airports."

"You sure you don't want me to come along?" Vines said.

"I think one of us at a time's about all Dannie can handle."

"Don't expect too much, Jack."

"No."

"Don't expect anything at all."

"All I expect is a visit with my last living blood relative."

Merriman Dorr, now no more than twenty feet away from the Mercedes, wore a brown leather flight jacket that Vines thought was either very old or the kind that was advertised as being "pre-distressed." He also wore dark aviator glasses, chinos, cowboy boots and a blue Dodgers baseball cap. When he was fifteen feet away, Dorr said, "That runway's a bitch."

"That mean we can't take off?" Adair said almost hopefully.

"I can take off from anything I can land on. You ready?"

Adair nodded.

"Then let's go," Dorr said, turned and started walking back toward the Cessna. Adair gave Vines a goodbye shrug and also headed toward the airplane, swinging his black cane.

Vines watched the takeoff from behind the wheel of his Mercedes. The Cessna headed out over the Pacific and turned south. When he could no longer see the airplane, Vines started the Mercedes and drove back to Durango.

He stopped first at a drugstore where he bought a can of Planters mixed nuts and two Baby Ruth candy bars, which would be his supper. To help him sleep, he bought a paperback novel by an author whose previous books had dealt with slightly depraved, extremely sensitive southerners to whom nothing much, good or bad, ever happened. In case the novel failed to put him to sleep, Vines stopped at a liquor store and bought an extra bottle of Jack Daniel's Black Label.

It was 6:20 P.M. when he reached the cream and green Victorian house. Vines parked in the street behind the Aston Martin and watched Dixie Mansur get out of it and walk back to his Mercedes. She wore white slacks and a dark blue cable-knit cotton sweater with a deep V-neck.

When she reached the Mercedes she bent down so she could speak to him through the open window. "Parvis made contact," she said.

"Already?"

"Already."

"You'd better come in and tell me about it."

"In the car?"

"The house."

Dixie Mansur straightened up, looked over the roof of the Mercedes at the old three-story showplace, bent down again and asked, "Who's home?"

"Nobody."

"You have anything to drink?"

"Bourbon."

"One of these days," she said, "you might buy a bottle of Scotch."

Vines gave her a tour of the downstairs. She was particularly taken with the parlor's dark heavy furniture and fat porcelain lamps. "It's like a movie set, isn't it?" she said.

"I don't know," Vines said. "I've never been on a movie set."

In the kitchen they emptied a tray of ice into a bowl, found two glasses, refilled the tray with water and put it back in the refrigerator's freezer. As they walked up the old carved oak staircase to the second floor, Dixie Mansur said, "I wouldn't want to live here."

"Why not?"

"Too many memories."

"What memories?"

"Of what happened before I was born," she said. "I don't like to think anything much happened before that."

In Vines's room they put the whiskey, the ice, the glasses, the mixed nuts and the candy on the walnut dresser. Vines placed the novel on the bedside table next to the small radio. Dixie Mansur looked around, inspecting everything, and said, "Where's Adair's room?"

"Down the hall," Vines said as he dropped ice cubes into the glasses, added whiskey and went into the bathroom for water. When he came back Dixie Mansur was seated on the bed, leaning against its headboard. He handed her a drink and said, "Tell me about it."

She tasted her drink first. "When we got back to Santa Barbara this afternoon, Parvis started working the phone. He made about a half dozen calls, maybe more, and was about to make another one when the other phone rang—his really private phone."

"And?"

"And it was them or him. Whoever."

"You listened?"

"He shooed me out."

"But you listened to those other calls he made."

"I got to listen to what he said but not to what the people he called said."

"What kind of pitch did he use?"

"I only heard one of them."

"You said you listened to them all."

"He only spoke English once. All the other times he spoke Farsi—you know, Persian."

"What about the call that came in on his really private line—the bingo call?"

"It started out in English."

"And switched to Farsi?"

"I don't know. He was still talking English when he shooed me out."

"But you did hear that one call he made in English, right?"

She nodded.

"What'd he say?" Vines asked. "I mean, did he start off, 'Hey, Al, have I got a sweet one for you'? What I'd like to know is exactly what he said."

"What's the matter? Don't you trust him?"

"Since it's my neck, I'm curious."

"I can't remember exactly what he said. Nobody could."

"As close as possible."

"Well, he didn't ask for anybody after the call was answered. He began by saying this is me—except he said, 'This is I' or maybe 'It is I, Parvis.' Then he said something about having extremely valuable information about certain officials in a southern California community, well known for its isolation, who were willing to part with two of their—I think he called them 'guests'— providing they—and I guess he was talking about B.D. and Sid—were reimbursed for their effort or risk or something like that. Then Parvis listened for a while and said, 'One million firm.' Then he said, 'Please see what you can do' and goodbye."

"What about when the bingo call came in?"

"He shooed me out, like I said. But when it was over he called me back in. He told me he'd made contact and it was important that you and Adair know so you could get ready. But he didn't want to call you and go through the hotel switchboard. And since he had to stay by the phone, he told me to drive over and tell you and Adair that he'd made contact. I asked him what if I couldn't find either of you, and he told me to keep looking till I did. Where is Adair anyhow?"

"Los Angeles."

"Doing what?"

"Seeing some people."

"When'll he be back?"

"Late."

"Mind if I wait for him?"

"Where?"

She patted the bed. "Here—unless your landlady objects."

"She won't."

"When'll she be back?"

"Around two-thirty."

"Then we've got plenty of time, don't we?" Dixie Mansur said, putting her drink down and slipping the dark blue cotton sweater off over her head and dropping it on the floor.

Convinced, for some reason, that she had never worn a brassiere in her life, Vines sat down next to her, put his own drink on the bedside table next to the small radio and kissed her. After the long bourbon-flavored kiss finally ended and Vines was unbuttoning his shirt, he said, "Is this also Parvis's idea?"

"Would you care if it was?"

"Not in the least," Kelly Vines said.

Twenty-eight

After the Cessna landed on the private dirt airstrip a mile or so south of the Ventura Freeway near the Kanan Dume Road in Agoura, Jack Adair decided it was best not to ask who owned either the strip or the fancy new Land-Rover that was waiting for them, its ignition key tucked behind a sun visor.

"Don't suppose you know where this Altoid nut farm is?" Merriman Dorr said as he started the Land-Rover's engine.

"I gave you the address."

"Out here in the boonies, an address seldom does much good."

Adair shrugged. "We could ask somebody."

"I never ask directions."

"Why not?"

"Because where I'm going's never anybody's business."

When Dorr finally found the road they wanted on a Thomas Brothers map, they crossed over the Ventura Freeway, heading north. A mile or so farther, Dorr turned left onto a narrow asphalt road with no shoulders that snaked up into some round drought-seared hills. The tan hills were sprinkled here and there with clumps of green oaks. But even the deep-rooted oaks, Adair thought, were beginning to look thirsty.

Adair was surprised that there was no chainlink fence surrounding the Altoid Sanitarium. At first glance, the place resembled an exclusive country club that somehow had misplaced its tennis courts and golf course. There was a fence of sorts that ran around what he guessed to be fifteen acres of rolling grounds, but it was a benign split-rail fence, useful for decoration and property lines, but useless against humans, rabbits, coyotes or reasonably determined deer.

Whoever had designed the sanitarium had managed to save many of the oaks. The gravel drive that went between a pair of fieldstone pillars and on up to the sanitarium's main entrance took sudden zigs and zags to avoid at least nine of the old trees whose trunks had been whitewashed.

The Land-Rover stopped in front of the recessed entrance door that was the size of a small drawbridge and fashioned out of thick redwood planks bound by hammered iron bands. Next to the door was a polished brass plate, no larger than an envelope, with small engraved black letters that read, "The Altoid Sanitarium." Below that, in smaller and, if possible, even more diffident letters, was the mild request, "Please Ring Only Once."

"How long d'you think you'll be?" Merriman Dorr asked.

"An hour. Not more."

Dorr looked at his watch, a workmanlike stainless-steel affair with a sweep second hand that Jack Adair somehow found reassuring. "It's six fifty-five now," Dorr said. "I'll be back for you at eight sharp, okay?"

"Fine," Adair said, climbed down from the Land-Rover, went up the two steps and rang the bell exactly as the brass plate suggested.

* * *

Danielle Adair Vines, the 35-year-old mental patient who sat at the far end of the small conference table in the cozy room with the big picture window, looked not much different to Jack Adair from the daughter he had last seen more than fifteen months ago. Paler, he thought, and not nearly as animated or maybe frenetic. But no big change really, which is exactly what that resident psychiatrist just told you. Nicely stabilized, he said. We soon expect marked progress.

Adair nodded and smiled at his daughter as he took a seat at the other end of the table. "How're you feeling, Dannie?"

She smiled back at him and said, "Who are you? Do I know you?"

"I'm Jack."

"Jack?"

"Jack Adair."

"I'm feeling very well, thank you, Jack."

"That's wonderful. Anything you need?"

"No. I don't believe so. Why?"

"Kelly sends his love."

"You mean Mr. Vines?"

"That's right. Kelly Vines."

"Mr. Vines is such a silly man. He comes to see me almost every month, I think. Sometimes he says he is Kelly Vines and sometimes he says he is someone else. Once he said he was a movie actor but I didn't really believe him." She smiled. "He's such a silly man."

"Do you get many other visitors?"

"The coyotes come sometimes. And the deer. The deer will come almost up to this window but the coyotes don't come nearly so close as that."

Adair nodded his appreciation of the visiting wildlife. "Did you ever get a visit or a call from Soldier Sloan?"

"Who?"

"Soldier P. Sloan."

"Whatever does the 'P' stand for?"

"Pershing."

"I remember him."

"Then he did visit you."

"He died."

"Yes, I know."

"Before I was born."

"Who died?"

"John Joseph 'Blackjack' Pershing. Born eighteen sixty. Died nineteen forty-eight."

Danielle Adair Vines rose slowly from her chair, clasped her hands loosely in front of her and, Adair thought, suddenly looked closer to 13 than 35. She cleared her throat, lifted her chin slightly and began to recite.

"'I Have a Rendezvous with Death,' by Alan Seeger, born eighteen eighty-eight; died nineteen sixteen." She cleared her throat again. "I have a rendezvous with Death / At some disputed barricade / When Spring comes back with rustling shade / And apple-blossoms fill the air.'"

She smiled shyly at Adair. "I know another one about the war your friend General Pershing fought in. It's called, 'In Flanders Fields.'"

"I think I know that one," Adair said. "It's also very nice. Very moving."

She sat back down in the chair and placed her still folded hands on the table. "Will Mr. Vines come to see me again?" she asked. "He's such a silly man."

"I'm sure he will."

"And will you be coming back?"

"If you like."

"I'll have to think about it. You're not silly like Mr. Vines, but I still have to think about it. And I am so very sorry about your friend."

"Who?"

"The one who died. General Pershing."

"Thank you, Dannie," said Jack Adair as he rose. "That's very kind of you."

The resident psychiatrist was Dr. David Pease, a 43-year-old twice-divorced Jungian, who held a twenty percent interest in the Altoid Sanitarium. He wore a green jogging suit and had a wedge-shaped head, some thinning curly gray hair and a pair of sooty eyes that blinked so rarely that Adair was almost willing to believe they had been painted on his face.

"Dr. Altoid still with you?" Adair asked.

David Pease shifted in the chair behind his desk, didn't blink, twitched his mouth and said, "Like Marley, Dr. Altoid has been dead these seven years."

"Died rich, I bet."

"Comfortable."

"How many more months do you think my daughter will have to spend here at six thousand dollars per month?"

"We can't provide you with a timetable, Mr. Adair."

"What about a guess—even a wild surmise will do."

Dr. Pease shook his head, the unblinking eyes never leaving Adair's face. "If I guessed, you'd take it as prediction. And if it were wrong, you'd understandably hold me to account."

"She's out of it, isn't she?" Adair said. "She's floating around out there in her own private galaxy."

"She's much better than she was."

"She doesn't recognize her own father."

"She must have her reasons."

"Or her husband."

"She recognizes Mr. Vines now. But not as her husband. She thinks of him as a harmless eccentric who visits her once a month."

"Can you cure her?"

"We can help her. We obviously have helped her."

"What if the money runs out?"

That made Dr. Pease blink. "Is that likely?"

"Considering that her father's just out of jail, her husband's disbarred and her brother's dead, it's what you might call a real possibility."

"What about her mother?"

"Her mother can't come up with seventy-two thousand a year."

"We'll keep Danielle as long as we can, of course. And if it should ever prove to be no longer possible, we will, if you like, see that she's accepted by a well-managed state facility."

"I didn't know there were any well-managed state facilities."

"Some are better run than others—like everything else."

"How long would the state keep her?"

"Until it's determined she's no longer a danger to herself or to others."

"That could be a week or ten days, couldn't it?"

"I wish you wouldn't try to pin me down, Mr. Adair."

Adair rose. "Either Vines or I will be here with the money on the fifteenth as usual."

Dr. Pease also rose until he reached his full height, which was a stooped six-foot-four. "She's worth every cent, Mr. Adair."

Jack Adair studied the unblinking Pease for several seconds, nodded and said, "Well, I suppose none of us reared our daughters to be bag ladies, did we?"

Adair waited for Merriman Dorr in the sanitarium's reception area, which resembled the lobby of a very expensive residential hotel. As he sat, shifting restlessly in a deep wingback chair, Adair fretted about his daughter, longed for a drink and repeatedly ran Soldier Sloan's cryptic notation through his mind: C JA O RE DV. But he could come up with nothing better than his original interpretation: See Jack Adair alone regarding Danielle Vines.

At exactly eight o'clock he hurried out the sanitarium's front door just as the Land-Rover pulled to a stop. Adair climbed into the front passenger seat and was turning around, reaching for something in the rear, when Dorr asked, "How'd it go?"

"Lousy," Adair said, facing the front again, the black cane in his right hand.

"So we don't stay overnight or anything?"

"No," Adair said, twisting the cane's handle to the right rather than the left. "We go back."

Dorr watched, obviously fascinated, as Adair removed the handle and the silver-capped cork, lifted out the glass tube and drank. As the whiskey's glow spread, Adair offered the tube to Dorr, who shook his head. "Not when I fly."

"Good," Adair said and had another drink.

After they passed the twin fieldstone pillars at the end of the drive, Merriman Dorr slowed the Land-Rover to a stop, looked both ways for approaching traffic and said, "Want to sell me that thing?"

"The cane?"

"The cane."

"It's already promised to somebody else."

"Who?"

"Sid Fork."

"That shit," said Dorr as he fed gas to the Land-Rover's engine and went speeding off down the winding narrow blacktop road that had no shoulders.

Twenty-nine

Because he had stopped to open a can of Budweiser, his third in three hours, Ivy Settles almost didn't see the pink Ford van as it sped along Noble's Trace, heading east toward Durango's city limits and, possibly, U.S. 101.

Settles had spent the last three hours cruising the streets of Durango on his own time in his own car. He was searching for the pink plumbing van and trying, without success, to lose the rage and humiliation that had almost engulfed him after the murder of Soldier Sloan.

The 51-year-old detective had nearly convinced himself it wasn't his fault that Sloan was dead. But Settles's powers of rationalization, which, like most policemen, were formidable, had failed him when it came to the short fat false Francis the Plumber. You let him walk, Ivy, he told himself. You. Nobody else. And that'll make your name in this town from now on. Ivy Settles? Sure. He's the one Sid Fork hired off the turnip truck.

Such dark thoughts finally had caused Settles to yell at his 37-year-old bride of six months, storm out of their two-bedroom house on North Twelfth, get into his four-year-old Honda Prelude, stop at a liquor store for a six-pack of Budweiser and cruise Durango for the next three hours, waiting for his rage to subside and his humiliation to go away.

He had begun his search for the pink van at 6:03 P.M. down near the Southern Pacific tracks. He worked his way out toward the eastern city limits, circling every block and driving down almost every alley. By 7:15 P.M., he had reached the city limits so he popped open another can of beer and repeated the search, this time from east to west.

By 9:02 P.M., he was back near the eastern city limits again and had decided it was time for a third beer. He had just opened the can at 9:03 P.M. when he glimpsed the pink van speeding east on Noble's Trace as it went past the 25th Street intersection.

Settles threw the full can of beer out the window, slammed the Prelude into first gear and chased after the van. When he had shifted into second, he opened the glove compartment and took out his .38 Chief's Special. Settles had had the revolver for twenty-one years but this was the first time he had ever really believed he might shoot some particular person with it—in this case, the fat false plumber. The thought ended his rage and humiliation and dangerously elevated his mood to one of near elation.

The Prelude had no siren but Settles had bought himself a red flasher that, after shifting into third, he plugged into the cigarette lighter. When he was no more than half a block from the pink van, he switched on the flasher and noticed he was two blocks past Durango's eastern city limits. It was an area of virtual wasteland that once had been promoted as an industrial park. The only industry ever to express any interest was a Go-Kart racetrack, which later changed its mind. The park had gone into bankruptcy.

After the red light began flashing, the pink van slowed,

pulled off onto the shoulder of Noble's Trace and stopped. Settles parked twenty feet behind the van and got out of the Prelude cautiously, the revolver in his right hand, a foot-long flashlight in his left. When he reached the driver's side of the van, he noticed that the Francis the Plumber magnetic stick-on signs had been removed, which didn't surprise him.

He was surprised to discover the van's driver was a dark-haired woman of 27 or 28 who stared at him with wide eyes that narrowed when the flashlight's beam struck them.

"Put your hands up where I can see them and get out," Settles said.

The woman nodded, raised her hands so he could see them and said, "How do I open the door if I keep my hands up here where you can see them?"

"I'll open it," Settles said, stuck the flashlight under his right armpit, reached for the door handle, turned it, opened the door two inches and stepped back four feet, his pistol and flashlight again aimed at the van door.

The woman came out slowly, her hands raised, palms forward. She wore jeans and a dark red T-shirt that said "I Shoot Anything" across its front in white letters. On her feet were blue and gray jogging shoes without socks. Her dark brown hair was cut fairly short and she was almost as tall as Settles, nearly five-nine. Her eyes, he noticed, were what he always thought of as "cow-brown." He also noticed that if she weren't so obviously frightened, she would be quite attractive, even pretty.

"Turn left and walk toward the rear of the van," Settles said.

Hands still raised, she turned and walked three steps before Settles told her to stop. "Turn toward the van," he said. After she had turned, he told her to lean on it. When she said it was too far away, he told her to lean on it anyhow. She almost fell toward the van, catching herself with her hands and forming a 60-degree angle.

After again sticking the flashlight into his right armpit, Settles patted the woman down, missing neither her breasts nor her crotch. But he did it quickly, impersonally, and the woman neither flinched nor said anything.

"Okay, stand up," Settles said.

The woman stood up. "Do I turn around?"

"Turn around."

She turned and the flashlight's beam caught her in the eyes again. She blinked and narrowed them. "What's your name?" Settles asked.

"Terri," she said. "Terri Candles."

"Terri with an 'i'?"

"With an 'i.'"

"What d'you do, Terri?"

"I'm a photographer."

"What kind?"

"Freelance."

"Like the T-shirt says, you shoot anything."

She nodded.

"Where d'you live, Terri?"

"Santa Barbara."

"What're you doing in Durango?"

"I don't think I was speeding."

"I said what're you doing in Durango, Terri?"

"I'm on assignment."

"Who for—the plumber?"

"What plumber?"

"Who were you taking pictures of in Durango, Terri?"

"A couple of kids. I'm good with kids."

"Where's your driver's license?"

"In the van. Want me to get it?"

"Later. Let's open the rear door first, see what's inside."

"It's locked. I'll have to get the key."

Settles thought for a moment and shook his head. "Let's

see if it's really locked." He waved her toward the rear of the van with the flashlight.

The handle of the van's single rear door was on the left. Settles positioned himself six feet away from it. "Open the door and tell whoever's inside to come out," he said.

"There's nobody inside and it's locked."

"Try the door anyway, Terri."

Her hand went to the rear door's handle and pulled it down. "It wasn't locked after all," she said.

"Open it nice and slow, Terri," Settles said.

She opened it quickly instead, moving with the door as it swung to the right. The flashlight revealed the double-barrelled shotgun first and then, above it, the remarkably ugly face of Francis the Plumber who stood, crouched over, holding the shotgun at hip level. Ivy Settles hesitated for a tenth of a second before he began to pull the trigger of his revolver. But by then the right barrel of the shotgun had fired and its load was knocking Settles backward. As he fell, his Chief's Special fired up into the air toward the stars and a full moon. The shotgun blast tore away much of the left side of Settles's chest and he died seconds after he fell to the ground.

The woman who said her name was Terri Candles moved from behind the van's open rear door and looked up at the short fat ugly man who was sometimes a false priest and sometimes a false plumber.

"Did I do okay, honey?" she asked him.

"You did fine," the man said and pulled the trigger that fired the shell in the shotgun's other barrel.

Thirty

A 32-year-old Ventura stockbroker, on his way to Durango in his BMW 325i convertible for a dirty weekend, was talking on his cellular phone to one of the women who would compose the ménage à trois when the pink Ford van whizzed past him, heading east, at not less than 80 miles per hour.

The stockbroker thought nothing of it and continued talking to the woman until a minute later, which made it 9:11 P.M., when he saw the two bodies, one a man, the other a woman, lying on the left shoulder of Noble's Trace at the edge of the failed industrial park. A Honda Prelude was parked nearby with its lights on.

The stockbroker slowed to stare at the two bodies, told the woman on the phone to forget about the weekend, hung up and drove very fast until he came to the first gas station in Durango. There, he dropped a quarter into a pay phone, dialed 911 and, refusing to identify himself, told whoever answered about the two bodies, the Honda and the pink Ford van that had sped past him at 80.

The stockbroker could have used his cellular phone to

make the call, but he dimly remembered someone warning him that all 911 calls are immediately traced—or something like that. And since he was already performing his duty by telling the police about the bodies, the stockbroker could see no reason for further civic involvement with Durango where he didn't even live anyhow.

He drove east on Noble's Trace, heading back toward U.S. 101, and looked quickly away to the left as he again passed by the bodies. When the stockbroker was a mile past them, he once more picked up his cellular phone, called a woman in Santa Barbara, mentioned he soon would just happen to be in her neighborhood and wondered if she'd like to go out for a drink and maybe a bite to eat. The woman, without apology or explanation, said no thanks.

The stockbroker drove on toward Ventura and home, listening to a tape of Linda Ronstadt singing Nelson Riddle arrangements and feeling not only very sorry for himself, but also uncomfortably virtuous.

Chief Sid Fork was on the end stool at the bar in the Blue Eagle, eating a cheeseburger and drinking a draft beer, when Virginia Trice pushed the phone over to him. Fork automatically looked up at the clock above the bar. The time was 9:23 P.M.

After Fork said hello, Detective Wade Bryant, the too-tall elf, identified himself and said, "Ivy just got blown away by a shotgun on the Trace two blocks past the city limits. A woman in her late twenties is also down and dead. Same way. Ivy's Honda is parked with its lights on."

"Which side of the road?" Fork asked.

"South. The sheriff got an anonymous nine-one-one and called us. The guy that called it in told 'em about the bodies and said a pink Ford van had passed him going like a bat out of hell the other way, east."

"Who's the woman?"

"No I.D. But she's around twenty-seven, twenty-eight, short brown hair, brown eyes, five-nine or -ten, and she's wearing a T-shirt that says, 'I Shoot Anything.' Just about everything between her belt and snatch is blown away."

"You there now?"

"Me and Joe Huff." Bryant paused. "You know something, Sid? It's the first time I ever saw Joe throw up."

"I'll be right there."

Fork hung up the phone and pushed it back to Virginia Trice, who said, "What's wrong now?"

"Ivy Settles."

"Dead?"

Fork nodded.

New grief seemed to press new lines into Virginia Trice's face. Her eyes filled with tears. Her lower lip quivered. She sniffed noisily and said, "That's just not . . . right."

"I know," Fork said. "Let me borrow a key to your house."

"Why?"

"Because I want to find Vines and if he's not there, I want to wait for him inside, not out in my car."

"He's got something to do with Ivy?"

"Something. But not what you think."

Sid Fork knew what to expect when he saw the Aston Martin parked in front of the floodlit Victorian house. He sighed, parked his own car in front of the Aston Martin, got out, almost nodded hello to Kelly Vines's blue Mercedes and started up the serpentine brick walk to the front door.

He used the key Virginia Trice had given him to enter the old house. Some lights were on downstairs, but after a quick look into the parlor and kitchen—both empty—Fork went up the oak staircase to the second floor and down the hall until he came to a door with light coming from beneath it.

He raised his fist to knock, hesitated, then knocked four times, very firmly, the way he thought a policeman should knock. A moment later the light from beneath the door went off.

"Goddamnit, it's me—Sid."

The light from beneath the door came back on and the door was opened by Dixie Mansur, who, from what Fork could see, wore nothing but a man's shirt and it carelessly buttoned.

"We thought you might be Parvis with a lecture," she said with a grin.

"Sure."

"What's up?"

"I have to talk to Vines."

"Why?"

Before Fork could invent an answer, Vines appeared at the half-open door, wearing only his pants. "Talk about what?"

"We have to go someplace."

"Where?"

"When we get there, you'll know what we have to talk about."

Vines's face stiffened, immobilizing his mouth and almost everything else except his eyes, which turned suspicious as, not quite realizing it, he turned a question into an accusation. "It's Adair, isn't it?" Vines said. "Something's happened to him."

"It's not Adair."

Vines's face relaxed first, then the rest of him, and he almost smiled. "I'll get dressed." As he turned from the half-open door, Dixie Mansur offered him the shirt she had just removed.

Vines thanked her, accepted the shirt and looked back at Fork, who, leaning against the doorjamb, was inspecting the now naked Dixie with a half-amused, half-exasperated expression that also contained, Vines thought, a trace of paternalism.

"We all leave together, Dixie," Fork said, "so get some clothes on."

"Why together?"

"Because if you leave later, you'll set off an alarm and the cops'll be here in four, maybe five minutes and arrest you for burglary, or maybe just housebreaking, and Parvis'll have to drive up from Santa Barbara, bail you out and, if he's smart, knock some sense into you."

"Set off what alarm?" she said.

"If you don't use a key to go in and out, it sets off a silent alarm."

"I still don't see what the rush is," she said, picking up her blue cable-knit cotton sweater from the floor and slipping it over her head.

"The rush is because I'm in a hurry," Fork said.

"It'd be far more civilized if we all had a drink first," she said, stepping into her white slacks.

Fork didn't bother to respond. Kelly Vines, now wearing shirt, shoes and pants, said he was ready to go.

"Wait a second," Dixie Mansur said, knelt beside the rumpled bed, found her white bikini panties beneath it, stuffed them into her purse, rose and said, "Okay. Let's go."

Thirty-one

The chief of police—and his two detectives who had once worked homicide in Detroit and Chicago—kept their eyes on Kelly Vines as he stared down at the dead woman who wore the dark red T-shirt with the white letters that read, "I Shoot Anything."

"Know her?" Sid Fork asked.

"Not exactly," Vines said, still staring at the woman.

"What's 'not exactly' mean?"

Vines looked at Fork. "It means I saw her once. In Lompoc. She was the one who opened the rear door of the pink Floradora Flowers van and took the pictures of me and Adair."

Fork nodded contentedly, as if confirming his own private theory, turned to Bryant, the too-tall elf, and said, "How d'you read it, Wade?"

Bryant tugged thoughtfully at his large right ear, which Fork had long thought resembled Mr. Spock's, shook his head in a small gesture of regret and said, "I think we rode Ivy a little too hard over there at the hotel this afternoon. I think we pissed him off royal. I think he went broody over it, got in his car, bought himself a six-pack, went looking for the pink van and just happened to find it. I think he used the flasher that's still plugged into his cigarette lighter to pull the van over. I think she was driving it, the girl. I think Ivy made the girl open the rear door so he could see what was inside. I think the plumber and his shotgun were inside. I know a shotgun killed Ivy and I know he got one shot off himself, but I don't know if he hit anything. I think the plumber was done with the girl and used the shotgun on her, maybe just to shut her up." Bryant paused, frowned, erased the frown and said, "That's what I think."

Fork turned to the black bald detective. "Joe?"

"The same—except I threw up."

Fork's sympathetic nod encouraged him to continue.

Indicating the two dead bodies with a nod, Joe Huff said, "They're nothing compared to what you'd see any Tuesday in Chicago. I got sick because I realized if I ever find that motherfucker, I won't even try and collar him."

"Just blow him away, huh?" Fork said.

"You know it. Thing is, I never got that mad before and I guess that's what made me sick. But when I got through throwing up over there behind Ivy's Honda, I still felt just as mad and I still feel that way right this minute."

"Who doesn't?" Fork said, again looked at the dead woman, then back at Huff. "See if you can find out who she is."

As Huff squatted beside the woman, his expression now detached, almost clinical, Fork recognized the throaty burble of an Aston Martin being driven in second gear. He turned and saw one of the uniforms bending down to look inside the British car. The uniform straightened up with a jack-in-the-box snap and waved it on.

The Aston Martin stopped just behind Ivy Settles's Honda, whose headlights no one had yet turned off. Dixie Mansur emerged from the driver's side, Mayor B.D. Huckins from the passenger side. Dixie still wore her blue cotton sweater and white pants. The mayor wore a navy-blue suit that wouldn't have been out of place at either a wake or a funeral.

Fork noticed that Huckins's full lips—devoid of all lipstick—were clamped into a thin stern line. But it wasn't her mildly aggrieved pothole complaint look. Instead, it was what he recognized as her total disaster look that she used to confront mud slides, raging brush fires, ruptured sewer mains and political treachery.

Both Wade Bryant and Joe Huff also recognized the look; murmured to Fork that they might as well go see if the uniforms had turned up anything useful, and slipped away into the night. Sid Fork decided he might as well try to preempt the mayor's attack.

"I forgot to call you again, B.D., and I'm awful sorry."

Stopping a yard away from Fork, the mayor first examined him carefully, then used a cold and formal tone to say, "That's perfectly all right, Chief Fork. Others called. UPI, AP and Reuters among them. They seem anxious to know all about our four murders in two days. Mrs. Ivy Settles also called after she heard about her husband's death on an L.A. radio station. She was extremely—what's the word?—distraught. But by then I could at least answer some of her questions because I'd been filled in and brought more or less up to date by Sheriff Coates. You know how diligent Charlie Coates is."

The chief of police decided a nod would be his wisest answer.

"Sheriff Coates is wondering if he should send in what he calls a task force to help us out," Huckins continued. "He seems to think our police department may be inadequate or, as he said, 'spread too thin' to deal with four homicides in two days. Sheriff Coates thinks that if Durango keeps this up, it'll soon be on the five o'clock CNN news, sandwiched in between east L.A. gangs and the

Israelis and Palestinians. Sheriff Coates is not at all sure Durango deserves that kind of notoriety. What d'you think, Chief Fork? Should the task force be invited in?"

Obviously confident of Fork's answer, B.D. Huckins strode past him to the body of Ivy Settles. She stared down at it for several seconds, biting her lower lip, then walked another five or six feet and stared down at the dead woman. "Who is she, Sid?"

Fork looked at Kelly Vines. "Tell her," he said and walked back to the Honda Prelude, reached through its open window and turned off its headlights.

"You knew her?" the mayor asked Vines.

Vines shook his head. "She was the one who took the pictures of Adair and me in Lompoc—and probably of you and Fork."

"The mysterious photographer." She looked down at the dead woman again. "Do they know who killed her?"

"They think it's the same short fat guy who was a priest when he killed Norm Trice, a plumber when he killed Soldier Sloan and God knows what when he killed these two."

"Teddy," she said.

"Teddy Smith or Jones. Whatever he's calling himself."

The mayor looked out across the failed industrial park, closed her eyes, took a deep breath, moved her lips slightly, let the breath out and said, "I was just counting the funerals I have to go to next week—thanks to Teddy."

"Three," Vines said, gave the dead woman a brief look and added, "Maybe even four."

"I wonder how many reporters there'll be?"

"As always, too many."

"We don't need that—their prying."

Vines studied the mayor, reached a conclusion and said, "Dixie didn't tell you, did she? If she had, you and I wouldn't be talking about public relations."

"Didn't tell me what?"

"That Parvis Mansur's made contact."

The mayor turned quickly and almost yelled at her sister, who was standing near the Prelude, talking cheerfully to a glum Sid Fork. Dixie Mansur turned slowly and, accompanied by Fork, strolled over to Huckins and Vines, giving the dead Ivy Settles an incurious glance and altogether ignoring the dead woman photographer.

"Mr. Vines tells me Parvis made contact," the mayor said.

Her sister nodded.

"You forgot to tell me. Or Sid."

"I didn't forget," Dixie said. "Parvis told me to tell Vines and Adair. Adair was out of town, so I told Vines. I like to do exactly what Parvis says. It makes life simpler."

"He didn't tell you not to tell Sid and me?"

"No. Why?"

Instead of replying, the mayor turned to the chief of police. "You and I have to decide right now if we're going to invite Charlie Coates and his task force in."

Sid Fork turned away to look across Noble's Trace at the same young uniformed policeman who had waved on the Aston Martin. The policeman was now bending over to lecture a dedicated gawker in a Thunderbird.

"Well?" the mayor said.

"If you invite Charlie Coates and his task force in, B.D.," Fork said, still watching the young policeman, "I quit."

"Don't threaten me, Sid."

"That's a guarantee, not a threat."

Before the mayor could make some possibly irrevocable decision, Kelly Vines interceded. "Like some professional advice?"

"From you?" she said.

Vines gave her his crooked, boyish grin, full of charm, the one Jack Adair knew to be a disguise. "My body's disbarred, not my brain."

"I'm sorry," she said and looked around. "Where?"

"My car," Sid Fork suggested.

"You want me along?" Dixie Mansur said.

"No," the mayor replied. "We don't."

"Good," Dixie said and started across Noble's Trace toward the young uniformed policeman who was again directing traffic.

The mayor and the chief of police sat in the rear of the four-door sedan. The disbarred lawyer sat in front, half-turned behind the steering wheel, his right arm resting along the top of the front seat's back.

"Don't turn the sheriff down cold," Vines said without preamble. "Stall him. When the media show up, give them your ten-minute scenic tour and make it last half an hour. Express grief, shock, horror and outrage about the murders. When they ask about motive, express bewilderment, but hint that arrests are imminent. Invite them to the funerals. Mention Durango's growth and investment potential until they're sick of it. Finally, call a press conference for the two of you and tell them again what you've already told them."

"Bore 'em to death, huh?" Fork said.

Vines nodded.

Huckins, after nodding her unenthusiastic agreement, said, "We can't stall Coates forever because he'll insist on a deadline. And unless we come up with the killer before it expires, we'll have to let him and his task force in."

"What about jurisdiction?" Vines asked.

"We're two blocks past the city limits," Fork said. "So it's my dead detective but his jurisdiction."

"Tell the sheriff he can send in his task force on the fourth of July," Vines said. "A week from Monday."

"Why the fourth?" Huckins asked.

"Because if Mansur hasn't closed the deal by then, it's not going to be closed. After that, even if he swears it's still on, neither Adair nor I will touch it."

It was obvious Sid Fork didn't like the date of the deadline. He glared at Vines, then at the mayor, gave his gray mustache a hard brush with his thumb and said, "You let a sheriff's task force in here on the fourth of July, B.D., and you can forget about being reelected on the eighth of November."

"Christ," Vines said. "Make it the fifth then."

Fork nodded, satisfied. "The fifth'd be a whole lot better."

B.D. Huckins turned to gaze out the car window at her sister, who was talking to the young uniformed policeman. "It doesn't really matter if it's the fourth or the fifth, Sid."

"The hell it doesn't."

The mayor turned to him and spoke in a voice that was slightly weary and extremely patient. A teacher's voice, Vines thought. "Charlie Coates doesn't want to send in a task force to help us find a killer. He wants to send in a task force to lift up the rocks and peek into our dark corners."

"Let 'em," Fork said. "You and me, B.D., we never took a dime from those hideout deals. The city got every last cent."

She smiled at him sadly. "Is that what you plan to tell Charlie Coates and his task force, Sid?"

Thirty-two

Kelly Vines sat behind the wheel of the Mercedes at the end of the abandoned Durango Municipal Airport's crumbling runway, waiting for the sound of the Cessna's engine and wishing he had brought along the Baby Ruth candy bars.

A 9:58 P.M. he heard the Cessna's engine as it made a low pass over the airport. Guessing its altitude at 250 or 300 feet, Vines switched on the car's headlights and flicked them up to bright. At 10:02 P.M. he watched Merriman Dorr make another perfect landing.

The Cessna taxied to within seventy-five feet of the Mercedes and stopped, but Dorr kept the plane's engine running as Jack Adair climbed out, made a wide berth of the spinning propellor and walked quickly toward the Mercedes, swinging the black cane. Before Adair reached the car, the Cessna had turned around, raced down the runway and disappeared into the night.

After Adair settled into the passenger seat, Vines switched off the headlights and asked, "How was she?"

"About like you said."

"She recognize you?"

"No."

"What else?"

"She thinks you're a very silly man," Adair said, unscrewed the cane's handle, removed the cork and silently handed the glass tube flask to Vines, who sighed before taking a swallow.

As he passed the glass tube back to Adair, Vines said, "Mansur made contact."

"He say who with?"

"He sent word by Dixie but she didn't seem to know much more than that."

"What else?"

"Well, there's Teddy, the plumber-priest."

"They caught him?" Adair asked, sounding less than hopeful.

"No, they didn't catch him, but he killed Sid Fork's bunco and fraud guy from Dallas, Ivy Settles."

"When?"

"About an hour ago. They also say that while he was at it, Teddy killed that woman photographer who took our pictures in Lompoc."

"Well, shit, Kelly," Adair said and lapsed into silence. Vines also seemed to have run out of things to say and the silence continued until Adair said, "From the beginning. Everything."

"All right."

It took Vines fifteen minutes to tell it. He began with his purchase of candy bars, mixed nuts, whiskey and the paperback novel, and ended with B.D. Huckins's gloomy assessment of the real purpose behind the sheriff's proposed task force.

Adair listened, asking no questions, until he was sure Vines had finished. Then he asked, "You know what I'm having?"

"Second thoughts?" Vines said.

"Exactly."

"Tell me about Dannie and we'll come back to your second thoughts."

"Well, she didn't know me from Adam's off ox and she thinks you're some silly but harmless gentleman caller."

"What about Soldier Sloan?"

"I made the mistake of asking her about Soldier P. Sloan and she immediately wanted to know what the 'P' stood for. I told her Pershing and suddenly she was back in junior high school, reciting the first verse of 'I Have a Rendezvous with Death' and asking whether I'd also like to hear the one about how poppies blow in Flanders fields."

Vines closed his eyes and said, "Which doctor did you talk to?"

"Pease. He thinks Dannie'll do just fine as long as we keep sending the six thousand a month. When I asked him what would happen to her if the money ran out, he said he'd see that she was placed in one of the state's better mental hospitals where they might keep her for a week or ten days. I believe I told him Dannie wouldn't make a very good bag lady."

"No," Vines said, opening his eyes, "she wouldn't." He drummed the fingers of his right hand on the steering wheel and asked, "Anything left in the tube?"

"Sure," Adair said and passed it to him.

Vines had another swallow of bourbon, coughed and passed the glass tube back to Adair. "So you think there's no possible connection between her and Soldier Sloan?"

"None," Adair said.

"Then Dannie's obviously not the DV in Soldier's 'C JA O RE DV.'"

"Obviously."

Vines again drummed his fingers on the steering wheel as he stared out at the night that began just beyond the Mercedes's three-pointed star atop the radiator. Finally, he stopped the drumming and said, "What about Venable?"

"Who?"

"Dixie Venable."

Adair bit his lower lip to keep from gaping, then opened his mouth just wide enough to say, "Jesus. Her maiden name."

"And the name Soldier first knew Dixie by."

Adair looked at Vines with total suspicion. "When did all this dawn on you?"

"Just now," Vines said.

"Who do we share this brilliance with?" Adair asked. "Dixie's sister? Her husband? Maybe with the chief of police?"

"With nobody," said Kelly Vines.

When Virginia Trice came over to their booth and said, "You got a call," Vines was drinking a draft beer and eating a bowl of chili that he thought had too much cumin in it and not enough chili pepper. Adair, his mouth full of a bacon, lettuce and tomato sandwich, shrugged helplessly at Vines, who asked, "Who's got a call?"

"Either one of you."

"Who's calling?"

"He wouldn't say," Virginia Trice replied, turned and went back to preside over the bar.

When Vines reached the bar, she had already moved the phone down to a spot in front of the last stool, which was four stools away from the nearest customer. Vines nodded his thanks, picked up the phone and said hello.

"Mr. Adair?"

"This is Vines."

"Good. It is I, Parvis Mansur."

"Right."

"I'm calling from a pay telephone in Santa Barbara so

please bear with me should I have to drop in more quarters."

"How'd you know we were here?"

Vines could hear Mansur's deep sigh. "Logic and luck. This is the fourth number I've called."

"Just curious."

"Did Dixie give you and Mr. Adair my message?"

"Yes."

"Did you inform B.D. and Sid?"

"Yes."

"Good. Approximately twenty-one minutes ago I received a call on my secure line, which obviously is no longer secure, hence this call from a pay telephone."

Wondering when he last had heard anyone say "hence," Vines said, "This call was from the same person?"

"Yes. This time a date was proposed or rather, I should say, insisted upon."

"When?"

"Four July. Is that satisfactory to you and Mr. Adair?"

"The date's okay. What about the place?"

"As we discussed, it must be a place to which, logically, the two of you could be lured. By that, I mean, it can't be under a tree in the middle of nowhere."

"Right."

"Do you have a suggestion? If not, I do."

Vines already had given considerable thought to where he and Adair were to be sold for $1 million. The place he had in mind featured a back door with an aluminum core sheathed in steel, but after deciding it would be prudent to listen first to Mansur's proposal, he said, "What do you suggest?"

"Cousin Mary's, primarily because of its location and its excellent security."

"Sounds okay."

"Good. I'm glad you agree."

"Who called you, Parvis?" Vines said, using Mansur's given name for the first time.

"The same man called both times. Obviously an American with a rather reedy tenor voice and no regional accent—at least none I could detect."

"How'd he get your phone number?"

"I thought it best not to ask."

The telephone buzzed and a recorded operator's voice interrupted, requesting the caller to deposit an additional fifty cents. Vines listened to the quarters clank down into the pay phone. When the clanking was over, Mansur said, "Are you still there?"

"Still. Did you talk to him about the price?"

"Yes, of course, and he agreed to it with a minimum of grumbling."

"No serious bargaining?"

"None."

"That's strange."

"I thought so, too, which is why I stressed there would be no sale until the exact, specific amount was confirmed."

"Until you've counted the money?"

"In essence, yes."

"What'd he say?"

"He said no problem."

"Anything else?" Vines asked.

"Did Dixie by any chance say where she was going after she left you?"

"When I last saw her she was with her sister."

"Good," Mansur said, sounding relieved. "That's splendid. You might call B.D. and Sid and inform them of these new developments."

"All right."

"Good night then, Mr. Vines."

"Good night," Vines said, broke the connection with a

forefinger, caught Virginia Trice's eye and used a nod to invite her down to his end of the bar.

"You have the mayor's home phone number?" Vines asked.

"It's unlisted."

"I know."

Virginia Trice looked up at the ceiling, back down at Vines and recited the number from memory. After Vines thanked her and began dialing, she moved farther up the bar.

The mayor answered with a hello halfway through the call's third ring.

"This is Kelly Vines."

"You must have the wrong number," B.D. Huckins said and hung up.

Thirty-three

After hanging up on Vines, the mayor returned to her chocolate-brown leather easy chair and smiled an apology at Sheriff Charles Coates, who perched on the edge of the cream 1930s couch, a cushion away from Sid Fork.

Sensitive about his average height, which he felt insufficient by southern California standards, the 42-year-old sheriff's backside rarely occupied more than six inches of anything it rested on. He usually sat as he sat now, leaning a bit forward, hands clasping his knees, heels slightly lifted—obviously all set for hot pursuit.

When standing, the sheriff looked neither short nor tall, possibly because of his glistening black cowboy boots with their one-and-a-half-inch heels. Once reporters had discovered he was height-conscious, they delighted in asking him how tall he was because of his unvarying reply: "Same as Steve McQueen alive and barefoot—five-ten and a quarter."

As B.D. Huckins sat back down in the leather easy chair, the six-foot-three, 28-year-old deputy sheriff asked whether she got many wrong-number calls. The deputy was Henry Quirt, who had been relegated to the only other chair in the living room—the one that was really more stool than chair and forced his knees up until they were almost level with his breastbone. The deputy sat on the low stool at the late night meeting in the mayor's house not only because he policed his section of the county from a Durango base, but also because Sheriff Coates had decided a witness might prove useful—even invaluable.

The mayor answered the deputy's question about wrong-number calls by replying, yes, she did receive quite a few of them. The sheriff said that although he couldn't prove it, he thought unlisted phone numbers got more wrong-number calls than listed ones. The mayor asked the sheriff whether she could get him and his deputy something, perhaps a beer.

"Not a thing, B.D., but thank you."

"I'd like a beer," Fork said, rising from the couch. "But I'll get it myself."

"Well, if you're having one, Sid, I guess I will, too," Coates said.

Fork looked at Deputy Quirt. "Henry?"

"No, thanks."

As Fork headed for the kitchen, Sheriff Coates said, "I apologize again for dropping by so late, B.D."

The mayor looked at her watch. "It's only ten forty-eight."

"But since I had to be over here in Durango anyhow—and wasn't that a terrible thing about Ivy Settles? Just awful. How's his wife taking it?"

"Hard."

"If there's anything at all I can do . . ." Coates left his offer dangling—incomplete, undefined and, in Huckins's opinion, meaningless.

"That's very kind of you."

"But the real reason I dropped by so late, B.D., is I need to talk a little politics."

"Who with?"

"Why, with you, of course."

Huckins kept her expression polite, her voice neutral. "Sid'll probably want to hear this."

"Wouldn't be surprised."

They sat in silence until Fork returned with two open bottles of beer and handed one to Coates. "Need a glass, Charlie?"

"What for?"

Huckins waited until Fork was again sitting on the cream couch and had drunk some of his beer before she said, "Charlie wants to talk a little politics."

Fork turned to examine the sheriff, as if for the first time. He inspected the glistening black boots, the tight tan whipcord pants and the forest-green Viyella shirt that was tailored to emphasize the flat stomach, deep chest and the shoulders that seemed a foot thick and a yard wide.

The chief's slow, careful inspection finally reached the sheriff's face with its landmark chin, bad-cop mouth, stuck-up nose that never sunburned or peeled and, finally, the blue eyes that crinkled on demand and were shaped like long teardrops. Topping all this was a wealth of dark brown gray-flecked hair that every seven days was trimmed to Marine Corps specifications.

"Politics?" Fork said after his inspection. "Christ, Charlie, you don't even have any opposition this year."

Coates nodded, studied the floor to demonstrate the gravity of what he was about to say, and looked up quickly, first at Fork, then at Huckins. "It can't go beyond these walls."

"I won't breathe a word," Fork said, "unless it'll do me some good."

Almost everything in Coates's face smiled except his mouth. "Still the merry prankster at forty, right, Sid?"

"Thirty-nine. And before you invite yourself into somebody's house, you oughta know if you can trust them or
not."

"B.D. knows the answer to that, don't you, B.D.?"

The mayor said, "Get to it, Charlie."

Coates edged forward another inch on the cream couch,
leaned another inch in Huckins's direction and spoke in
the hushed tones of the seasoned conspirator. "Old man
Sloop's going to step down as county supervisor in nineteen ninety."

"Why?" she said.

"To pursue other interests."

The mayor shook her head. "Billy Sloop celebrated—or
at least observed—his sixty-eighth birthday last week.
He's been a county supervisor for fourteen years and
doesn't have any other interests to pursue. So how much
have you got on him, Charlie?"

"Enough."

"Why tell me?"

"Because I'm going to announce for his job and I want
your endorsement."

"When're you going to announce?"

"Two days after the election—November tenth."

"Why then?"

"Because that's the day Billy's promised me he'll let it
out that he won't be running for reelection in nineteen
ninety after all, and my announcement will give me the
jump on everyone else."

"And you want my endorsement?"

"Sure do, B.D."

"You know I never endorse anyone except at the city
level."

"Thought you might make an exception."

The mayor sighed. "Cut the crap, Charlie. What d'you
really want?"

"I want to help you clean up Durango."

"It's not dirty," Fork said.

The sheriff turned to the chief of police, making no effort to hide his contempt. "Four murders in two days? A serial killer on the loose? If anybody else gets killed here, they'll start calling it Beirut, California. I can bring my task force in and nail that sucker in ten days max, Sid, maybe even seven."

"That's not fast enough," the mayor said.

Coates's look of contempt vanished, replaced by one that made him seem honestly puzzled. "I don't follow you, B.D."

"It's simple. Durango is an incorporated municipality that provides its own law enforcement."

"I don't need any civics lesson."

"Politics, not civics. You said you wanted to talk a little politics so that's what I'm doing. Let's begin with Durango. It has an elected mayor who's its chief executive. Me. I hire its chief of police, who's sitting right next to you. Sid. I hire him with the City Council's approval and he reports to me. That means law enforcement is ultimately my responsibility. That's what I'm elected to do and if I can't do it, the city will elect itself a mayor who can. But if I invite the county sheriff and his task force in to do what the police chief and I're supposed to do, then even the dimmest voter'll get the idea that B.D. Huckins and Sid Fork are incapable of maintaining law and order, which would give this same dimmest voter a fine reason to vote for a new mayor who'd hire a new chief of police. You following me so far?"

Coates only nodded.

"I like living in this town, Charlie. I like being its mayor. I know maybe two thousand people in Durango by their first names. I belong here and can't even imagine living anywhere else. What's more, I plan to go on being mayor for as long as I can get elected because I'm a damn good one—the best this town ever had. But what you're asking me to do is commit political suicide by jump-starting your campaign. Charlie Coates for county supervisor—the man who cleaned up Durango in a week or maybe ten days. Well, that's not fast enough, Sheriff, because the killer, whoever he is, will be arrested by Durango cops and put behind Durango bars in Durango's jail by the fourth of July and that I can absolutely guarantee you."

The mayor paused, smiled almost sweetly and said, "So there's really no logical reason to bring in your task force, is there?"

It was B.D. at her best, Sid Fork decided. On the attack, not giving an inch, her voice low and as cold as ice water and those gray eyes drilling right through old Charlie's thick skull. Fork decided to lend a hand.

"I don't know about that guaranteed July the fourth deadline, B.D.," he said.

"Why not?" Huckins said, faking a note of asperity to make it sound as if she had no idea what Fork's answer would be.

"Because we're going to have that sucker in jail by the second of July—the third at the latest."

Sheriff Coates advanced another inch on the cream couch, reducing the width of his perch to approximately four inches. "How long've we known each other, B.D.?"

"Nineteen long years."

"More like twenty. I remember I'd just started on the same job Deputy Quirt's got when you and Sid and the rest of 'em rolled in here from Frisco in that old GM school bus you'd painted up like an Easter egg. You parked where you shouldn't've—on Seventh next to City Park—and the next morning I just happened by, woke everybody up and told you to move it before the city cops busted you. I even told you where you could park the thing. Remember that, Sid?"

"Not really."

"We go back a long, long way, B.D.—you, me, Sid and

Dixie. You got to be mayor; I got to be sheriff; Sid got to be chief of police; and Dixie, well, I guess Dixie got to be rich. But wasn't there another guy with you all back then? Funny-looking short guy. Ugly. Called himself Teddy, I think. Teddy Smith? Jones? Something like that."

"Something like that," the mayor said.

"Wonder what ever happened to him?"

"No idea."

"After the rest of your bunch left for Colorado, the four of you all moved into that old shack out on Boatright, didn't you? Then Teddy just sort of disappeared—like he'd jumped into the ocean and drowned or something."

"He jumped on a bus," Fork said.

"Wonder where he went?"

"No telling."

Coates shook his head sadly, as if at some old friend's mysterious disappearance, and turned to the mayor. "B.D., if I thought bringing a task force in to find a crazy killer'd hurt you politically, I'd've never even suggested it. I didn't think it would then and I still don't. But I'll accept your judgment."

"Good."

"Thing is, what if something happens and our killer's not behind bars after all come July fourth?"

"There's another possibility, Charlie," Fork said.

"Possibility of what?"

"Of his being dead by the fourth."

"Shot while resisting maybe?"

Fork shrugged.

"Not as much ink and airtime in that, Sid. Thing to do is bring him to trial and let it run forever."

The sheriff rose, placing his empty beer bottle on the coffee table that had been fashioned from the old steamer trunk. Huckins leaned forward and slipped a coaster beneath it. Staring down, watching her, Coates said, "I'd still like an answer, B.D."

"To what?"

"To my 'what if' question. What if, despite all Sid's efforts, the killer's neither behind bars nor dead by the fourth of July? What if he's still loose out there?"

"Then I'd reconsider inviting your task force in."

"And if we collared him?"

"I'd have to rethink my endorsement policy."

The sheriff beamed, crinkled his eyes and suddenly snapped his fingers as if he had just remembered something. He even said, "Damn," causing Sid Fork to wonder whether the sheriff really had any future in politics where a modicum of acting ability is as necessary as money.

"Almost forgot, Sid, but we found that pink Ford van up on One-Oh-One at a rest stop. Wiped clean as a whistle except for what ninety-nine percent of 'em always forget—the little lever that moves the driver's seat up and back. Got three good ones off the left hand plus a partial thumb. The state and the Feds are both checking 'em out and if we get a make back, I'll let you know."

The deputy, Henry Quirt, was now up and looming over Coates's right shoulder. "You told me to remind you of that telex we got from Lompoc, Sheriff."

Coates snapped his fingers again, causing the chief of police to decide that the sheriff's performance really needed a lot of work. "Shit-oh-dear," Coates said. "Forgot that, too. Seems the FBI'd like to talk to a couple of guys about something or other that happened at the Lompoc Federal pen yesterday or the day before—I forget which. But the guys' names are Kelly Adair and Jack Vines."

"The other way around," Quirt said.

Coates thought, nodded and said, "Yeah. *Jack* Adair and *Kelly* Vines. Anyway, Quirt and I, just on the off chance, stopped by the Holiday Inn on our way up to your place, B.D., but it seems Adair and Vines checked out around four this afternoon right after that old guy Sloan got it—can't say I blame 'em—but didn't leave any forwarding. So if you bump into 'em, Sid, ask 'em to give the Federales in Santa Barbara a shout."

"There a warrant out for them?" Fork said.

"No, the Feds just want to dialogue a little." He turned to Huckins. "Of course, I can't say if anybody else is after 'em or not. But on the other hand, everybody's got enemies, right, B.D.?"

"So they say."

Coates thanked her for the beer, said good night and left, trailed by his six-foot-three deputy. After the sheriff's black Lincoln town car with the twin whip antennae pulled away, B.D. Huckins turned from the window to Sid Fork.

"He knows it's Teddy," she said.

Fork nodded.

"But that's not why he wants to bring his task force in."

"No."

"What he really wants is to prove we've somehow been fiddling the books, send us to jail and ride that right into the county supervisor's office."

Fork thought about it, nodded and said, "It might work. But not if I find Teddy."

"Well. Can you?"

Fork moved over to Huckins, tilted her chin up and kissed her. "I don't have to find Teddy," he said. "All I have to do is make him want to find me."

Thirty-four

The thirty-nine-year-old frame and stucco house was on the southeast edge of Durango in the Explorer subdivision that consisted of three short streets named Lewis, Clark and Fremont. There would have been more houses on streets named after other explorers if the novice developer, a former high school history teacher with a modest inheritance, hadn't run out of both money and buyers during the recession of 1949.

At 12:20 A.M. Sid Fork was parked on Fremont under a fragrant thirty-nine-year-old magnolia, waiting for the light to go off in the third house from the corner. It was a TV set's bluish light and, since the house boasted no dish antenna, Fork was almost certain that those inside were watching a rented videocassette on their VCR. With luck, he thought, it might even be a short one—maybe a forty-five-minute X-rated feature.

After the bluish light went off at 12:32 A.M., Fork gave the occupants another twenty-nine minutes to go to bed and perhaps even to sleep. By 1:01 A.M. he was pounding on the front door. It was opened less than a minute later by a sleepy-looking Henry Quirt, the deputy sheriff, who wore a white T-shirt, pale blue boxer shorts and aimed a short-barrelled .38-caliber Smith & Wesson revolver at the chief of police.

"Christ, Sid, it's one in the fucking morning."

"Mind pointing the piece someplace else?"

After Quirt lowered the pistol to his side, Fork said, "I was already in bed myself, Henry, when it just hit me all of a sudden."

"What?"

"Be better if I told you about it inside."

Before Quirt could respond, a woman's voice called from the rear of the house. "Who is it, honey?"

Quirt turned his head to call his answer. "Sid Fork."

"What's *he* want?"

Quirt hesitated before calling his second answer, "Business." He looked back at Fork, all sleepiness gone, and said in a voice that only the chief of police could hear, "It is business, isn't it, Sid?"

Fork waited in the living room for the deputy sheriff, who had said he wanted to put some clothes on. Out of habit, Fork inventoried the room, pricing its contents that included a matching couch and easy chair that were protected by clear-plastic slipcovers. Of more interest was the triangular maple whatnot stand in one corner whose five shelves held nine chrome-framed photographs, at least two dozen miniature china cats and kittens and five conch-like seashells that Fork guessed were from Florida.

There were four nicely framed prints on the walls, all of them pastoral scenes, which Fork placed in nineteenth-century Europe, probably France, and decided he didn't much like. He scuffed the edge of his right shoe along the beige nylon carpet, put its price at $4.95 a square yard wholesale and moved over to the built-in bookcase that contained a Bible, a fairly new set of the Encyclopaedia

Britannica and nine paperback novels that turned out to be Harlequin romances.

The room's focus, however, was on its home entertainment center—a large oak stand with staggered shelves that held a 21-inch Sony TV set with an attached VCR and a complicated-looking audio system that could play LP records, tapes and compact discs. Two La-Z-Boy recliners were aimed at the center. On top of the TV set was a boxed videocassette. Fork went over, read the label, which said it was "Debbie Does the Devil," and tried to remember whether he had ever rented it.

He turned from the entertainment center just as Quirt entered the living room. The deputy now wore jeans, the same T-shirt and a pair of thick white ribbed athletic socks. Although Fork scarcely glanced at the socks, Quirt seemed to think he should explain them. "I don't wear shoes in the house when the kid's asleep."

"Wayne must be what now—two?"

"Two and a half."

"How's Mary Helen?"

"Okay if we keep our voices down and don't wake up the kid."

They sat on the plastic-covered furniture, Fork taking the chair, Quirt the couch. "Some meeting we had, huh?" Fork said.

Quirt shook his head, as if in appreciation. "That B.D."

"After you and the sheriff left I went home and went to bed. But it's been one hell of a long lousy day and I just couldn't get to sleep. Mostly, I was thinking about Ivy Settles, who was one fine cop even if he didn't look like much."

"Ivy was okay."

"So I was lying there, tossing and turning and thinking about Ivy and Carlotta—you know Carlotta?"

Quirt said he knew Carlotta Settles.

"At least she'll get a decent pension. Anyway, I was lying

there, worrying about her and wondering who in the world I could get to replace Ivy when all of a sudden it just hit me."

"What?"

"You."

Quirt leaned back on the couch and studied Fork. The chief of police was pleased that the tall deputy hadn't said, "Me?" He was further encouraged by the flicker of cunning in Quirt's dark brown eyes.

"Go on," Quirt said.

Fork obviously was in no hurry. "If Charlie Coates runs for county supervisor two years from now like he said, who d'you think'll be our new sheriff?"

"That dickhead Jim Grieg."

"Don't get along with Lieutenant Grieg so good, huh?"

"I get along with anybody I have to get along with, Sid."

"Think Charlie Coates'll make a halfway decent county supervisor?"

"Supervisor's just a stop."

"On the way to where?"

"Coates is forty-two," Quirt said. "If he gets elected supervisor in ninety, he'll be forty-four. Two years as supervisor and he'll make a free-ride run at Congress. If he wins, fine. If not, he's got two years left as supervisor and he'll be only forty-six. He'll use those next two years to build up his name recognition and war chest and then make another run at Congress when he's forty-eight. But if he doesn't make it to Washington either time, he'll just give up and get rich instead."

"He tell you all this?"

"He takes me along to be his rememberer. That's why I was at B.D.'s tonight. I got an awful good memory, Sid."

"Charlie ever say anything about taking you along if he gets to be supervisor or goes to Washington? Maybe to carry his bags, meet his plane, do his remembering?"

"He might've."

"How d'you like Durango, Henry?"

"I like the weather."

"Think you might like it back in Washington?"

"I was born in Washington. My old man was with the Department of Commerce. It was a hundred and three there today. The humidity was ninety something."

"Never been to Washington," Fork said, paused and frowned, as if trying to make some difficult decision. He kept the frown in place, letting the suspense build until Quirt grew restless. It was then that Fork asked, "You said you could get along with anybody you had to get along with, right?"

Quirt nodded.

"Wonder if you could get along with B.D. and me if I offered you thirty-five a year, detective rank, a take-home car, free dental and medical and four weeks annual leave a year?"

"I could get along with you and B.D. fine, Sid, but I'd have to go along to do it, wouldn't I?"

Fork made himself look puzzled. "Don't quite follow that."

"I mean, you want something from me. Right now. Tonight."

Fork changed his expression from puzzled to hurt. "I don't play that way, Henry, and neither does B.D. The job's yours. You can start Monday, like I said, if you can quit the sheriff that soon. But I'd better be absolutely honest with you. If anybody ever dumps B.D., I expect to be the first one fired and the new mayor'll probably get rid of all my people and bring in his own. But that's just the way things work, isn't it?"

Henry Quirt leaned forward on the couch, managing to look both skeptical and wise. "What d'you want from me that'll help B.D. stay mayor forever?"

"Nothing. Like I keep saying, the job's yours."

"No more bullshit, Sid."

"Well, now that you brought it up, there are those prints Charlie Coates told me and B.D. about—the ones they lifted off of that pink Ford van. Charlie's already got a make on 'em, right? Despite what he said."

"Right."

"You get a look at the make?"

Quirt nodded.

"And with that memory of yours . . ."

"I remember it, Sid. All of it."

"Now I'm not asking you to tell me who belongs to those prints. And I want you to understand that it's got nothing to do with the job and the take-home car and the thirty-five a year because that's all set. And anyway, I can't ask you to do something you can't do in good conscience."

Looking more skeptical and wise than ever, Quirt said, "I don't hear my conscience saying much of anything, Sid."

"Well, now, that's fine. So when d'you want to come to work—Monday?"

"Better make it the fifteenth of next month—just in case Sheriff Charlie turns up something else B.D. can use."

Thirty-five

At 2:04 A.M. on that last Sunday in June, Kelly Vines and Chief Sid Fork once again sat side by side on the couch with the woven-cane back in Virginia Trice's Victorian parlor.

Mayor B.D. Huckins sat opposite them, her legs tucked beneath a straight-back chair and crossed at the ankles. Jack Adair sat on the low chair with the worn plush seat—hair mussed, shirttails half-out and bare feet in the cordovan oxfords he still hadn't bothered to tie because it was Adair who had raced down the stairs at 1:52 A.M. to answer the insistent doorbell. Vines, then only half-awake, had dressed while Adair was in the kitchen, making coffee.

Huckins put her cup and saucer down and said, "Virginia not home from work yet?"

"Not yet," Adair said.

"We need to talk about something."

"Something that can't wait, I take it," Adair said.

She nodded. "But first I want answers to some questions."

"First thing I wish you'd do, B.D.," Sid Fork said, "is quit acting so goddamn mysterious."

The mayor's gray eyes were still on Adair when she said, "Shut up, Sid."

The chief of police opened his mouth to reply, thought better of it, slumped back on the couch, stuck his feet out and jammed his hands down into his pants pockets, looking, Kelly Vines thought, extremely pissed off.

Still gazing at Adair and obviously indifferent to how Fork felt, Huckins cleared her throat and said, "You never told us what happened to the boy and girl—Jack and Jill Jimson—after your supreme court overturned their guilty verdicts and ordered a new trial."

"They were retried in another county."

"A change of venue then?"

"Combine Wilson argued for it and got it. The Jimson kids were tried a second time a hundred and thirteen miles from home and acquitted."

"But didn't that bribe the old justice took, what's his name, Fuller—"

"Mark Tyson Fuller."

"Didn't that taint the supreme court's decision?"

"The state decided there was no bribe."

"What did it call that five hundred thousand dollars in shoeboxes on the dining room table?"

"Four hundred and ninety-seven thousand," Adair corrected her, "not to mention the five hundred thousand in my closet that they didn't find."

"Let's stick to the Fuller case," she said. "If it wasn't a bribe, what did they call it?"

"A double murder," Adair said. "And also a very expensive and elaborate scheme to make it look like a bribe."

"This is official—and not just your theory?" Huckins said.

"It's what was decided after an extensive investigation by city and state police. Actually the state police were the attorney general's investigators who were brought in because, after all, old Mark was a state supreme court justice."

"Why didn't you tell us this before?" Huckins said.

Adair's blue eyes were kitten-innocent as he looked at Kelly Vines and asked, "Didn't we go over all this during lunch at the roadhouse?"

"No," Vines said.

"Why not, Mr. Vines?" she said.

Vines shrugged. "It's a matter of public record."

"The public record in a distant state."

"Maybe I should've said common knowledge."

"Sounds to me like some folks for some reason don't trust other folks," Fork said.

The silence that followed was growing uncomfortable when Jack Adair, using what he regarded as his voice of sweet reason, broke it with: "We're about to reach an impasse that maybe I can prevent, Mayor, if you'll indulge me for a minute or so."

After considering the request, she nodded.

"According to both state and city police," Adair said, "the killer who rigged the deaths of old Justice Fuller and his wife to look like suicide and murder, respectively, was either careless, stupid or hadn't watched enough TV. As every nine-year-old now knows, thanks to television, when you fire a semiautomatic pistol it leaves a residue on your hand. There wasn't any on Justice Fuller's hand. Therefore, he couldn't have shot either his wife or himself." Adair looked at Vines. "The murder weapon, as I recall, was a thirty-two-caliber Llama, right?"

"The XA model," Vines said.

"The police traced it to a Tampa gun shop," Adair continued, "where it'd been bought by a Mr. T. S. Jones, whose name, address and driver's license proved false."

"What about that letter Fuller wrote—his confession?" Huckins asked.

"The police decided it was dictated to him. They're convinced the shooter threatened to kill old Mrs. Fuller unless her husband wrote exactly what he was told. After he wrote the dictated confession and signed it, the cops think he was forced to remove his lower plate and use it as a paperweight—a bizarre touch—and shove his chair back from the table. The killer then shot Fuller, went into the living room and shot Mrs. Fuller, who was so far gone she probably didn't even realize what was happening. The killer then returned to the dining room, wrapped Fuller's hand around the pistol to leave some prints and let the gun fall to the floor. It was, the cops said, a very amateurish piece of work—except for the false teeth on the suicide note, which they thought was kind of cute, and the three thousand dollars missing from the five hundred thousand that made it look as if Fuller had already spent it. The cops also liked that a lot."

"What if the cops had found that half million in your closet?" Huckins said.

"If that'd happened, I suspect they wouldn't have been nearly so diligent in their investigation of the Fullers' deaths and might well have accepted the written confession at face value. And as for me, well, I'd've still been doing time."

"So you're saying that no one was bribed," Huckins said.

"I'm still living off that half million Kelly found in my closet and shipped down to the Bahamas."

"But that wasn't a bribe in the legal sense, was it?"

"What would you call it—a gift?"

"I'd call it found money," Sid Fork said. "But I'm kind of flexible."

There was another silence, briefer this time, that Huckins ended when she asked Adair, "Where are they now?"

"Jack and Jill?" He looked at Vines. "I'm not sure. New York?"

"London," Vines said.

"When we were out at Cousin Mary's today—yesterday now—except for Sid, of course, and you avoided telling me— "

"Neglected, not avoided," Adair said.

"When you didn't tell me what you've just now told us, I remember your saying that if the two Jimson kids died, their share of the gas revenues or royalties would go to their stepmother. Is that correct?"

"Yes," Adair said. "And if the stepmother died, her share would go to Jack and Jill."

"Once I'd found out that bribe was a fake," Sid Fork said, "you could bet the rent I'd've had me a talk with that stepmother."

"Kelly's the authority on her," Adair said.

All three looked at Vines, but it was the mayor who said, "This time, Mr. Vines, please don't leave anything out."

Vines ignored her and looked to his right at the chief of police. "How hard is it to fake a suicide when a gun's the death weapon?"

"Damned near impossible what with all the forensic expertise there is nowadays," Fork said. "Best way to fake a suicide is shove the victim out of a high window around three in the morning and don't leave a note or anything else behind."

Vines turned to the mayor. "After the cops told our somewhat dim attorney general that the Fullers' deaths were probably a double murder, he did nothing until he figured out what would give him the most political mileage. Finally, he decided that having a bribe-proof supreme court was the way to go—even though its chief justice by then was having a little trouble with the IRS."

"Not so little," Adair said.

"So the A.G. ordered a full-scale investigation that would, in his words, leave no stone unturned. One of the stones most in need of turning was, of course, the stepmother. So a two-man team of experienced investigators was sent down to question her. Soon after the team came back and made its report, the attorney general called a press conference to announce that the deaths of Justice and Mrs. Mark Fuller weren't suicide-murder after all, but rather what he called 'a diabolical double murder' and that neither Justice Fuller nor Chief Justice Adair had ever been bribed. Two days later, just before the two investigators were to question the stepmother again, her Cadillac ran off the road at an estimated seventy-eight miles per hour and into a cottonwood tree."

"Killed her, too, I bet," Fork said.

"Broke her neck. An autopsy showed a point-one-six-percent alcohol in her blood, which made her more than legally drunk. An autopsy of the Cadillac by a team of mechanics hired by the attorney general revealed what he described—at still another press conference—as 'an inexplicable failure of the car's steering mechanism.' When a reporter asked if that meant somebody had messed with the tie rods, he said he couldn't comment until further tests were made, and went on to announce that the stepmother, over the past five months, had withdrawn almost two million dollars in cash from her several bank accounts. After that, everybody thought they knew where the money in the shoeboxes came from and the tie rods were almost forgotten."

"Pretty good motive," Sid Fork said. "She puts up two million to win how much—fifteen million, twenty?"

"If both the Jimson kids died, she'd get all the gas royalties," Vines said. "The last I heard they were valued at anywhere between fifty and a hundred million dollars."

"If she could've made it look like those two kids had successfully bribed the supreme court to keep them out of the gas chamber—"

"It's lethal injection in my state," Adair said.

"Okay," Fork said. "Out of the needle room. But if that'd

241

happened, I don't think there's a court in the land that'd lift a finger to keep the kids from being executed."

"I'm afraid you're right," Adair said.

"And if Mr. Vines hadn't found that half a million in your closet," said B.D. Huckins, "I think it still could've worked."

"I'm afraid that's right, too," Adair said.

"Anyway, it sure has a happy ending, doesn't it?" Sid Fork said. "The two kids are acquitted. The state supreme court turns out to be honest after all, except for that little problem its chief justice had with the IRS. And when they finally got around to figuring out the 'who profits?' angle if the kids'd been executed, it turns out to be the wicked stepmother. That about it, Mr. Vines?"

"Just about."

"Then tell me this," Fork said. "Did they ever try and come up with the sucker who did the scut work? The one who zapped the old judge and his wife, then dressed up like a priest to stick that half a million bucks in the judge's closet and maybe even messed with the tie rods on the stepmother's Caddie?"

Before Vines could answer, B.D. Huckins looked at Adair and said, "What was the stepmother's name?"

"Marie. Marie Jimson."

"Before she was married—her maiden name?"

"Marie Contraire."

Sid Fork's face went almost white just before the blood raced up his neck and turned his ears a cardinal red. He jumped to his feet, pointed an accusatory finger at Huckins and roared, *"Goddamnit, B.D.!"*

The mayor gave him her sweetest smile. "I just wanted you to hear it in context from them and not from me."

The red was fading to pink as Fork, still glowering, sat back down and said, "That was one shitty thing to pull."

"Shut up and listen some more," she said and turned to Adair again. "Because Sid wasn't with us when we met with Parvis at Cousin Mary's, I gave him a condensed version of what we talked about. Obviously, I left out a few details."

"Like the stepmother's maiden name," Fork said.

She ignored him and shifted her gaze to Vines. "When you called earlier tonight, I was in some delicate political negotiations with the sheriff and that's why I hung up on you. I apologize."

"No need."

"Later, Sid came up with some very important information, which is the real reason we're here."

She's giving him all the credit for something, Vines thought as he looked at Fork. "What'd you turn up, Chief?"

It was not a modest smile that spread across Fork's face. "This guy that B.D. and I knew a long time ago—the one who dresses up like a priest and a plumber and all—and who we knew as Teddy Smith or Jones?"

"The killer," Vines said.

"Yeah. Him. Well, I found out his real name."

"How?"

"From fingerprints he left on that pink van."

"Stop milking it, Sid," Huckins said.

His proud and happy smile still in place, Fork looked from Vines to Adair. "Well, the guy's real name isn't Smith or Jones—although that's no big news. His real name's Theodore Contraire."

Fork watched with evident enjoyment as surprise rearranged the faces of Adair and Vines. It was Vines who recovered first and asked, "Her brother?"

Fork nodded. "Who else could she trust with something like that? According to his sheet, he has—or had, I guess—a sister three years older than him whose name was Marie Elena—like the old song—Contraire."

"How long's his sheet?" Vines said.

"Nine arrests and two convictions. he spent two years in

243

Angola down in Louisiana and nine months in the L.A. county jail for aggravated assault."

"What'd he give as his occupation—just out of curiosity?"

Fork grinned happily. "Actor."

"Congratulations, Chief," Adair said.

"Well, it took more charm than brains," said Fork, trying to sound modest but not succeeding. "All I had to do was convince some guy to do something he wasn't quite sure he wanted to do."

Vines rose, went to the window, looked out, noticed the unmarked four-door sedan that was parked down the street and wondered whether it was the black detective or the too-tall one who was keeping the night watch. He turned from the window to B.D. Huckins.

"When you hung up on me," he said, "I was calling to tell you your brother-in-law had phoned to say that the date and place of the switch are set. July fourth at Cousin Mary's."

Huckins nodded her approval. "Good. Merriman always closes on the fourth. What time?"

"Mansur didn't say."

"It'll have to be in the afternoon."

"Why?"

"Because Sid and I have to be in the parade in the morning."

Thirty-six

After he gave the pan a small flip, Jack Adair's first omelette in eighteen months folded over perfectly and Virginia Trice said, "Mine always falls apart right about now and I wind up with scrambled eggs."

Adair glanced over his right shoulder to find her standing in the kitchen entrance, leaning against the doorjamb, her arms folded tightly against her chest, as if to keep the quivering at bay. Adair thought the smudges under her eyes were larger and darker than they had been that afternoon when she'd played reluctant landlady. Three-way exhaustion, he decided, confident of his diagnosis. Physical, mental and emotional.

"Better sit down and have some," he said. "I got carried away and used six eggs." Turning back to the gas stove, which he guessed was as at least as old as he, Adair asked, "Long day?"

"The longest," she said and sat down at the pickled-pine kitchen table.

Adair moved a few steps to his right, keeping an eye on the omelette as he poured coffee from the Bunn automatic into a mug. He placed it on the table in front of her and went quickly back to the stove.

"Now comes the tricky part," he said, "which'll turn out to be either a breeze or a disaster."

The omelette slid, as if trained, from pan onto plate. Adair quickly cut it in two, placing half on another plate, which he served to Virginia Trice along with silverware and a paper napkin. "Toast is in the oven," he said.

"There's a toaster over there by the can opener."

"I know, but I like to do it in the oven under the broiler."

He opened the old stove's high door, used a pot holder to pull out the broiler grill and speared the four pieces of toast with a long-tined cooking fork. He served the toast on a plate along with a small open tub of margarine. "I couldn't find any butter," he said as he sat down across from her with his share of the omelette.

"We don't use butter because Norm worried about his cholesterol," she said, spreading margarine over a piece of toast. "But I guess he could've gone ahead and eaten all the butter he wanted, couldn't he?"

"I guess."

She tasted the omelette and said it was perfect. Adair said he thought it could use a little salt and pepper. She said she didn't use much salt anymore. They ate in silence after that, Adair trying to think of something to say that didn't sound like forced small talk. He was rescued from what was beginning to seem like an insurmountable task when Virginia Trice said, "When's the last time you fucked a woman?"

Adair went on spreading margarine over his last small piece of toast. "Seventeen months and four days ago."

"How long were you in Lompac?"

"Fifteen months."

"You didn't have one final fling?"

Adair used knife and fork to pile the last bit of omelette on the last of his toast, vaguely pleased that they had come out even. He ate the final bite, swallowed and said, "My legal problems prior to incarceration were such that sex became a matter of supreme unimportance."

"Something like saltpeter, huh?"

"Possibly."

"What'd you do for sex in jail?"

"I did without and two hundred sit-ups a day. Of course, there was also a normal amount of masturbation. At least, I trust it was normal."

She put her knife and fork down, pushed away the plate with its half-eaten omelette, and leaned on the table with folded arms, staring down at its waxed surface. "I feel like I've just been sent to jail."

"That won't last."

Still staring at the table, she said, "I must've had four or five hundred customers in today. I opened at eight and closed at two-fifteen, two-thirty, around in there. Nine of the guys who came in to say how sorry they were about Norm tried to hit on me. Married guys. Good friends of his. When I was showing you and Vines your rooms this afternoon, I'd almost decided not to go back to the Eagle."

"You learned an invaluable lesson today," Adair said. "The assholes are everywhere."

"I've lived in this town four years now, going on five, and that's longer'n I ever lived anywhere. I know a lot of people because I'm Norm's wife and before that I worked in the Eagle for him. But he's the only real friend I had here and now he's dead. So after I closed up tonight, I was sitting there at the bar with a gin and tonic that I don't even like and wondering how I was going to last till morning when somebody knocks at the door—and it's like two forty-five by then."

She looked up at Adair, as if for either comment or encouragement. Adair nodded and said, "You answered the door?"

"Well, I go and ask who's there first because, you know,

it's late and I've got all the day's cash and I don't wanta take any chances. So guess who it is?"

"No idea."

"It's B.D."

"The mayor."

"Yeah, and she comes in and wants to know if I'd like to stay at her place tonight or as long as I want to. So you know what I do?"

"You cry."

"Bawl like a baby. But she's just as nice as she can be and seems to understand when I tell her I can't stay with her."

"Why not?"

"I don't know. But I guess it's because I kept thinking, What'll you tell Norm? Does that make any sense?"

Adair said he thought it did.

"Well, when I finally get in the car and start home, it's all of a sudden like I'm going to jail. I mean it's like I've gotta spend a year or two all by myself up in that room on the second floor. Like it's the law or something."

"It's not, of course," Adair said. "At least, not yet."

"Well, it sure feels like it," she said, looking away and up toward the kitchen's most distant corner. She was still inspecting the far corner when she said, "So d'you wanta sleep with me tonight?"

"Why me?"

She looked at him—rather gravely, he thought—and said "Well, you're nice and you're older and since I'm asking you, instead of you making a move on me, it means it's my choice, doesn't it? And if I can make a choice, then I must not be in jail after all."

"It also means you can choose somebody else," Adair said.

"We don't have to—*do* anything—unless you want to. I just wanta wake up and find somebody there. Somebody nice."

"I'm very flattered," Adair said.

She smiled for the first time—a very slight smile. "I think you just said no thanks, Virginia."

Adair smiled back. "But if you're still feeling the same some other night, well . . ."

She rose slowly and stood, staring down at him curiously. "What you're doing is giving me one more choice, aren't you?"

"I can't give what you already have."

She smiled again, more confidently this time. "I'll think about it, Mr. Adair," Virginia Trice said, turned and left the kitchen.

Adair rose, picked up the plates, mugs and silver and carried them to the sink. As he ran the water and added the Ivory Liquid, he promised himself to wash and dry everything slowly, concentrating on each plate, mug, fork, spoon and knife. This would keep him from thinking of what it would be like, sitting on the edge of the bed up in Virginia Trice's room, slowly taking off her clothing, one item at a time.

After she left the studio apartment of the tall young uniformed policeman who had directed traffic out on Noble's Trace where Ivy Settles and the woman photographer had been shot to death, Dixie Mansur drove home to Santa Barbara and its Montecito enclave. It was there that she and Parvis Mansur lived in the sprawling field-stone house with the blue tile roof on an acre of ground that was surrounded by a twelve-foot-high chain link fence.

As she slipped the coded plastic card into the slot that opened the sliding steel gate, she tried to remember the young policeman's name. It was either Sean or Michael, she thought, deciding he was just about young enough to have been born at a time when most male babies seemed to be named either Sean or Michael. But what she remembered best about him was the mess his apartment had been.

She drove the Aston Martin through the gate and on up the concrete drive to the four-door garage. She pressed the switch beneath the dashboard that signalled her garage door to rise. Once it had risen, she drove in and parked next to Parvis Mansur's white Rolls-Royce.

As she entered the library, Mansur looked up from his book, down at his watch, and up again. "You might've called," he said.

Dixie went over to the bar and poured herself a glass of sherry. "I started to," she said, taking a sip, "but after I talked to Vines and told him what you told me to tell him, I went over to B.D.'s and after that things got a little hectic."

"In what respect?"

"Remember that photographer—the one who wanted to do a freelance feature on the house for some grubby monthly?"

"I remember that you talked to her and turned her down. A Miss Hornette, wasn't it?"

"Hazel Hornette—although she liked to be called Hazy. Anyway, she's dead."

"An accident?"

"She was shot dead out on the Trace about two blocks east of the city limits. A Durango cop was also killed. One of the out-of-town ones that Sid hired. Ivy something."

"Ivy Settles," said Mansur, who had made it a point to learn the names of all four detectives Sid Fork had hired for what Mansur thought of as the chief's personal Savak. He put down his book, Palmer and Colton's *A History of the Modern World*, the fifth edition, rose and walked over to the bar, where he mixed himself a weak Scotch and water. After a swallow, he turned to Dixie and asked, "You saw them then—the remains?"

"I was with B.D. when the sheriff called and told her

about it. She was in a hurry to get there so we went in my car. They hadn't been moved so, yes, I saw the bodies."

"I'd like you to tell me the rest of it, Dixie, and do take your time. You might start from when you first saw Kelly Vines."

She gave him a concise and reasonably factual account of how she had spent the afternoon, evening, night and morning hours, and also of what she had seen and heard and done, leaving out the sex she had enjoyed with Vines and the sex she had experienced, if not enjoyed, with the tall young uniformed policeman whose name, she now remembered, was Sean and not Michael.

After she had finished, and after Mansur had asked all the questions he thought he needed to ask, she said, "This is tied in somehow with that deal you've arranged for the fourth, isn't it?"

Mansur thought about it, nodded and said, "It would appear to be."

"Then on the fourth I'm going to be out of town."

"Why?"

"Because if anything goes wrong, or if anything happens to you or Sid, I want to be with somebody someplace else."

Mansur smiled approvingly. "You want an alibi."

"You could call it that."

"I really can't blame you. Whom d'you have in mind?"

"I thought I'd drive down to San Diego Saturday, stay with the Moussavvises and come back late Monday when it's all over."

"They'll be glad to see you, especially Reva, but the traffic's going to be bloody awful."

"That's why I thought I might take the Rolls—unless you plan to do your go-betweening in it."

Mansur chuckled. "I can think of nothing more inappropriate."

"That's what I thought."

"Take it, of course," he said and looked at his watch.

"We'd best get to bed, hadn't we?" He paused to smile at her—a smile full of hope. "Would you like to sleep in my room tonight, or are you too tired?"

"I'm not tired at all," Dixie Mansur said.

Thirty-seven

From the June 28, 29, 30 and July 2 editions of *The Durango Times*:

> Services for Norman Trice, 46, owner of the landmark Blue Eagle Bar, were held Monday at Bruner Brothers Mortuary.
>
> Twenty-three out-of-town me dia representatives and approximately 200 mourners heard Mayor B.D. Huckins deliver a brief but moving eulogy. Mr. Trice, a native of Durango, is survived by his
> (*Cont. on Page 3*)
>
> A memorial service was held Tuesday at the First Methodist Church for Detective Ivy Settles, 51, of the Du-

rango Police Department. A brief but moving eulogy was delivered by Chief of Police Sid Fork.

Among the more than 100 persons attending the services were Mayor B.D. Huckins, Sheriff Charles J. Coates and representatives from 17 California police departments. Five out-of-town reporters were also present.

Settles is survived by his
(*Cont. Page 5*)

The body of Hazel Hornette, 28, a Santa Barbara freelance photographer, was identified here Wednesday by her aunt, Marlene Hornette, 52, also of Santa Barbara.

Following cremation, private services will be held at sea by the Santa Barbara Neptune Society.

Graveside services for Brig. Gen. Soldier P. Sloan (RCAF-Ret.), 71, were held Friday at the Evergreen Cemetery with prayers offered by Fr. Francis Riggins of Santa Margarita Catholic Church. A brief but moving eulogy was spoken by Jack Adair, formerly of Lompoc.

In attendance were Mayor

> B.D. Huckins, Chief of Police
> Sid Fork, Kelly Vines, for-
> merly of La Jolla, and Mrs.
> Parvis Mansur of Santa Bar-
> bara.
>
> General Sloan left no survi-
> vors.

Adair and Vines walked away from Soldier Sloan's grave on Thursday morning after the final prayer and headed for the blue Mercedes. A man, dressed in a tan poplin suit, got out of a black Mercury sedan parked near the Mercedes and walked toward them.

The man's right hand was reaching for something in either his shirt pocket or the breast pocket inside his coat when Sid Fork materialized in front of Vines and Adair, blocking the man's approach.

Fork had dressed for the graveside services in his old tweed jacket, ironed jeans, white shirt and black knit tie. His right hand was jammed down into the jacket's right pocket.

Staring at the man in the tan suit, Fork said, "Sure hope that's either a cigarette or some I.D. you're reaching for, friend."

The man in the tan suit nodded. "After I bring it out ever so slowly, it'll say I'm with the Department of Justice."

"Nice and slow then."

The man produced a folding I.D. case and handed it to Fork, who studied it, looked up and said, "Claims you're Leonard Deep and that you're an assistant deputy U.S. attorney out of Washington. What it doesn't say is if you're here on official business."

"Personal," Deep said. "With Mr. Adair and Mr. Vines."

Fork turned to them and said, "You want to talk to the Justice Department about something personal?"

"I think so," Adair said, looking at Vines. "Kelly?"

"Sure. Why not?"

"Then B.D. and I'll see you out at Cousin Mary's for lunch," Fork said, handed the I.D. back to Deep, turned and walked toward the mayor, who was standing beside her Volvo, listening to Father Riggins.

"Where'd you like to talk, Mr. Deep?" Vines asked.

Deep looked around the cemetery. "That bench over there in the shade looks comfortable."

To reach the bench they had to pass by Soldier Sloan's grave, which was being filled in by two workmen with shovels. Deep paused to read aloud the inscription Vines had composed for the headstone: "'Soldier Pershing Sloan, 1917–1988, Few Deserve Such a Friend.'" Deep looked up at Adair and Vines and said, "I think Soldier would've approved. Like him, it's nicely equivocal."

"You knew Soldier?" Adair said as he and Deep sat down on the bench and Vines leaned against one of the pines that provided the shade.

"Let's say that over the years his long and interesting career came to our attention."

At 40, or close to it, Deep had the body and moves of a slowly aging athlete who, in his youth, Vines guessed, had passed up contact sports for the loner's favorites of running, swimming or diving. Vines decided Deep had probably been a snob jock and was possibly just as smart as he looked.

"You here to talk to us about Soldier?" Adair said, his voice as innocent as his kitten blue eyes.

Deep's reply sounded almost diffident. "The FBI in Santa Barbara would appreciate it if you'd give them a ring."

"That's what Chief Fork told me," Adair said. "I'll have to do that when I get a moment."

Deep smiled as if he knew he was being lied to shamelessly and didn't really care. Vines decided to find out why and said, "Suggesting that Jack call the FBI makes your trip sound more official than personal."

Deep studied Vines before he said, "I'm here because of Paul Adair."

"What about Paul?" Adair demanded.

"This may not be much comfort, Mr. Adair, but I can assure you Paul didn't commit suicide."

Adair nodded slowly. "That's no small comfort and I thank you for telling me."

"I also want you to know we've finally located the two Mexican prostitutes who signed sworn statements that they heard two shots as they were going up the stairs to Paul's room in Tijuana. They've now refuted those statements and deny they either were on their way up to his room or ever heard any shots."

"This comes from where?" Vines said.

"From an FBI investigation ordered by the attorney general who had great respect for Paul."

"Well, that's nice of the attorney general," Adair said, "and I appreciate your telling us Paul didn't commit suicide because Kelly and I'd wondered how he managed to shoot himself in the mouth twice with a forty-five. Then, too, knowing Paul's sexual orientation, we never put much stock in his sending down for a pair of female prostitutes. They were female, weren't they, Mr. Deep?"

Deep gave his head an almost amused tilt to the right and said, "You knew he was gay, of course."

"Ever since he announced it at the breakfast table to his mother, his sister and me on his fifteenth birthday."

"You also knew, Mr. Vines?"

"Yes, but I still preferred his sister."

"Whom you married."

"So I did."

Deep sighed and said, "I was shattered by Paul's death. It was a great personal loss."

"We all felt rotten," Adair said. "Especially Kelly, who had to go down there and identify his body."

"He was absolutely brilliant," Deep said. "If Paul had lived, he could have—"

"He's dead, Mr. Deep," Adair said.

"And we finally know who killed him," Deep said and waited, as if for some emotional outcry.

But Jack Adair only nodded and said, "You mean Theodore Contraire, right? Also known as Teddy Smith or Jones."

Leonard Deep lost a little of his almost studied poise, but recovered it quickly and said, "I'd very much like to know how you learned about Contraire."

"Chief Fork figured it out and told us. Contraire's the one who's apparently been killing all these folks in Durango, including Soldier Sloan, which got me and Kelly pretty upset because we'd both known Soldier for years. Chief Fork, of course, doesn't have the FBI's resources but he's shrewd and persistent. Seems to me they ought to get together with him and compare notes."

"I'll recommend it," Deep said as he rose from the cemetery bench.

"You and Paul were good friends, I take it?" Adair said.

"Extremely close."

"Well, I'm glad he had someone."

"Another couple of questions, Mr. Adair—completely unofficial?"

Adair nodded.

"Why're you in Durango?"

"On the day I was to get out of Lompoc, somebody put a price on my head."

"I heard. Twenty thousand dollars."

"So I figured Durango'd be as good a place as any to hide out or lie low or whatever you want to call it."

"Who recommended it?"

"Soldier Sloan."

"What was Soldier doing here when he was killed?"

"He never got the chance to say."

"If I were either you or Mr. Vines," Deep said, "I'd get out of Durango as quickly as possible."

"Kelly and I're leaving on the evening of the fourth."

"Why not before?"

"We don't want to miss the parade," Vines said.

Thirty-eight

Merriman Dorr's small office in Cousin Mary's was two doors down the corridor from the poker room where the weekend table-stakes games were played. The office was about the size of the average living room rug and contained a large Chubb safe, three bar-locked steel filing cabinets and two wingback chairs.

There was also a desk—a child's desk Dorr had salvaged from the old schoolhouse—with a wooden top that lifted up, a round inkwell and a fold-up seat he had moved back a foot or so to make room for his knees.

Dorr was now seated at the desk, shaking his head at B.D. Huckins, who sat in one of the wingback chairs, her legs crossed and her navy-blue dress pulled well down over her knees.

"Sounds like gore on the floor to me, B.D.," Dorr said after he stopped shaking his head no.

"Five thousand, Merriman, for the use of two rooms and your safe for one hour."

"If you need two rooms and a safe, that means you've got two people or two groups of people involved. One of 'em's got the goods and the other's got the money and nobody trusts anybody. If one of 'em forgets to bring the money or the goods, then there's liable to be some bang-bang. And if that happens, five thousand won't even come close to paying for the misery I'll get from Charlie Coates or maybe the DEA."

"I don't need to tell you it's not drugs."

"Yeah, but it's something that needs two rooms and a safe for an hour, and that means big bucks're changing hands because, if they weren't, they could do it down near the teeter-totters in Handshaw Park."

"Ten thousand," she said. "Final offer."

"In advance."

She hesitated, nodded reluctantly and said, "All right."

Dorr rose from the child's desk, smiling. "Now how's this sound for lunch, B.D.? A ham loaf made out of real Virginia ham; fresh peas, new potatoes, an endive salad and, for dessert, homemade peach ice cream?"

"If it comes out of your ten thousand, it sounds fine," Huckins said.

Once again lunch had been served at the round table in the large room with no windows. When they had all finished their peach ice cream, except for Kelly Vines, who hadn't wanted any, Parvis Mansur lit a cigarette, blew smoke at the ceiling, smiled his most genial smile and said, "Shall we begin, B.D.?"

The mayor looked at Vines and said, "Merriman wants ten thousand in advance." She paused. "Today."

"What do we get in return?" Vines asked.

"A safe and two rooms—this one and the poker room. And since you're paying, you get first choice."

"I'd like to see that poker room first," Vines said.

"Merriman'll let you see it after he gets his ten thousand."

"I know what it looks like," Sid Fork said. "It's got the

standard poker table and chairs, a couple of couches, a little bar, a refrigerator, a toaster oven, a commercial coffee maker, a bathroom and no windows."

"What about the door?" Vines asked.

"Steel door."

Vines looked at Jack Adair. "What do you think?"

"I like the steel door."

"So do I," Vines said and turned to Huckins. "Where's Merriman?"

"In his office."

Vines pushed his chair back from the table and rose. "Then I might as well go pay him his money."

After he knocked and the voice said come in, Vines entered Merriman Dorr's small office and looked around curiously. "Nice safe," he said. "I also like your desk."

"Will I need to open the safe?"

"I think so," Vines said, went over to Dorr, took a thick white No. 10 envelope from his jacket breast pocket and placed it on the desktop. Dorr picked it up, lifted its flap and looked inside. "Think I'll count it," he said.

Vines nodded, turned, went to one of the wingback chairs, sat down and watched Dorr count the $10,000.

"All there," Dorr said when the count was finished.

"Tell me something," Vines said. "What's the contingency plan?"

"In case of what?"

"In case the sheriff raids the game."

Dorr shrugged. "Out the back door."

"And into the arms of the deputies? I don't mean that plan. I mean the real one."

"Well, sir, if I was sitting in that game—although I never do—and heard Charlie Coates and his deputies trying to beat down the poker room door, which oughta take 'em at least four minutes, maybe five, well, I'd pick up my money and head for the bathroom that doesn't have a bathtub, but does have a tin shower stall."

Dorr rose, went to the safe, turned his back on Vines to protect the combination and began turning the dial.

"Then what?" Vines asked as Dorr tugged open the safe door and placed the money envelope inside.

Dorr left the safe door open as he turned back to Vines and said, "Hardly seems worthwhile to close it and then open it up again for less than a thousand, does it?"

"Leave it open and I'll put a thousand on your little desk. You tell me what happens in the shower stall. If I like it, you put the thousand in the safe. If I don't, you only put five hundred in."

"You'll like it," Dorr said.

Vines took ten one-hundred-dollar bills from his wallet, placed them on the child's desk, returned to the wingback chair, sat down and nodded at Dorr. "Let's hear it."

"Once I got inside the shower stall with all my clothes on," Dorr said, "I'd turn the cold water handle to the right and push pretty hard. The metal panel would open up on an old flight of wood stairs that leads down to the school basement. On the landing there's a flashlight. I'd turn that on, shut the shower panel real tight, go down the stairs, take a seat and wait."

"For what?"

"For the sheriff to leave."

"No way out of the basement then?"

"It's just a hidey-hole, Mr. Vines. Only way out's the way you come in."

"It'd be better if there were another way out."

"But there's not."

"Pick up your thousand," Vines said.

After Kelly Vines returned to the round table to report he had arranged for the two rooms and the safe, Parvis Mansur took over the discussion.

"The simplest of ruses is usually the best," he said. "So the one I'll use to lure Mr. Vines and Mr. Adair here on Monday next, the fourth of July, is a holiday poker game."

"At least that's what you'll tell whoever's willing to pay a million dollars for the pair of us," Adair said.

"Correct."

"What time does the game start?"

"Three in the afternoon."

"And what will you tell him—this guy who keeps calling you?"

"You mean about the procedure?"

"Yes."

"Well, first I'll speak of money."

"Good," Sid Fork said.

"I shall also emphasize—rather strongly, I might add—that nothing will happen until the money has been tallied and secured."

"What's the deal on the safe?" Fork asked Vines.

"Dorr's agreed to leave it open and let Parvis lock the money inside."

"So when it's all over, Merriman'll unlock it and hand over the million?" Fork said.

Vines nodded.

"Seems to me if something happened to some of us," Fork said, "old Merriman could just say, 'What money?'—couldn't he?"

"What an interesting thought, Chief," Adair said.

"I think while all this is going on," Fork said, "Merriman and I'll play a few hands of gin out at my house—just to pass the time."

"Extremely wise," Mansur said.

"Well, let's see now," Adair said. "Mr. Mansur has counted the money and locked it away in the safe. Now what?"

Mansur said, "Next I turn to the person or persons who've paid me the money and hand over the key that unlocks the poker room where you and Mr. Vines are ostensibly waiting to commence your game."

"You've locked us in?" Vines said.

"I'm afraid so—for the sake of realism."

No one said anything after that for several seconds until B.D. Huckins quietly asked, "What happens then, Mr. Vines?"

"It all depends," he said.

At 12:09 A.M. on Saturday, July 2, the chief of police rose naked from the mayor's bed and pulled on the Jockey shorts that were lying on the floor next to the jeans and white shirt he had worn to Soldier Sloan's burial.

"Like me to get you something before I go?" he asked B.D. Huckins, who lay on her back, the sheet up to her chin, staring at the bedroom's textured ceiling that always reminded Fork of three-week-old cottage cheese.

"Maybe a glass of wine."

"Zinfandel?" he asked as he zipped up the jeans and began buttoning the shirt.

"Fine," the mayor said.

Stuffing the tails of his shirt down into the jeans, Fork said, "Maybe I ought to stay, B.D."

She shook her head. "I need time to think."

"About what?"

"Just think."

"I'll get the wine," he said.

When he came back with two glasses of Zinfandel, Huckins propped herself up against the bed's headboard, letting the sheet slip almost to her waist. Fork smiled at her bare breasts that he long ago had decided were perfect.

"When I see 'em like that," he said, handing her the wine, "sort of accidentally, I still think exactly what I thought twenty years ago: she's got the best-looking set of jugs in California."

"Jugs," she said, looking down at her breasts with what could have been either detachment or indifference. "I guess you could call them that since their main purpose is to supply milk to the young I'm probably never going to have."

"That bother you?"

She sipped the wine, as if reflecting on Fork's question. "I'm thirty-six, Sid. Another four or five years and—"

"You wanta get married?"

"I don't need to get married to have a kid."

Fork finished his wine, put the glass down on the bedside table and said, "Lemme ask you something else, B.D."

She nodded.

"Did it ever sort of happen to cross your mind that we could take that million and just tell Durango goodbye, good luck and *hasta la vista*?"

She stared at him with eyes that—perhaps because of the dim light—had taken on the color of gunpower. "That's one of the things I need to think about."

At 12:49 A.M. on that same Saturday, Virginia Trice arrived home after closing the Blue Eagle early to find Jack Adair again in the kitchen of the old house. He had just finished making two toasted Spam and cheese sandwiches when she said, "You really like to cook?"

"I like to eat," Adair said, placed the sandwiches on two plates and served them on the pine kitchen table.

"Looks good," she said, sitting down.

"Milk okay?" he asked, opening the refrigerator.

"Fine."

Adair served the milk, sat down at the table, took an enormous bite of his sandwich and chewed it with obvious enjoyment. As they ate the sandwiches and drank the milk, she told him how a waitress at the Blue Eagle had quit that afternoon without notice. It could've put her in a bind, she said, because it was the first of the month and the government checks were arriving.

"But it didn't?" he asked.

"In Durango? An hour after she quit five girls came in to apply for her job. I told each one I'd call her tomorrow—today now—and tell her yes or no. That way they don't have to sit around waiting for the phone to ring."

"That was a decent thing to do."

"When I was a waitress I learned pretty quick that this country's got a real shortage of decency."

She reached into her small brown leather purse, hesitated, looked at Adair and said, "You smoke?"

"Used to."

"Mind if I do?"

"Not at all."

She took a pack of filtered Camels from the purse and lit one with a disposable lighter. "I started again on Tuesday right after the funeral. I'd been off for sixteen months."

"Well, they can be a solace."

"I've been thinking about what you said about choice—how you can choose to do something or not do it—like I chose to start smoking again. But then I decided there aren't that many choices when you get right down to it. If you're sick, you can't choose to get well. And you sure as hell can't choose your parents and all the crap that goes with that. So the more I thought about it the more it seems like you don't get to make the big choices, just the little ones."

"Such as?" Adair said

"Such as crossing the street almost on an impulse that later turns out to be the biggest choice of your life."

"Because of subsequent events," he said.

"Yeah. Because of what happens. So I decided to make a choice. I don't know if it's a big one or a little one. But I decided to ask you, no strings attached, if you'd like to go to bed with me tonight?"

Adair smiled what he hoped was his most winning smile. "I'd be delighted."

Kelly Vines, lying in bed, looked up from page 389 of his 406-page novel of mild southern decadence when he heard Adair's voice and Virginia Trice's giggle as they went past his room. He waited for the now familiar sound of Adair's door to open and close. Instead, he heard a door open and close farther down the hall. It was, he decided, the sound of the door to Virginia's room.

Vines smiled, put his book down, took a handful of mixed nuts from the open can on the bedside table, rose and went to the window that overlooked the street. The anonymous sedan was parked two houses down. Glancing at his watch, Vines saw it was a few minutes to one.

He stood, eating the nuts one at a time, as he stared out the window and waited for the shift to change. At one minute past one, another anonymous sedan parked in front of the other car. A very tall man got out, went back to the rear car, bent down—apparently to say a few words—and returned to his own car.

The rear car switched on its lights and left. Vines finished his handful of nuts, returned to the bed, picked up the novel and, sitting on the edge of the bed, finished it. But because the novel had failed to put him to sleep, he reached for the old standby remedy and poured almost three ounces of Jack Daniel's into a water glass.

He drank it slowly, wondering as he often did on sleepless nights where he would be a year from now, presuming, of course, he told himself, that a year from now you'll still be around.

He finished the whiskey, turned off the light and lay down. When he looked for the last time at his watch's glowing dial it was a little past three and Jack Adair had still not returned to his room.

Thirty-nine

At a little past 9 A.M. on Sunday, July 3, Dixie Mansur kissed her husband goodbye and drove away in his white Rolls-Royce, heading south on U.S. 101 toward San Diego, where, Parvis Mansur believed, she planned to spend the holiday weekend with their friends, Mr. and Mrs. Reva Moussavvis.

Because of heavy holiday traffic, Dixie didn't reach Ventura's beachside Holiday Inn until a little past ten that morning. She removed an overnight bag, locked the white Rolls and checked into a prepaid room that had been reserved for her under the name of Joyce Mellon.

Once in the room she tossed the overnight bag on one bed, sat down on the other, picked up the phone and tapped out the three numbers of another room in the hotel. When a man's voice answered with a hello, she said, "You ready?" After the man replied he was, she said she would be right down.

Dixie Mansur's room was 607 and the man's room was 505. She went down the stairs, along the corridor and knocked at the door. It was opened by Theodore Contraire, who sometimes wore a priest's outfit, sometimes a plumber's, and now wore a pale blue smock that could have belonged to either a pharmacist or a hairdresser.

Once Dixie was inside the room and the door was closed, the five-foot-one Contraire reached up, grabbed her by the shoulders and forced her head down to his so he could mash their lips together in a long, long kiss that entailed a lot of wet tongue work.

The kiss ended as abruptly as it began. Contraire wiped his mouth with the back of his hand and said, "We're running a little late."

"I had to fuck Parvis before I could leave."

"Over here," he said, indicating a long low dresser with a large mirror. She sat down on a padded bench and Contraire switched on the four lights he had rigged up to illuminate the mirror.

Staring at herself, Dixie said, "Christ, I look awful."

"You're gonna look even worse," he said. "Older. Maybe ten years older. I'm gonna start with the contacts. Here."

He handed her a small plastic case. She removed the contact lenses from it and inserted them quickly.

"Been practicing," he said with grudging approval.

"All week."

"Okay, now you got brown eyes instead of blue."

"I like blue better."

"Not with dark brown hair, you don't." Contraire stuck four bobby pins in his mouth, pulled Dixie's blond hair back and expertly pinned it into a smooth helmet. He picked up a shoulder-length brown wig from the dresser, used a brush on it and carefully fitted it to her head.

After inspecting his handiwork with obvious satisfaction, he picked up a squat white bottle with no label, removed its cap, poured a small amount of thick beige liquid onto his fingertips and began working it into her face and neck. "It takes two minutes, that's all," he said.

When he finished, she had acquired a moderately deep tan.

Dixie inspected herself critically in the mirror. "I look different but not much older."

Contraire, looking over her shoulder into the mirror, ran the thumb and forefinger of his right hand down the faint parenthetic lines that began at the base of Dixie's nose and went to the corners of her mouth. "When you get older," he said, "these get deeper. So here's what we do."

Using what appeared to be a well-sharpened eyebrow pencil, Contraire delicately increased the visibility of the two parenthetic lines. The results made Dixie say, "I'll be damned."

"Put these on," Contraire said, handing her a wire-framed pair of green-tinted glasses whose lenses were only slightly larger than half-glasses. She put them on and they promptly slipped down her nose. She shoved them up. They slipped down again.

"When you're talking to him, keep shoving 'em back up. It'll drive him nuts."

Dixie turned her head as far to the right as she could and still examine herself in the mirror. Turning her head to the left, she did the same. "I look almost forty with these dumb glasses."

Contraire removed the top from a large jar of cold cream. "Okay," he said. "Take it all off, then put it back on and let's see how fast you can do it."

She did it twice before he was satisfied. He placed the wig, the tinted glasses, the contact lenses and the cosmetics in a plain white paper shopping bag. From the pocket of his smock he took a sheaf of hundred-dollar bills bound with a red rubber band.

"Six thousand exactly," he said, dropping it into the shopping bag.

"What about the map?" Dixie said.

He brought that out from the other pocket of his smock.

271

It was hand-drawn on a sheet of plain white paper. Dixie studied it, nodded and said, "What kind of car?"

"Two-year-old black Cadillac Seville sedan." He smiled, displaying the gray teeth. "Real conservative." He stopped smiling and frowned, as if he had forgotten something. "What about your clothes?"

"I bought a frumpy summer suit at the Junior League thrift shop in Santa Barbara."

"That oughta do."

"Should I call him from here?"

"Christ, no. From a pay phone."

"Don't you want to hear my voice?"

Contraire grimaced, as if he had just been accused of negligence. "Sure I want to hear it. I was just about to ask you."

"Here goes then," Dixie said. "Hello, there. I'm Mrs. Nelson Wigmore? Kelly Vines's cousin? And I'd like to find out if I can do something that's really rotten?"

Contraire again nodded his approval. "Don't forget those rising inflections. But it sounds pretty good—like about halfway between New Orleans and Mobile."

"I practiced with a tape recorder."

Contraire frowned again, as if trying to think of something else he had forgotten. Nothing apparently came to mind so he asked a question instead. "How're B.D. and Sid and them taking it?"

"They still don't know diddly. Except Sid did find out who Hazy was. Why'd you have to fix her anyway?"

"Why? Because you brought her in when we needed a photographer and she could've tied you in with me, that's why. And after she saw me fix that cop from the back of the van, well, what'd you expect me to do except what I did?"

"You could've done something different."

"You're making it sound like I wanted to fix her, like I was dying to or something. Maybe you oughta know that by then Hazy and I had a nice little something going."

"Fuck off, Teddy."

"You fuck off, Dixie."

It was often the way they said goodbye.

Dixie Mansur drove out of the Ventura Holiday Inn parking lot and two blocks farther on found a Texaco gas station with a bank of pay phones. She got out of the Rolls, locked it again, dropped her quarter and tapped out the eleven-digit number. When her call was answered, the operator cut in with instructions to deposit an additional $1.25 for three minutes. Dixie instead dropped in seven quarters.

After the quarters stopped clanging, the man's voice on the phone again said, "Altoid Sanitarium."

Dixie shifted into her southern accent and said, "May I speak to Dr. David Pease? This is Mrs. Nelson Wigmore? Mr. Jack Adair's niece?"

Forty

When his stainless-steel Omega Seamaster said it was exactly 6 A.M. on Monday, the fourth of July, Merriman Dorr grabbed the rope with both hands, pulled down hard and rang the old schoolhouse's cast-iron bell.

By the ninth pull, which now was more yank than pull, the big bell's clangor and peal were being answered by the distant howls of at least two dozen dogs. Dorr rang the old bell faster and faster, yipping and howling back at the dogs and occasionally bursting into snatches of "The Battle Hymn of the Republic," "Dixie" and "God Bless America."

He rang the school bell for exactly ten minutes. At 6:10 A.M. he marched to the old schoolhouse flagpole, ran up the Stars and Stripes and stood at rigid attention, reciting the Pledge of Allegiance. Still at attention, Dorr gave the flag a snappy salute and a look of utter adulation. He also gave it a glorious smile that easily could have been worn by either a devout patriot or, as some suspected, a nut.

After a smart about-face, Dorr marched back to the front

entrance of Cousin Mary's, still wearing his Glorious Fourth smile, but thinking now of breakfast that would include fresh orange juice, pork sausages, blueberry pancakes, two or three eggs, lightly basted, salt-rising bread toast, and at least three cups of coffee. After that he would go downtown and watch the parade.

The parade began forming at 9 A.M. down near the Southern Pacific tracks and Durango's former train depot, which had lost its purpose, if not its usefulness, when the railroad concluded there was no longer any profit in hauling humans.

The depot had been transformed into Durango's Tourist and Cultural Center. This lasted until the city discovered that it served precious few tourists and provided no culture to speak of. After scrapping the center, Durango rented the depot in rapid succession to a head shop, a sushi bar, an adult book store, a Tex-Mex cafe and an acupuncturist. All of them failed. The depot now housed the city's Venereal Disease Control Center, which Sid Fork and others usually referred to as the clap clinic.

The parade would have begun as scheduled, at 10:30 A.M., if 12-year-old Billy Apco's mother, a single parent, hadn't had to deal with a flat tire on her Ford Bronco that took her and Billy fifteen minutes to change. But since Billy was the one who beat the bass drum in the Kiwanis-sponsored Fife and Drum Corps, the consensus was to delay the parade's start until he arrived.

The parade's route would take it straight up North Fifth Street through the heart of the business district until it reached Handshaw Park at around noon, where it would disband and Mayor B.D. Huckins, speaking from the bandstand, would deliver what *The Durango Times* had said would be "brief patriotic remarks." The mayor's audience would be lured to the park by the promise of free hot dogs and soda pop, courtesy of the Safeway and Alpha

Beta supermarkets, and five-cents-a-plastic-cup beer for adults, a traditional courtesy of the Blue Eagle Bar.

Jack Adair and Kelly Vines, glasses of draft beer in hand, stood outside the Blue Eagle, waiting for the parade. A little behind them and to their left was Detective Joe Huff, looking far less bald and a bit less professorial because of his Chicago Cubs baseball cap and huge cigar. To the right of Vines and Adair was Detective Wade Bryant, the too-tall elf, whose height enabled him to see over the heads of the parade watchers who were lined up one-deep at the curb.

Leading the parade was a color guard composed of American Legion and Veterans of Foreign Wars members, all of them old enough to have fought in either World War Two or Korea. After the guard came the Pretty Polly's Sandwiches and Pies float, one of the nine commercial floats in the parade. Then came "The Wild Bunch," a geriatric biker's club whose members all rode Harleys, followed by the Durango Palomino and Philosophical Society, which boasted some beautiful mounts; the Kiwanis Fife and Drum Corps, with Billy Apco banging away on his big bass drum; the splendidly costumed Gay Vaqueros, who were excellent riders and outrageous flirts; more floats; the mayor, riding on the folded-down convertible top of a 1947 Chrysler Town and Country; the chief of police, waving from the back of a 1940 Buick Century convertible; the members of the City Council, riding together and grinning like fools in an open carriage drawn by two fine bays; a troop of Boy Scouts; a bicycle club; fourteen clowns who belonged to the Chamber of Commerce and gave away Hershey Kisses and Fleer's bubble gum; and, finally, twelve barely pubescent baton twirlers who twirled to the strains of "Colonel Bogie" as played and whistled by the Rotary Club's Drum and Bugle Corps.

After the parade went by, Adair, Vines and Virginia Trice walked to Handshaw Park, trailed by Detectives Bryant and Huff. They ate free hot dogs and drank five-cent beer while listening to the city attorney introduce Mayor B.D. Huckins.

Quoting Tom Paine, Abraham Lincoln, Dwight Eisenhower and Bruce Springsteen, Huckins gave what Jack Adair decided was the best eight-minute all-purpose political speech he had ever heard.

"She's not only got a good voice and a great delivery," he told Kelly Vines, "but she also knows a secret that ninety-nine percent of today's politicians have either forgotten or never knew."

"Which is?" said Vines, slipping into what he was beginning to regard as his customary straight man role.

"She knows how to leave them wanting more," Adair said. "And any politician who can do that these days can get reelected forever unless, of course, as the ex-governor of Louisiana says, they find him in bed with either a dead woman or a live boy."

At 12:31 P.M., just after her sister finished her brief patriotic remarks in Durango's Handshaw Park, Dixie Mansur turned off U.S. 101 at the Kanan Dume Road exit in Agoura and crossed over the freeway to the Jack in the Box where Theodore Contraire had said the black Cadillac Seville would be parked.

As promised, the 1986 Cadillac was parked behind the restaurant. Dixie got out of her husband's white Rolls-Royce, locked it and, carrying the same plain shopping bag Contraire had given her, went into the Jack in the Box and entered the women's toilet.

No one in the place noticed the brown-haired woman in the wrinkled, frumpy-looking tan linen suit and the green-tinted glasses who came out of the toilet five minutes later. Nor did anyone ever remember that she went around to the rear of the restaurant and got into the black Cadillac instead of the white Rolls she had arrived in.

The key to the Cadillac was in the ashtray, just as Contraire had said it would be. Dixie started the engine, checked the gas gauge, which registered full, backed out, crossed over U.S. 101 and, after less than a mile, found the winding narrow blacktop road with no shoulders that led up into the brown hills.

Dixie had left San Diego and the home of her weekend hosts, Mr. and Mrs. Reva Moussavvis, at seven that morning, cutting her visit short with the plausible excuse that she was growing more and more worried about the holiday traffic.

At exactly 12:46 P.M., which made her one minute late, she turned the Cadillac into the Altoid Sanitarium, went past the twin stone pillars, up the zigzag drive and parked the Cadillac directly in front of the massive redwood door. She slid over into the passenger seat and inspected herself in the sun visor's vanity mirror, pushing the tinted glasses up her nose and watching them slide back down. She also examined her new brown eyes, courtesy of the contact lenses, and her newly lined and tanned face, which she decided was one of modern chemistry's minor wonders.

Confident that she looked as if she were easily pushing 40, Dixie got out of the Cadillac and rang the bell twice, ignoring the engraved brass plate that asked visitors to please ring only once.

Now seated across the desk from Dr. David Pease, who wore a purple and orange Hawaiian shirt over white duck pants, Dixie Mansur said, "We were just stunned when we got that letter in Aberdeen from Dannie's mama. Nelson and I had no idea."

"Nelson is your husband, I believe."

"Nelson Wigmore? Like I told you on the phone? In the oil business? With Oxy? That's what we were doing in Aberdeen for four years."

"In Scotland."

Dixie pushed the tinted green glasses back up her nose. "Didn't I say Scotland? I reckon I'm just used to everyone in the business knowing if you say Aberdeen, you mean Scotland and North Sea and not South Dakota. But anyway, Dannie's mama is my Aunt Lena and Jack Adair's my uncle, even if they are divorced and have been since way back in seventy-two. But this letter I got from Aunt Lena said she heard that Uncle Jack and Kelly Vines—who's sort of my cousin by marriage?"

Dr. Pease nodded his understanding as Dixie pushed the glasses back up her nose.

"Well, she'd heard, Aunt Lena, I mean, that because of all that trouble Uncle Jack and Kelly had, they might not be able to afford to, well, you know, keep Dannie here any longer. So I talked to Nelson about it?"

"And what did he say?"

"And Nelson said, Shoot, you tell 'em not to worry about their bill. So then I talked to you yesterday and you said it would cost six thousand a month? And Nelson said why don't we just start taking care of it right now? So here I am and do you mind being paid in cash?"

"That's quite acceptable, Mrs. Wigmore," Dr. Pease said.

Dixie picked up a large woven-fiber purse from the floor and began rummaging through it, pausing three times to shove her glasses back up her nose. She finally found the envelope from Shearson Lehman Hutton addressed to Mr. Nelson Wigmore on Camden Drive in Beverly Hills. She slid the unsealed envelope across the desk to Dr. Pease, the address up. After he had glanced at the name and address and was looking inside, Dixie said, "Could I have that back, please?"

An almost startled Dr. Pease started to return the envelope. But Dixie shook her head. "Not the money, sugar; just the envelope. It's got an address and a phone number I need on the back."

Trying to remember the last time anyone had called him

sugar, Dr. Pease removed the sixty hundred-dollar bills and handed back the envelope. Dixie tucked it into her large purse and said, "Would it be okay if I drop by on the fifteenth of each month, a day or two either way, and maybe say hello to Dannie after I pay the bill?"

"Would you like to see her now?"

"Oh! Could I really?" Dixie said, pushing her glasses back up for what Dr. Pease estimated was the dozenth time. Dixie's expression suddenly went from pleased to concerned. "You think she'll know me? Aunt Lena says Dannie doesn't even recognize Kelly or Uncle Jack."

"Regardless of whether she recognizes you," he said, "it might prove beneficial if you saw her."

Dixie pushed the glasses up again. "You know, Dr. Pease, I was just thinking? What if I took Dannie out and bought her a chocolate sundae or something? Just for an hour or so? And the next time I'm here to, you know, pay the bill, maybe I could take her out for lunch and a little drive? That wouldn't hurt anything, would it?"

Dr. Pease glanced at the money, looked up at Dixie and smiled. "I can't say that it will help, Mrs. Wigmore. But I'm quite confident it won't hurt anything."

Pushing her glasses back up again, Dixie frowned, leaned forward and almost whispered, "She's not, well, violent or anything, is she?"

"Of course not."

"I didn't think so." Dixie sighed. "Dannie was always just the sweetest, gentlest thing you ever saw."

Danielle Adair Vines finished her chocolate fudge sundae as Dixie turned into the motel that was just off U.S. 101 and near the Kanan Dume Road, which led to the ocean and Malibu.

"I thought we'd go in here an maybe look at television and have something cool to drink."

"I'm terribly sorry," Danielle Vines said, "but I don't remember your name."

"Betty."

"Yes. Betty. Right."

"And maybe a little later," Dixie said as she pulled the Cadillac into the parking space in front of room 141, "we could call Jack and Kelly."

"Who?"

"Jack Adair and Kelly Vines."

"Oh, yes, of course. Mr. Adair. He's very nice. But that Mr. Vines is such a silly man."

Forty-one

After the gray Volvo sedan reached the fifth hairpin turn up on Garner Road, B.D. Huckins took a right into Don Domingo Drive and headed for Chief Sid Fork's measle-white house at the end of the cul-de-sac.

It was Merriman Dorr, seated next to the mayor, whose pilot's eye spotted the catastrophe first and said, "Hey, Sid. Somebody went and chopped down all your cactuses."

Sid Fork shot forward in the back seat, staring with disbelief through the windshield at his twelve immense, if ailing, saguaro cacti that had been felled, obviously by a chain saw, leaving a dozen one-foot-high stumps.

"Son of a bitch," Fork said, much as he might say a prayer.

"Now who the hell'd want to do something like that?" Dorr asked.

Neither Huckins nor Fork replied as the mayor turned slowly into the chief's driveway and stopped, but kept the Volvo's engine running.

"Stay here a minute," Fork said, getting out of the

sedan's rear, taking his time, a .38 Smith & Wesson Bodyguard Airweight revolver now in his right hand. He strolled past the felled cacti without a glance, keeping his eyes on the front door of his house.

When he reached the door he found it had been left slightly ajar. Fork stepped back and kicked it open, flattening his back against the brick wall on the right. He waited almost a full minute, the revolver pointed up and held in a two-handed grip. When nothing happened, he ducked through the open door in a crouch and disappeared from view.

Fork reappeared two minutes later with a stricken expression and his revolver dangling, apparently forgotten, at his right side. With his left hand he made a curiously defeated gesture that beckoned Huckins and Dorr.

The first thing they saw when they entered the living room was the far wall. All the framed pictures had been stripped from it and dropped to the floor where someone had apparently jumped up and down on them. Spray-painted on the wall was a greeting that read, "Snout says Hi!"

The mayor inspected the rest of the living room, saw nothing else that had been vandalized and said, "This it?"

Fork shook his head. "The big bedroom."

Followed by Dorr, the mayor went down the short hall and into the larger of the two bedrooms that housed the Fork Collection of American Artifacts. The sixty-two pre-1941 Coca-Cola bottles were all smashed. The ninety-four varieties of "I Like Ike" campaign buttons had been dropped to the floor and pounded with something, possibly a hammer. The last editions ever printed of the extinct magazines had been ripped apart. Maple syrup had been poured over the mounted barbed-wire display. All of the glass insulators, Fork's special pride, had been smashed.

"Jesus," Dorr said and again asked, "Who'd want to do this?"

"Kids probably," Huckins said. "During the parade when none of the neighbors were home."

They went back to the living room to find Fork leaning against one wall and glaring at the opposite one with its spray-painted greeting of "Snout says Hi!" The revolver was no longer in sight. Fork's arms were folded across his chest, giving him an almost defensive posture.

Huckins turned to Dorr and said, "Why not wait for us in the car, Merriman? We'll be out in a minute."

"Yeah," Dorr said, nodding his understanding. "Sure."

After he had gone, the mayor went over to the chief of police and put a gentle, reassuring hand on his shoulder.

"Let's go, Sid. There's nothing you can do here."

Fork ignored her and continued to glare at the opposite wall.

"Teddy did all this to make you come after him," Huckins said. "So he can kill you."

He looked at her. "Who told him, B.D.?"

"Told him what?"

"About my collection of—stuff."

"That's no secret."

Fork shook his head stubbornly. "Somebody told him."

"Maybe he's got a partner," she said. "Maybe it's even somebody here in town."

"After I fix Teddy," Fork said, "then I'll fix his partner."

Kelly Vines parked the blue Mercedes behind Cousin Mary's at 2:45 P.M. on Monday, July 4, exactly as Parvis Mansur had instructed. Vines got out first. Then came Jack Adair, who stood, leaning on his black cane and looking around the restaurant's rear parking lot that was empty of cars save for the blue Acura Legend coupe that Mansur had said he would be driving.

Vines and Adair started toward the rear steel-sheathed door. It was opened before they could reach it by Parvis Mansur, who wore a nervous, excited air and his raw-silk bush jacket.

"You didn't wear coats," he said by way of greeting. "Good."

"As instructed," Vines said.

Eyeing Adair's black cane, Mansur said, "That a sword cane?"

Adair handed the cane to him and said, "Turn the handle to the right, not the left."

Following instructions, Mansur removed the handle, smiled at the sight of the silver-topped cork, drew it out, raised the cane and sniffed. "Bourbon, right?"

"Nerve tonic," Adair said.

Mansur put the cane back together and returned it to Adair. "You probably want to inspect the poker room first."

"Alone," Vines said.

"Yes, of course. Alone."

The poker room was almost as Sid Fork had described it. There was a seven-player table covered with green baize. There were also seven comfortable chairs drawn up to it. There were three leather couches (instead of two by Fork's count) that were long enough to nap on; a bar, nicely stocked; a coffee maker; a large GE refrigerator with an automatic ice-maker; a toaster oven; a cabinet full of plates, glasses, cups, bowls and flatware; a long narrow table where the buffets were presumably laid out; a six-line phone; and no windows.

"What about the john?" Adair said.

Vines nodded toward a closed door at the rear of the room. "Let's check it out."

The bathroom was large enough for a urinal, a toilet, a

sink, and a metal shower stall with a green rubberized shower curtain that hung on plastic ivory-colored rings. Vines pushed the shower curtain to one side, looked down and saw that the floor was cement with a metal drain. He reached into the shower, grasped the cold water faucet and turned it to the right, jerking his arm back as if to avoid the spray. But there was no spray.

"Suspicious bastard, aren't you?" Adair said.

"Cautious," said Vines as he stepped into the shower and gave a hard push to the metal wall that held the faucets and shower head. The wall swung away, revealing a three-by-three foot wooden landing. A large five-cell chrome flashlight was held in place on the landing by a bracket.

They used the flashlight to go down a steep flight of wooden stairs made of unfinished pine lumber. There was no banister. The stairs led down to a small room with concrete walls and floor. The room contained a wooden bench, a chemical toilet, a five-gallon sealed plastic bottle of Arrowhead drinking water, two metal cups and nothing else.

Vines played the flashlight around the room, exploring the ceiling and all four corners. "No escape hatch," Adair said.

"No."

"Let's get out of here."

When they reentered the poker room the telephone was chirping softly. Vines picked it up and said, "Yes."

"Mansur here. I'm calling from the private dining room. The phone, either this one or the one in Dorr's office, will be our communications channel. If necessary, we can even set up a conference call although I don't foresee that necessity."

"What about the safe?" Vines said.

"It's open and completely empty."

"Any sign of the money man?"

"None. But he still has five minutes. After he arrives and I've tallied the money, I'll lock it in the safe, hand him the key to the poker room and take my leave."

"Are you saying we're already locked in here?" Vines asked.

"Yes. Of course."

"We weren't expecting that. At least, not yet."

Mansur sighed deeply. "You must remember that I was to have lured you here, Mr. Vines, on the pretext of a poker game. I am supposedly acting as agent for B.D. and Sid, who're selling you to whoever appears with the money. If our little playlet is to have any credibility, I can't have you and Mr. Adair running up and down the hall, now can I?"

"Parvis," Vines said.

"Yes?"

"What if he doesn't have the money?"

"Then I'm prepared to defend myself. And you, too, of course." There was a brief pause that ended when Mansur said, "Sorry to cut this short, but he's here."

After the line went dead, Vines hung up the poker room phone and turned to Adair. "He's here."

"And we're locked in."

"You want a drink?" Vines said.

"No. Do you?"

"No."

"What a couple of liars," said Jack Adair.

Theodore Contraire, who sometimes called himself Teddy Jones or Smith, came into the private dining room in Cousin Mary's dressed for the Fourth of July as a Vietnam veteran. He wore camouflage fatigues, jump boots, a fatigue hat and, cradled in his right arm, an unaltered and therefore illegal M-16 that was aimed at Parvis Mansur.

"You're Parvis, right?"

"I'm Parvis."

"Where's Adair and Vines?"

"Where, I might ask, is the money?"

"What money?" said Theodore Contraire.

Forty-two

Mansur, his hands now clasped behind his neck, walked into Merriman Dorr's small office, followed by Contraire and the M-16. Contraire looked around, taking in the two wingback chairs, the safe and the child's desk. "Cute," he said. "What's in the safe?"

"Nothing."

"Open it up and let's see."

Parvis moved to the safe and pulled the heavy door open.

"Hands behind your neck," Contraire reminded Mansur, backing up to get a better view of the safe, whose interior space was approximately three feet high, two feet wide and three feet deep.

"Big bastard," Contraire said.

"Yes."

"All cleaned out, too. Not even a shelf left. Hold a million bucks with no trouble at all, even if it was in twenties and fifties."

"Twenties and fifties will be perfectly acceptable."

"I guess I didn't make myself clear," Contraire said.

"There's not gonna be any money. But there is gonna be something worth a whole lot more'n a million to somebody."

"What?"

Contraire used the M-16 to indicate the child's desk. "Sit down over at that kiddie's desk. Once you're there you can take your hands down and fold 'em together on top of the desk like you did in grade school."

"I never went to grade school, as you call it," Mansur said. "I was privately tutored."

"Sit down any way and I'll sit in one of these chairs over here and we'll wait for the phone to ring."

"Merriman has an unlisted number in here," Mansur said.

"There's no such thing as an unlisted number."

The telephone rang two minutes later at exactly 3:05 P.M. Aiming the M-16 at Mansur with his right hand, Contraire picked up the ringing phone with his left and said, "It's me."

He listened, smiling his gray-toothed smile at Mansur, who, still seated at the child's desk, his hands folded on its top, smiled politely back.

"Hold on," Contraire said into the phone. To Mansur he said, "I bet you can turn this into a conference call—you and me in here, whoever's just called, and Vines and Adair in the poker room. You can do that, can't you, Parvie?"

Mansur nodded.

Cradling the phone's receiver between his ear and left shoulder, Contraire used his now freed left hand to pick up the rest of the telephone and place it in front of Mansur, who tapped out four numbers on the Touch-Tone buttons.

Nodding and smiling at Mansur, Contraire said into the receiver: "Hear it ringing? Now let's see which one answers."

Vines picked up the phone on its fourth chirp and said, "Yes."

"Who's this?" a man's voice said.

"Kelly Vines."

"Well, look, Kelly, I'm gonna put Parvie on for a second so he can tell you what the score is. Okay?"

"Yes."

There was a wait of a second or two until Mansur came on and said, "There's no money."

"No money?" Vines said, lifting the phone an inch or so from his ear so Jack Adair could also listen.

"No. He's here and there's an M-16 pointed at me. I might add that the safety's off. He has someone on the telephone whom he wishes you to speak with. That's all I know."

There was another pause before Contraire came back on and said, "You get all that, Kelly?"

"Yes."

"Okay, let's see if you recognize the next voice you hear."

The next voice Vines and Adair heard said, "Hello, Mr. Vines. How are you today?"

"I'm fine, Dannie. And you?"

"I've had such a nice outing. We took a short drive and I had an ice cream sundae and now we're having a little rest before I go back."

"Someone's with you then?" Vines said.

"Betty's with me."

"Betty who?"

Vines could hear his wife's voice through the hand she must have placed over the phone. "I'm sorry, but I don't remember your last name."

There was an indistinct, muffled reply, a pause and Danielle Vines was again speaking to her husband. "Betty Thompson."

"May I speak to Miss Thompson?" Vines said.

Contraire cut in. "Sorry, Kelly."

"Who was that, Mr. Vines?" Danielle asked.

"A friend."

"Is Mr. Adair with you? Betty said I could also talk with Mr. Adair, who I think is quite nice."

Vines handed the phone to Adair, who closed his eyes, massaged them with the thumb and middle finger on his left hand, and said to his daughter, "Hello, Dannie. This is Jack Adair."

"How are you today, Mr. Adair?"

"I'm fine, Dannie. Where're you calling from?"

"I'm in—"

There was the sound of a phone being hung up. But Contraire was still on the line. "That's enough chitchat, Jack. You wanta talk to me or do you wanta put Vines back on?"

"I'll talk to you," Adair said, holding the receiver away from his ear so Vines could listen.

"Well, it's like this, Jack. I need to get some answers from you guys face-to-face and, if I don't get 'em, well, I'm afraid Dannie's not gonna make it back to the nut farm. So what I want you to do is tell Parvis to give me the key to the poker room."

"What happens to him after he gives you the key?"

"Nothing happens to him. Why would anything happen to him? Well, sure, I might lock him in the dining room there, but it's got a nice little bar where he can sit and drink himself shitfaced until it's all over."

"Put Parvis on," Adair said.

"Mansur here."

"Can he hear me?"

"No."

"He wants you to give him the key to the poker room."

"I know."

"If you don't give it to him," Adair said, "he'll kill you."

"Understood."

"If you give it to him, he'll also kill you."

"That's not altogether certain."

"Ever play poker?"

292

"Yes."

"Well, put your best poker face on because you're going to need it. I'm going to ask you a question that I don't expect you to answer. What I expect you to do is say goodbye, hang up the phone and do whatever you think best. Is that clear?"

"Yes."

"Here's the question," Adair said. "If you were to die today, who would inherit your estate?"

There was silence. Adair counted to six before he heard Parvis Mansur gently hang up the phone. After Adair recradled the poker room phone he turned to Vines and said, "What else could I say?"

"Nothing."

"You think they'll let Dannie go?"

"I doubt it," said Kelly Vines.

Mansur rose from the child's desk and said, "I think my wisest course is to hand you the key without further ado."

"That's very wise, Parvie."

"But to give you the key I must reach into the right pocket of my jacket. In the event you think this is a trick or a subterfuge, you're welcome to reach into the pocket yourself."

"Tell you what," Contraire said. "You go stand over there in front of the safe."

"Very well," Mansur said and crossed to the spot Contraire had indicated with a wave of the M-16.

"I'm not gonna reach into your pocket, Parvie," Contraire said. "The reason I'm not is because I figure that when you were with Savak you learned all sorts of cute and dirty stuff."

"I was never with Savak," Mansur said with stiff dignity.

"None of you rich towelheads ever were—just like none of the krauts were ever with the SS either. I don't blame you. I'd say the same thing myself. But I'm still not gonna walk over there and reach into your pocket because you're gonna turn around, take the key out of your pocket and put it on top of the safe."

"Now?"

"Now."

Mansur turned around, facing the safe. His right hand, neither fast nor slow, dipped into his bush jacket pocket. He spun around, firing through the pocket at Contraire. The round, which sounded like a small caliber, missed Contraire and instead hit one of the two wingback chairs. Contraire shot Mansur in the left thigh and, taking his time, shot him again in the left shoulder. Mansur groaned, staggered and crumpled to the floor.

Contraire bent down and took a nickel-plated .25-caliber Sterling automatic, the old 300 model, from Mansur's pocket. A purse gun, Contraire thought as he stuck the weapon into one of his own pockets. The same hand went back into Mansur's pocket again and came out with a key.

"Can you crawl?" Contraire asked.

"Yes," Mansur whispered. "I don't know."

"I think you better make up your mind that you can crawl into the safe there."

"No."

Contraire made his voice sound patient and reasonable. "You gotta understand something, Parvie. I don't mind you taking a shot at me. I'd've done the same thing. So I'm giving you a chance. You crawl into the safe and it'll be the first place Sid and B.D.'ll look for the money. Maybe you won't even be dead by then, if you take real tiny little breaths. But if you don't crawl in there, I'm gonna have to put a round through your head."

It took Mansur nearly five minutes to fit himself into the safe. His knees were up to his chin. His face was a mask of bewilderment and pain.

Contraire squatted down in front of him. "You okay?"

"Why?"

"Why what?"

"Why did she do it?"

"Dixie?" Contraire said. "Because she's nuts about me and has been ever since she was twelve."

"But why?" Mansur whispered.

"Must be my looks," Contraire said, rose, slowly closed the safe and, after it was closed and locked, gave the combination dial a couple of spins.

Forty-three

When the black Cadillac sedan was almost halfway up the narrow twisting road with no shoulders that led to the Altoid Sanitarium, Danielle Adair Vines turned to Dixie Mansur and said, "I've had such a wonderful time, Betty, I don't want to go back."

Dixie, concentrating on a sharp curve, didn't look at her. "That's nice."

"I don't think you understand, Betty. Or maybe I didn't make myself clear—although I'm much better at that than I used to be."

Dixie gave her a brief glance. "Understand what?"

"That I'm not going back to Dr. Pease. I think I'll go visit Mr. Vines and that nice Mr. Adair instead."

"After I drop you off at the entrance, you can do what you want."

"But if I go back there, Dr. Pease won't let me leave. So why don't we just return to that nice motel and I'll call Mr. Adair? Or you can call him for me. Then I'll wait for him in the motel."

"Sorry," Dixie said.

"You mean you won't?"

"That's right. I won't."

"Oh dear," Danielle Vines said, grabbed the steering wheel with both hands and wrenched it to the left just as the Cadillac entered a sharp right-hand curve. Dixie Mansur fought for control of the wheel but the wife of Kelly Vines had either too much strength or too much desperation. Dixie instinctively slammed on the brakes as the Cadillac veered toward the guardrail.

The brakes and the guardrail together slowed the Cadillac but failed to stop it. The heavy car flattened the rail and plunged down the 45-degree slope, bursting its two front tires. Neither woman had time to scream or cry out before the car smashed into a large old oak at 34 miles per hour.

The old tree, growing on the steep slope, had low spreading branches. Some almost touched the ground. And one of them, a dead branch, shattered the Cadillac's windshield on the driver's side. It also penetrated Dixie Mansur's throat near the base of her neck, killing her almost instantly.

Danielle Vines, shaken, bruised and bleeding from a deep cut on her right cheek and a bad scrape on her left hand, managed to force open the passenger door and scramble out of the car. She was on her hands and knees, still dazed, when she heard the man's voice call, "You okay, lady?"

She looked up to see the man standing by the flattened guardrail, staring down at her. She noticed he wore a grayish-green uniform of some kind.

"I—I think so," she said. "But I don't think poor Betty is."

Karl Seemant looked at his watch. It was 3:35 P.M. Seemant was an exterminator for the Agoura Pest and Varmint Control Co. and had been responding to a frantic call from the Altoid Sanitarium when, two dozen yards or so behind the Cadillac, he had watched it crash through the guardrail. The sanitarium had placed the frantic call after discovering its patients were afflicted with a mysterious plague of fleas.

Since it was the fourth of July and Seemant was being paid holiday double time, he decided the best thing to do was use his truck's cellular phone to call either the sheriff or the Highway Patrol, wait around until they showed up—or maybe an ambulance—and then charge the time he waited to the Altoid loony bin, which, everybody said, had more money than it knew what to do with.

Theodore Contraire unlocked the poker room door in Cousin Mary's quietly. After he opened it just a fraction, he put the key back in his pocket, kicked the door open and charged into the room, his M-16 on full automatic.

Contraire's eyes raked the room, making full use of their peripheral vision, just as he had been taught at that two-week Reconnaissance and Survival course he had attended in southern Alabama at a cost of $4,250 in tuition.

"No games!" he shouted. "I don't like fucking games!"

The door at the far end of the poker room opened slowly. It revealed Jack Adair, sitting on the toilet, his pants and shorts down around his ankles, one hand resting on the curved handle of the black cane.

"I'll be out shortly," Adair said and closed the door.

Contraire raced to the door, banged through it and poked the M-16's muzzle into Adair's left ear. "What the fuck's going on here?"

"I'm discovering why fear is nature's most reliable laxative," Adair said.

Contraire chuckled, removed the M-16's muzzle from Adair's ear, stopped chuckling and said, "Where's Vines?"

"Where's my daughter?"

"By now she oughta be back at the nut farm—so where's Vines?"

"I don't follow you."

"He's not fucking here!" Contraire yelled.

"But why should he be?" Adair asked. "I certainly wouldn't ask him to accompany me to the toilet. Nor would he volunteer. So he must be in the poker room where I left him."

"He's not there, goddamn it!"

"You don't suppose he's done a flit, do you?" Adair said. "Had his own key maybe? And after I was in here and preoccupied, he was out the back door and away. That's so very like Kelly, who's never really been one for self-sacrifice. Can't say I blame him, of course, but still he could've invited me along."

Contraire had long since stopped listening to Adair's musings. He was concentrating now on the shower stall and the green curtain drawn across its entrance.

"He's behind the shower curtain there."

"I assure you he's not," Adair said.

"He's in there with maybe a broken beer bottle or something so when I stick my head in he'll scoop out my eye."

"I can almost see it."

"Hey, Vines!" Contraire called. "Come on out!"

But when Vines didn't, Contraire switched the M-16 to single fire and sent three rounds through the shower curtain. The shots made Adair's ears ring.

When nothing happened after several seconds, Contraire said, "Well, maybe he's not in there after all."

"Or it was a very quiet death."

Contraire looked at his watch. "I got three thirty-eight and my lease on this place runs out at four. So we got thirty-two minutes to talk about this and that."

"Twenty-two, I believe," Adair said.

Contraire frowned, did some mental arithmetic and said, "Yeah. Twenty-two. That's plenty."

"Since you seem to be planning some sort of colloquy, why don't we hold it in the other room where it's far more comfortable?"

"I like you just like you are, Judge, with your pants and drawers down around your ankles. No sudden dashes that way."

"May I at least flush the toilet?"

Contraire sniffed. "Yeah. Maybe you better."

Adair reached back and pressed down the handle. The old toilet made a roar and a gurgle that Kelly Vines could hear from where he crouched on the hidden three-by-three-foot landing of the wooden stairs that led down to the bolt-hole basement. The toilet's thunder was also loud enough to conceal the faint sound the shower wall door made as Vines slipped through it into the stall itself and stood, motionless, behind the drawn shower curtain, breathing through his mouth.

Adair looked back up at Contraire and asked, "Could I have a drink?"

"If you got a glass, there's a faucet."

"I was thinking of whiskey."

"You want me to go bring you a whiskey?"

"I have my own," Adair said, picked up the black cane and shook it so Contraire could hear it gurgle.

"Yeah, Dixie was telling me about that thing."

"Any objections?"

Contraire shrugged.

Adair twisted off the cane's handle, removed the cork, then the glass tube and drank. He offered the tube to Contraire, who shook his head and said, "Maybe you put some kind of poison in there."

"Then I'll soon be dead," Adair said, replacing the tube, the cork and the handle.

"But maybe you've got an antidote hidden somewhere."

The implausibility of his last statement made Contraire hasten to add, "Anyway, I hardly ever drink on the job."

"Would that there were more like you."

Contraire leaned against the wall, the M-16 cradled in his arms, and studied Adair. "You know who I really am?"

Adair nodded. "You're the guy Sid Fork ran out of town back in sixty-eight after he caught you, gin bottle in hand, with twelve-year-old Dixie tied to a bed."

"That was all her idea, not mine. Dixie's kind of kinky. Always was. Always will be."

"You're also the brother of Marie Contraire who died after her car ran into a cottonwood tree when its steering failed—rather mysteriously, I'm told."

"Got any idea of how much I'd've inherited from Marie if the state'd overdosed those two Jimson brats like it was supposed to?"

"Millions."

"Millions and millions and millions."

"I'm curious, " Adair said. "When you were putting together this—well, this scheme to turn Dixie into a rich widow—did she get in touch with you or did you get in touch with her?"

Contraire formed a thin-lipped smile that quickly turned into a smirk. "Since sixty-eight, me and Dixie were never out of touch. At least, not for long. You gotta understand—and I'm not bragging now either—but I'm the only one that can keep up with her in the sex department. We both go for the same kind of stuff."

"And poor Parvis, I assume, is now dead?"

Contraire again looked at his watch. "Has been for prid near an hour. After I shot him I locked him in the safe, so it wouldn't have been more'n five minutes, ten tops, before he ran out of air or bled to death."

"How much will Dixie inherit?"

"Ballpark figure?"

Adair nodded.

"Maybe thirty million. That's not near as much as I'd've got from Marie if all that'd worked out. But thirty's not peanuts either."

"So what happens next?"

"Well, Dixie comes home from her visit and is all shocked and shook up and sad when she finds her husband's dead because he let himself get mixed up in some screwy deal the mayor and the chief cooked up. The sheriff's gonna be all over them two—Sid and B.D.—so they're gonna stonewall. And you sure won't say anything, being dead, and neither will Vines when I find him. So that doesn't leave hardly anybody who really knows what the fuck's been going on."

"What makes you so sure about the mayor and the chief?"

"Dixie figures she can buy 'em both for maybe a million or two." Contraire frowned. "How'd you find out about Dixie anyway?"

"It was Vines who first suspected her—thanks to Soldier Sloan."

"I kept telling her if she didn't quit messing around with that old fart, I'd have to do something about him and I did."

"Did you also have to do something about my son?"

"Now there was one smart cookie. You know he almost had the whole thing figured by the time he got down to Tijuana there. I sometimes think fags are smarter'n people."

After looking at his watch again, Contraire said, "Doesn't look like Vines is coming back after all." He flicked the M-16 to full automatic and aimed it at Adair's chest.

"One last drink?" Adair asked with an obviously forced smile.

Contraire smiled back, apparently enjoying himself. "Make it a quick one."

Adair twisted the handle of the cane again. But this time he twisted it to the left rather than the right. He also coughed just loudly enough to prevent Contraire from hearing the cane's faint click. After the click, Adair shook his head sadly, looked up and said, "I guess I don't want that last drink after all."

"Tummy a little upset?" Contraire said, chuckled, but suddenly stopped chuckling when another thought occurred to him.

"That was just bullshit, wasn't it—about you knowing something that was worth a million dollars? You just cooked that up and fed it to B.D. and Sid after Dixie got Soldier to steer you up here."

"But who was the steersman and who the steered?" Adair said.

"Maybe it was about fifty-fifty. But you didn't know squat. Nothing worth a million anyhow. So what was really in it for you and Vines—me? Getting even?"

"You killed my son. Helped destroy my daughter's mind. Managed to land me in a Federal penitentiary for fifteen months. So, yes, I must've had revenge in mind. As for Kelly, well, he'll have to speak for himself."

It was Vines's cue. He shoved the rubberized green shower curtain all the way to the left. Its plastic rings created a racket that made Contraire start and spin toward the stall. As Contraire turned, Adair jerked the handle from the cane and with it came a seven-inch-long stiletto that resembled an ice pick. Now on his feet, but in a crouch, his pants and shorts still down around his ankles, Adair plunged the thin blade into Contraire's right buttock.

Contraire yelled, shifted the M-16 to his left hand and used his right one to grasp his wounded buttock. Vines burst out of the shower stall and grabbed the M-16, shoving its barrel toward the ceiling. Contraire—or his reflexes—fired a burst into the air. Vines kicked at Contraire, aiming for the short man's kneecap and hitting his crotch instead. Contraire snorted and Vines, using both hands, tore the M-16 from his grasp.

The short heavy man with the remarkably ugly face sucked in as much air as his lungs would hold and doubled over. He stayed that way for at least twenty seconds, his left hand cradling his balls, his right hand still pressed against the wound in his right buttock. Vines thought it was an extremely awkward posture, which, for some reason, reminded him of a pretzel.

When Contraire finally straightened, all evidence of pain was gone, concealed by a mask of indifference. He looked down at the bloody stiletto in Adair's right hand.

"How's that fucker work?" he asked with what seemed to be professional curiosity.

"You turn the handle to the left instead of the right until you hear a click," Adair said. "The click means a tongue-in-groove catch has fastened on the blade."

Contraire nodded, as if in appreciation, and looked at the M-16 Vines was aiming at him, much as he might aim at a not-quite-dead snake.

"You gotta pull the trigger to make it work, dickhead," Contraire said.

Vines nodded, as if in thanks for the reminder, wrapped a forefinger around the trigger, aimed the M-16 more carefully at Contraire, glanced briefly at Jack Adair and said, "Well?"

There was a long pause before Adair said, "No."

"Why not?" Vines said, his eyes on Contraire.

Adair sighed. "Because, Kelly, it's against the law."

Forty-four

Contraire, his hands now locked behind his neck, came out of the bathroom first, followed by Vines with the M-16 and Adair with the black cane, its curved handle back in place, its stiletto sheathed.

They were moving silently toward the poker room's steel door when the telephone chirped. Adair answered it with a hello. Contraire, hands still locked behind his neck, turned to look at Adair, who was again massaging closed eyes with thumb and middle finger as he listened, the corners of his mouth curved down into twin hooks. Kelly Vines kept his eyes and the M-16 on Contraire.

After listening for almost thirty seconds, Adair asked his first question. "When did it happen?" After nodding to his unseen caller, he asked, "And you're sure she's all right?"

There was another listening pause before Adair said, "I don't quite know what to say except that I'm very, very sorry. Does Chief Fork know?"

The answer made Adair frown and say, "I see." After abruptly hanging up the phone he turned slowly to Theodore Contraire and said, "Dixie Mansur's dead. She was killed in an auto accident while driving Dannie back to the sanitarium."

Contraire had to digest the news. But Vines said, "How's Dannie?"

"She's all right. A little shaken and bruised but all right. They have her under sedation at the sanitarium."

Instead of digesting the news of Dixie Mansur's death, Contraire rejected it with a small knowing smile and a headshake. "What're you guys trying to pull?"

"That was the mayor on the phone," Adair said, his voice patient. "The Highway Patrol just called her after they couldn't locate Parvis. They have Dixie's driver's license. Her credit cards. They say she was wearing a wig. She's dead."

Contraire swallowed, looked away and managed to get the word out, "Dead?"

"Yes."

"That's not fair."

"No," Adair said. "Probably not."

Contraire slowly brought his hands down from behind his neck and used them to rip open the top of his camouflage battle fatigues, exposing his bare chest that was matted with thick graying hair. "Do me a big favor, Vines, and pull the fucking trigger."

Vines shook his head and, still looking at Contraire, said to Adair, "What do we do with him, Jack?"

"We let him go."

"Why?"

"Because it's the wisest thing to do."

"I'm not feeling very compassionate."

"I didn't say compassionate. I said wise."

"Which door do we use—front or back?"

"The front."

"Let's go, Teddy," Vines said, "with your hands back up behind your neck."

The three of them went down the long hall, past Merriman Dorr's office with its large Chubb safe that still contained the body of Parvis Mansur, and on past the private dining room that had no windows. Contraire was in the lead, hands still behind his neck and limping slightly, favoring his right leg—the only sign of physical pain he had displayed since they left the bathroom.

Behind Contraire came Vines with the M-16. And behind Vines was Jack Adair, following slowly, swinging his black cane in time with his steps, an expression of unresolved doubt on his face.

When they reached Cousin Mary's front door, Contraire stopped and said, "Can I take my hands down before I bleed to death from the butt?"

"What you can do, Teddy," Vines said, "is open the door slowly and go out. Once outside, you can do anything you want."

Contraire lowered his hands. He used the left one to grasp the doorknob. He stuck his right one down into the same pocket that still held Parvis Mansur's small .25-caliber automatic.

"Well," Contraire said, "I guess I won't be seeing much of you guys anymore."

Before Vines or Adair could reply, Contraire was opening the door, darting through it and snatching the small semiautomatic from his pocket.

Not looking at each other, Vines and Adair remained behind the closed front door of Cousin Mary's, waiting to hear what happened next.

Sid Fork, the chief of police, crouched behind the hood of his Ford sedan and used both hands to aim his five-shot Smith & Wesson Bodyguard Airweight revolver at the front door of Cousin Mary's. He shouted neither "Freeze!" nor "Police!" when Theodore Contraire burst through the door, the small semiautomatic in his right hand.

Fork instead shot Contraire in the left shoulder, which

rocked the short heavy man back and made him grunt as he returned the fire, hitting the Ford's rear side window. Fork shot Contraire again, this time in the stomach. Contraire looked down at the wound in his bare stomach almost curiously, looked up and again fired back, this time hitting the Ford's front door panel.

Fork watched as Contraire sank to his knees, firing the small semiautomatic for the last time into the earth. Taking careful aim, Fork shot him in the chest. Contraire looked up, smiled slightly, as if to say, "That's the one," and toppled over onto his right side. Sid Fork walked around the hood of the Ford, reached Contraire and shot him in the head.

After the swarm of media arrived, and after Sheriff Charles Coates congratulated Chief Sid Fork—on camera—for "having solved the Durango serial murders and for having made the killer pay the ultimate price"— almost choking on the words—Mayor B.D. Huckins took Charlie Coates aside and informed him—some said warned him—that she didn't want to see him inside the city limits until after the November election, if then. After that the four of them—Huckins, Fork, Vines and Adair— met a little after 10 P.M. on the fourth of July in the mayor's living room.

She sat in her favorite chocolate-brown leather chair. Vines and Adair were on the long cream couch. Sid Fork perched on the only other chair in the room, which was really more stool than chair.

B.D. Huckins sat slumped down in the chocolate-brown chair, holding a glass of wine with both hands and staring at the far wall when Fork said, "I've got this kind of dirty feeling—like I've been used and jerked around by some-body a whole lot smarter'n me."

"You have been," the mayor said. "All of us have. By Dixie."

Adair gave his throat a judicial clearing and said, "While you were holding your press conference, Kelly and I called in a few favors from an attorney we know."

"Christ," Fork said. "That's all we need—another lawyer."

"Why?" Huckins said.

"We retained him to represent you," Adair said.

"I don't need a lawyer."

"Nevertheless, we retained him in exchange, as I said, for past favors."

"Must've been some favors," Fork said.

Huckins looked at Vines. "Why do I need a lawyer, Mr. Vines?" she said, as if seeking a second opinion.

"To find out whether Dixie left a will."

"And equally important," Adair said, "to determine the provisions of Parvis's will."

"Dixie didn't have anything," Huckins said. "Well, she did have some clothes and jewelry and that nutty car, but that's all."

"I might as well be blunt," Vines said. "From what we can determine, Dixie died after Parvis died. The lawyer we retained interrupted the holiday of some people in Santa Barbara and called in some favors of his own. He's discovered that Parvis left everything to Dixie except for a few relatively minor bequests to some pet charities."

"Parvis had pet charities?" Fork said.

Vines ignored him and spoke to Huckins. "Dixie had also made a will. She left everything she owned to Parvis. But in the event that Parvis died before she did, Dixie left everything to you."

"You see, Mayor," Adair said, "we've established that Dixie died after Parvis did. And during those last forty-five minutes or that hour of her life, she was the sole legal heir of Parvis's estate, which now goes to you."

"Unless," Vines said.

"Unless what?" Fork said.

"Unless it can be proved that Dixie conspired to murder Parvis." "And the only evidence of that is right here in this room."

"I get everything Parvis had?" Huckins said. "Is that what you're saying?"

"In essence," Adair said.

"How much?" the mayor asked.

"Well," Adair said, "Teddy was in a position to know and he said it was around thirty million."

"What I mean," B.D. Huckins said, "is how much do you guys want to keep quiet about Dixie?"

Adair later swore that somewhere beneath the long silence that followed he could hear the choler in the room coming to a boil and the hostility sizzling in an equally imaginary pan. He even swore he could taste some rancor and smell the bitterness. He also thought it would never end.

But it did when Sid Fork sighed, rose slowly, went over to stand in front of Huckins and stare down at her until he said, very quietly, "Goddamn it, B.D. That was the dumbest fucking thing you ever said in your life."

Huckins closed her eyes and nodded. "I know. I knew as soon as I said it. I must've said it because I wanted to blame somebody for Dixie. But there's nobody to blame."

She opened her eyes and looked first at Jack Adair. "I apologize, Mr. Adair." She next looked at Kelly Vines. "And I apologize to you, Mr. Vines. I'm very sorry."

Adair smiled. "I guess the first thing you'll have to learn, Mayor, is that rich folks don't ever have to explain or apologize for anything."

On their way down to the Blue Eagle in Vines's Mercedes, Jack Adair said, "You want to come in and say goodbye to Virginia?"

"I'm not much on goodbyes, Jack."

"Well, I'll say it for you."

"How long do you think you'll stay on?"

"Until I have someplace else to go. For the time being, I'll help out at the bar and turn her house into a bed-and-breakfast inn since, as she says, it already looks like one anyway."

"With chocolates on the pillows by courtesy of your host, genial Jack Adair."

Adair grinned as the Mercedes stopped in front of the Blue Eagle. "I'll borrow Virginia's car tomorrow, drive down to Agoura and see Dannie."

"Tell Dr. Pease I'll keep the money coming," Vines said. "Somehow."

"Any idea of where you'll light?"

"None."

Adair got out of the car, closed the door and bent down to look through the window at Vines. "When you do, let me know."

"Okay," Vines said and drove away.

Four blocks later, Kelly Vines took Garner Road up to the fifth hairpin turn and drove down Don Domingo Drive until he came to the small measle-white house whose front lawn was adorned with six very large and very ugly igneous boulders and the foot-high stumps of a dozen giant saguaro cacti.

Vines parked at the curb, cut his headlights, switched on a dash light and took a no-longer-valid professional card from his wallet. He scribbled a note on the back of the card and wrapped it around the black cane, binding it in place with a rubber band.

He got out of the Mercedes, walked up to Sid Fork's front door, leaned the cane against it and returned to his car. After that he took Noble's Trace until it reached the twin on-ramps to U.S. Highway 101. Just before he got to the ramps, Vines pulled over, parked and sat there, trying to decide whether to go south toward Guadalajara or north toward Nome.

* * *

Sid Fork left B.D. Huckins at 2:04 A.M. on Tuesday, July 5, arrived home at 2:09 A.M. and smiled when he found the black cane leaning against his front door.

In his living room he removed Kelly Vines's business card and read what had been written on its back: "Turn to the left and pull."

Fork turned the curved handle of the cane to the left until he heard a faint click. He pulled. The handle came off, transformed into a seven-inch stiletto. Fork grinned and touched the point to see how sharp it was. He reinserted it into the cane, turned the handle this time to the right, again removed it—along with the silver-capped cork—and poured a small measure of Jack Daniel's Black Label whiskey into a glass.

He sat down in an easy chair, sipped the whiskey and thought about starting a new collection of American artifacts. Maybe the Fork Collection of Strange and Terrible Weapons of Death. Or something along that line.